Eva Woods grew up in a small Irish village and now lives in London, where she dodges urban foxes and tuts at tourists on escalators. She ran the UK's first writing course for commercial novels and regularly teaches creative writing.

Also by Eva Woods

How to Be Happy
The Lives We Touch
The Ex Factor
The Thirty List

THE MAN
I CAN'T FORGET

Eva Woods

sphere

SPHERE

First published in Great Britain in 2019 by Sphere

1 3 5 7 9 10 8 6 4 2

A CIP catalogue record for this book
is available from the British Library.

ISBN 978-0-7515-7584-2

Typeset in Baskerville by M Rules
Printed and bound in Great Britain by Clays Ltd, Elcograf S.p.A.

Papers used by Sphere are from well-managed forests
and other responsible sources.

Sphere
An imprint of
Little, Brown Book Group
Carmelite House
50 Victoria Embankment
London EC4Y 0DZ

An Hachette UK Company
www.hachette.co.uk

www.littlebrown.co.uk

THE MAN
I CAN'T FORGET

To the memory of my grandparents

EVE

The first time I saw him was not in romantic surroundings. Far from it – it was in the rec room of Sunnyside Independent Living Centre, the care home that I work in, in the town of Bishopsdean in Southern England. It's what you call a 'commuter town', which means it exists mostly so that people can travel there to sleep. And it does feel like a place people only go to close their eyes. Quiet, characterless. Comfortable, in its way, I suppose.

On that particular day – a chilly, grey one in March, the kind where the sun seems too tired to shine properly – Daniel O'Donnell was playing on the stereo and at least one person had definitely had an accident in their chair (or else done a dirty protest at the music). I was trying to find the source of the smell, sniffing round like a beagle, when Magda came in.

Magda (indeterminate age, jewel-rimmed glasses, if not the world's actual worst driver then at least in the top ten) is my boss, the 'senior lifestyle facilitator' here at Sunnyside, which means she wears suits from George at Asda instead of the wipe-clean scrubs the rest of us have on. More than once I've thrown myself in front of her to block flying bodily fluids, like the President's bodyguard taking a bullet (for example when John Hinckley Jr shot Ronald Reagan in 1981, but did you know he also shot three other people, including the President's Press Secretary, who was called James Brady and who died of his injuries years later?). I noticed that Magda had at least four pens stuck into her huge messy bun, which meant today was 'one of those'.

'Eve,' she said, sniffing distractedly, 'we have a new resident. This one is . . . different.'

'Different how?' I steered her away from the battlefield that was the rec room. 'And did you remember to renew your car tax?' Magda is the scattiest person I know – several times I've seen her looking for a resident's file or a cup of tea or her glasses, when they're actually in her hand at the time. I help her out as best I can – she calls me her human Filofax, which Julie the kitchen coordinator (twenty-seven, loves acrylic nails and her phone, hates vegans and anyone with dietary requirements), says makes her sound 'dead ancient, like from the eighties or something'.

'Oh, fudging hell, I didn't.' Magda doesn't like to swear in front of the residents, as if they're children instead of adults in their seventies and eighties. 'Do you have a pen?'

'Um, there's some in your . . . ' Too late, she had taken mine from my scrubs pocket and scrawled a note on her hand, then shoved my pen into her hair, making five in total. 'Different how?' I asked again, saying a quiet farewell to the pen, which had been one of my favourites (style 99E, ballpoint, branded with the NatWest logo). We've had all sorts of residents over the years. All different nationalities, languages, religions – even Mr Smith the Satanist, who was very sweet if you ignored the smell from his room.

'Well, he's got no memory at all. The police found him wandering down the M25, no phone or ID, no keys or cash or anything. He can't remember his name or where he lives or – you know, anything.'

2

I nodded. This was unusual, but not as much as you'd think. 'Oh, and he's . . . '

Behind her, dressed in clean blue scrubs, and carrying a small Tesco bag of possessions, was the most handsome man I had ever seen in my life (bumping to number 2 actor Jonny Dunne, who I spotted when I worked for a week as a waitress in a Pizza Express in Covent Garden, and to number 3 an unknown man I saw busking at Leeds train station in 1997). The new resident wasn't much more than forty, I was sure, and had a faint red mark on his forehead, like an injury. And he was smiling, nervously but sincerely. 'Hello.'

'He's so young!' I blurted to Magda. That really did make him unusual. The youngest resident we had otherwise was Mrs Burke, who was only sixty-eight but had already forgotten her husband and all her children, everyone except the family Pekinese, Roger, who she asked after on a daily basis.

Magda said, 'He'll be staying here until they can find out who he is. They need the hospital bed he was in, and he's nowhere else to go. Lovie, this is Eve, who'll take care of you.'

'Hello.' He took my hand and shook it firmly, then looked at his own, as if slightly confused at what he'd just done. His was large and square, with long fingers. 'I'm – sorry, I don't know my name. But I'm very pleased to meet you. This is – I'm sure it's a lovely place.'

Magda and I exchanged a quick look. We try to make SILC as nice as we can, but our budget is about 10p a day per resident, and there's no disguising the constant smell of boiled food and bodily fluids.

'Did he hit his head?' I asked her quietly.

'They don't know. He can't remember a thing.'

3

'There's nothing they can do?'

Magda shook her head, making a pen fly out of her hair. It was yellow, with bumblebees printed on it. I caught it like a baseball fielder (there are seven of these on a baseball team, did you know? Four infielders and three outfielders) before it took someone's eye out. 'They don't know how to make memories come back, lovie.'

Or make them go away. I of all people should know that.

'So we've got him till he remembers or the police work out who he is. Someone'll report him missing, I'm sure.'

A handsome, young-ish man? Someone like that would surely have a whole world of people missing him. Colleagues, friends, a family.

'Does he really have no name? I can't just call him nothing.' I watched him bumble across the room, shaking hands with residents. Most of them irritably told him to get out of the way of the TV, which was showing *Location, Location, Location*, a popular choice here (I think the residents enjoy the *schadenfreude* that they'd all been able to buy their houses for ten pounds back in the 1950s, while these poor suckers on TV are paying half a million for a cupboard in South London). One or two burst into tears, a standard response to anything new, and Miss Cole shyly handed him a half-chewed biscuit.

Magda said, 'The police call him Adam. It's a joke! Adam and Eve, ha ha!'

I laughed dutifully, although I didn't think it was all that funny. Adam and Eve are perfectly good names, and it's just a shame that some mythological people who couldn't control themselves have ruined it for the rest of us.

Magda leaned in closer, so that I could see the cracks in

her bright pink lipstick. 'I thought you could make him your next client.'

I lowered my gaze. A mistake, because it only let me see how dirty the carpet was. After lunch it all gets a bit 'feeding the cow to the raptors' in here (*Jurassic Park*, 1993). 'I don't know, Magda. My plate's a bit full at the moment.' The truth was, the idea of making Adam a client terrified me. Maybe because he didn't know me yet. Didn't know what I could do, the things that made me different. The idea of letting him find out those things made me want to bolt for the hills, out the smudged patio door and down the road past the housing estate, keep going to the M25 and on to the coast. It was one thing working with the other residents; most of them were never going to recover, and their knowledge of what I could do would be forgotten with them. The risks were low. Adam was different. He would hopefully return to himself, go back to his life. And then he might tell someone, and they'd tell someone else, and before I knew it I could lose everything I'd built so carefully for almost twenty years.

Magda looked disappointed and I felt a stab of guilt. 'Suit yourself, lovie. But if you change your mind, he's going to be with us for the foreseeable. Oh, and I think Mrs O'Reilly's had an accident, can you clear it up?'

The first thing I remember is yellow. A yellow dress, a yellow square of sun on the carpet. Yellow Lego bricks. Then later, a waffle-knit blanket, the kind you might drape on a baby's cot, in the same soft yellow as ducklings or the first sunshine of spring. Although I was six, someone had placed this blanket over me, maybe to soften the stark whiteness of the hospital bed I was in.

Bits of me hurt in a way I was confused about – my hands, my stomach. I felt ... rearranged. My brain was hurting too, but I didn't understand if that was on the inside or the outside. There were people at the door, and I can't remember their faces or if they were men or women, but I remember what they said.

Has she been told yet?

No. Poor little thing. Nothing'll ever be the same now.

EVE

Something everyone learns as they get older is this – your memory can't be relied on. Things slip away, like keys down a grate. That PIN number. The name of the girl who sat beside you in Maths in Year Ten. The colour of the flowers on your wedding day. Memory is not automatic, as any schoolkid knows, sweating in exams trying to recall the metal that makes leaves green (it's magnesium, if you're wondering).

Imagine now that your memory is all too reliable. That you can summon up any name, any fact, the face of a dead parent, the wag of a long-gone dog's tail. That you can remember past days in so much detail it's like sitting down to watch a home movie. Great, right?

Wrong. But I'm getting ahead of myself.

I've worked in Sunnyside Independent Living Centre for more than seventeen years. I've noticed what happens when you do this kind of job, the 'low-skilled' kind: people automatically think it's the only job you ever could have had. One time, this couple who had a relative here (Mr and Mrs Mendoza, drove a Jaguar and did their best to hide the fact it was leased, called the evening meal 'supper' except when they forgot and said 'tea') were having an argument about what the currency of Croatia was – they were going on holiday the next day and he maintained it had the euro, while she thought she'd read that it didn't.

I was passing with a bedpan and I just said, 'The currency of Croatia is the Kuna, first established in 1941, and then again in 1994, after the fall of Yugoslavia!' Just a little fact, seeing as I had it to hand and they didn't. I thought they might find it interesting.

Well, the looks they gave me! They even asked Magda was I 'one of those Rainman-type people who can remember all the numbers and things'.

I should have known. I should have learned that lesson years ago – people don't like it if you can remember too much, especially things they've forgotten themselves. It's part of the reason I struggle meeting a new person. It's all so clean and fresh to start with – no facts about them crowding my head, which happens every time I see someone I know – but then you're just waiting for the moment when they go, *Oh I love pickles me*, and you remind them that on 4 February 2003 they picked the gherkin from their McDonald's burger and threw it away into a bin and said it was disgusting, like a slimy bit of vinegary tongue. With every new person, I scold myself to keep a lid on my memory, pretend I don't know that they've told me a story before or that I can recall the name of their tennis partner, who they only mentioned once five months ago. Eventually I always give myself away, and I see it cross their face: *She's a freak.*

So when I first met Adam, I skirted him warily. Someone brand new, who didn't know about me and my ... skill. All I could tell was he was very handsome, and I guessed around forty years old. There were touches of silver like frost in his hair and the stubble on his face. We'd had people brought in before who'd been sleeping rough, who like him had no ID or phone or wallet, but you could always tell by their weather-beaten skin, their dirty broken nails and wild hair. Adam looked well cared

8

for, his nails trimmed, his hair cut. And yet he was a missing person no one seemed to be looking for. Was he actually missing, if we knew where he was, but not where he belonged? To us he was more . . . found. Like an umbrella left behind on the bus.

Here's what we knew about 'Adam'. The police officer who brought him in, Raheem (thirty, plays five-a-side football every Tuesday, middle child of seven), let me have a read of the file while he was sitting in the kitchen eating the extra rice pudding from lunch. Several months of observation (the six times Raheem has been here in the past year) have led me to believe that he has a crush on Julie, the kitchen coordinator. Six times is, after all, a lot for the police to be at a nursing home. One time he came because Ms Jerman got out and was wandering in her nightgown singing songs from *Cabaret*, and once because Captain Philips thought someone had stolen his war medals (we found them buried in the garden), but the other visits were surely spurious.

This time was a genuine mystery. Adam – I had decided to go along with calling him that since I didn't know his name – had been found four days ago, running down the embankment in the middle of the M25 several miles from here. It was 1.23 a.m., so luckily there wasn't much traffic on the road, or he could have been killed (in 2016, 448 pedestrians were killed by cars in the UK). He had a head injury on his right temple, and was bleeding from his scalp, which could explain his memory loss.

The police report was very clear that Adam had been *running* – not wandering, as Magda had said. Like someone with a purpose. Except when they asked him, he had no idea where he was running to. Or what he was running from. On further questioning, he didn't know his name or address or phone number. He had no shoes on, but was wearing socks from John Lewis that had penguins on them (from the recent Christmas range, I recalled, which led me to deduce they'd been a present) and rolled-up jeans from AllSaints, an expensive shop, and a T-shirt with the band The Killers (formed in 2001 in Las Vegas) on it. He didn't have a wallet or a phone or keys. Of course they checked the CCTV from the motorway (his socks weren't dirty, so he couldn't have run very far), but the place he'd been found was in a security-camera black spot.

Adam had been taken to a specialist brain unit in London while the police went through missing persons' records, checked his fingerprints on databases, and did house-to-house calls near where he'd been found. So far, they'd come up with nothing. Raheem said that if he didn't remember who he was in a few weeks, they'd launch a TV appeal. It was hinted in the report that he could have escaped from a car or a van or something, like maybe he'd been kidnapped or someone was after him, so they didn't want to show his face on TV just yet, in case it put him at risk.

There were a few small clues as to the mystery man's identity. In the pockets of Adam's jeans had been found a total of five things.

1. A small Lego brick, green, two holes.
2. A dry-cleaning ticket, or something like it, with the number 67 printed on it.
3. A striped pebble shaped like a humbug sweet, the old-fashioned kind.
4. A biro with the logo of a bird on it, no writing.
5. One diamond ring on a platinum band.

I shut the manila folder, feeling both curious and frustrated. Whoever had taken down the report was a details person, like me, but there were so many unanswered questions. What did Adam say when they found him? What direction was he running in? I'd need to know these things if I was going to help him.

Not that I was going to, of course. I'd already decided that. As I said, this was just curiosity.

RACHEL

Waking up alone – love having the big bed to myself! ;)

The morning began as they all had since it happened, five days ago and counting. She shot awake, her body drenched in fear and shame. Like 'the horrors' you got after a night of drinking, when you woke up convinced you'd done something terrible, and texted round all your friends, and even when they reassured you you'd been lovely, charming, that everyone thought it was hilarious when you climbed on the bar and danced to the Spice Girls, you still had this niggling doubt that you'd insulted someone or broken something or maybe, just possibly, killed a person?

But this was much worse. Because she *had* done something. At least, she might have. She didn't even know for sure. There was still nothing online. Was it the kind of thing that would get online? She'd tied herself up in a series of different mental scenarios, imagining a hundred contradictory stories with the ingenuity of J.K. Rowling. What she didn't know was what kind of story she was in. Perhaps he had left her – she was the put-upon wife in a stirring woman-starts-cupcake-business story, and when Simon eventually crawled back she would be far too busy hooking up with her new love, David Tennant. What she'd found on his phone that terrible night would support this possibility. Rachel had asked herself over and over had she really seen it. She could have checked, since his phone was sitting on the dresser in their room, beside his wallet and keys, but she didn't know the passcode. And how could he be managing without those things?

Unless he had other bank cards, accounts she didn't know about. At this stage, her imaginings would morph into a high-stakes thriller, a domestic noir where the woman found out her husband had lied to her all along. He had secrets. He'd been hiding money, getting ready to divorce her. He'd upped and left his life, shrugging it off like an old coat. She couldn't imagine doing that. Hers was so tied down, with Hannah and the house, the milk deliveries, the organic veg box, the cleaner who came on Wednesdays, the gardener who did alternate Fridays. Some days she felt like Gulliver, pinned to the ground by a million little threads. Had Simon been able to snip through his own? Would he do that to Hannah, even if he'd do it to her?

There were other stories she could be in. He could be a spy. His whole life was a sham. He'd been targeted by a secret government organisation and left the country, but would come back for her when he could. He'd been living in witness protection. He'd faked his own death. Been abducted by aliens.

Just as she was coming to the same conclusion as every other day since it happened – that she knew absolutely nothing, and would never have a career as a fiction writer – her alarm went off.

Hannah put down the spoon she was using to eat her granola (Rachel made it herself without added sugar; just one of the many small things she'd done over the years to try to be good, be right, and now all of that was going up in flames).

'Mummy.' Hannah had a strong, confident voice, strident

13

as a Tory politician, Margaret Thatcher or Andrea Leadsom or one of those pull-yourself-together-no-whining types. It sat strangely on a seven-year-old.

'Yes, darling?' Opposite her, Rachel was eating toast, for the first time in two years. Usually she had a boiled egg and avocado for breakfast, avoiding carbs. She was almost dizzy with the taste of the bread, the hot butter dripping and mingling with sweet jam. Her mind was spiralling, as if several different people were having an argument inside it. *Call the police, you idiot. I can't call the police, for God's sake! Anyway, there's no need. Go and look for him. Call his work.*

'Why are you different, Mummy?'

'Hmm?'

'You're eating toast. And you're not dressed.'

It was true, she was still in her Boden pyjamas at the breakfast table. 'It's nice to have a break sometimes.' Hannah narrowed her eyes at her mother, and quite right too. Rachel didn't believe in breaks. Breaks were really no different from cracks.

'Is it because Daddy's away?' Hannah, thank God, had not been at the house that night – Rachel woke up sometimes in a cold sweat, realising how very much worse things could have been if she had. She'd told her Daddy was away on business, but Hannah would be expecting a call or FaceTime before too long.

'That's right – I thought we could take it easy, while he's away.' *Which might be for ever.*

'Does that mean I still have to do homework and violin practice and tae kwon do?' How over-scheduled her daughter was. How many things they did to fit in here in Little Sudbury. Organic gardening (Rachel hated gardening! Soil under her nails and aching knees). Mandarin lessons. Pilates, book club.

Group holidays in Devon. She remembered last half-term, when they'd gone away with Miranda and Lorcan and their bratty twin boys, Edward and Horatio, and Hannah had bossed the kids into acting in a play about serial killers (the babysitter had given her unsupervised access to Netflix), resulting in probably life-long trauma, and Lorcan and Miranda had fought every day and drunk too much Pinot Noir at night, and after the holiday it transpired they were on the brink of divorce and this had been the thing to push them over the edge.

'Never again,' Simon had muttered. Was that them now? The couple on the brink of divorce – or worse, already over it and she just didn't know? *The Woman Whose Husband Disappeared, by Rachel Kempner. Coming March 2019.*

She looked at Hannah across the table, her curly hair in messy plaits, wearing the Ninja Turtles T-shirt she'd insisted on buying from the boys' section of John Lewis, because 'it's silly to have boys' and girls' clothes, Mummy', and a smudge of milk across one cheek. Her latest Lego project, a model of the Eiffel Tower, but built from scratch as Hannah considered kits to be 'cheating', was spread out over the living-room floor. Rachel's heart hurt, thinking of what might be ahead. 'Not if you don't want to.' Hannah gaped at her; clearly, she hadn't expected that gambit to work. But at least it would keep her distracted while Rachel figured out what to do, and the less they saw the school-mum brigade, the better.

And so Rachel spent the day like the one before, scanning news sites, clicking into her phone every five seconds, seeing only the endless stream of WhatsApps from the school mums about parking and cake sales, and Rachel's nemesis, Janine Hewson-Taylor, warning about a possible outbreak of nits in

Year Five (there was nothing like a crisis to make you realise how few real friends you had left, and as for family – forget about it). Listening to the sickening thud of her heart in her chest, answering all of Hannah's questions with a distracted, 'Hmm?' The fear was there when she loaded the washing machine, when she picked Hannah up from school and sorted the carrots from the organic veg box, looking for one that most resembled an animated Disney character: *You could be a killer. You could go to prison.*

Because that was the other alternative, another story she might be living in right now. He hadn't been in touch because he was dead. And that meant she was a murderer.

EVE

I haven't told you yet what it is I do. Yes, officially, I work here as a care assistant, doling out cups of tea and refereeing disputes about whether to watch *Loose Women* or *Homes Under the Hammer* in the rec room. I've done that ever since I turned up in Bishopsdean at the age of seventeen, frightened and running, with no bank account and only one pair of shoes. Magda took pity on me, and I'm so grateful for that I'll clean up any amount of spilled lunches (or worse) until the day someone tells me to stop.

But I have an unofficial job too. You see, a lot of the residents have memory problems. It could be minor, like not knowing the name of that actor in that film about that thing, or as major as not knowing what year it is or recognising their own children. I try to help them find their memories, using a combination of interviews, research, sensory stimulation, and my own personal knowledge of how memory works.

You may have worked out by now that my memory isn't quite the same as other people's. To explain it, it's easier if I use the thing Theresa said when I was ten, irritation scratching at her voice: *Eve, you're like one of those hoarder people on the telly, except in your brain. Can you not just forget for once?*

But I can't. Basically I remember everything that's ever happened to me since the age of six. I had a bit of a sad time before I ended up here, and realised I could use my strange memory to help people with holes in theirs. But don't feel sorry for me. I like my life – my little ordered flat with the lock on the door, nights in with my TV programmes, making rounds of the residents every two hours, serving up meals at seven, eleven and five, counting out meds each morning and night, watching *Doctors* every day, laundering sheets, scrubbing pots. My life makes sense. I can help people.

When I'd finished reading Adam's file, Raheem was scraping out the rice-pudding bowl, while Julie looked on, scowling (her natural expression). 'Careful, you'll take the pattern off.'

'Can't help it. How d'you get it so creamy, man?'

Julie sniffed and went back to stirring the soup for dinner, though I could tell by the slight lift of her pencilled-in eyebrows that she was pleased. The real Julie starts quite far under the surface, what with her false nails and hair extensions and make-up. I'll never forget the day Mr Andrews, who grew up in Australia, started screaming that there was a poisonous spider in the cock-a-leekie soup, and we fished it out, only to find it was Julie's left eyelashes.

'Find anything, Columbo?' Raheem said, when I gave him back the file. I didn't see what I had in common with an older man in a trench coat (a role filled by Peter Falk, but initially offered to Bing Crosby, fun fact).

'Maybe. The things he had in his pockets – where are they?'

'Evidence locker, most likely,' Raheem mumbled, through pudding.

'Would it be possible to get them? I mean, they do belong to Adam. Are you searching hard to find out who he is?' I couldn't help but think that Raheem had other things to do than sit here eating all the rice pudding.

He belched slightly. 'Cuts, innit. We'll do our best, like, but if no one filled a misper report . . . '

'Thought you weren't helping this one, Eve?' said Julie, who was dishing out squares of cheesecake on to white plates. As soon as one meal ends here, another begins. I often think that sugar and tea are all that keep us from a full-on *Walking Dead*-style rampage by the residents.

'I'm not. I just – he could take a quick look at the items, couldn't he, and see if he remembers? If Raheem wouldn't mind coming back again.'

'I don't mind,' he said eagerly, and Julie turned away to her desserts, blushing. I smiled to myself. 'How come you're not helping him, then?' Raheem takes a keen interest in my work, seeing as they get quite a few dementia cases down at the police station, wandering round the shops in their nighties or ripping off all their clothes in the middle of McDonald's.

'No reason. I just – I'm busy.' I left the room then to avoid further questions.

It's difficult for me to maintain casual acquaintanceships, because I remember everything that people tell me, and like I said, comparative strangers find it odd if you can recall that they don't like the blue Wagon Wheels but do like the red ones, when you only met them once ten years ago. But my stand-offishness doesn't stop people at SILC from sticking their noses in. On my way to the rec room I passed Charity (forty-three, born in Trinidad, partial to Rolos), our visiting nurse, who has her own small office beside Magda's. 'Afternoon, Eve. I'm pray-ing you find it in your heart to help the new resident!' She was laying out a tray of pills in little plastic cups.

'Oh, er, thank you, but there's no need.'

'Why's she not helping?' That was Anthony, the part-time porter (twenty-seven, oldest of four kids, doesn't like peas), coming to fetch the tray of pills. He's at the local university doing a PhD in Gothic Literature, and I guess he feels he has to look the part, because he always has on white make-up and eye-liner, and has seventeen different piercings (that are visible to the eye at least). I test him sometimes on quotes from *Dracula* and the like, as his viva is coming up this summer.

I was irritated. It was no one's business why I didn't want to help Adam. 'I just don't think I can, is all. He's an extreme case – no memory at all.'

Anthony wrinkled his chalk-white forehead. 'You helped Mr Maginty remember the name of his dog when he was little. That dog's been dead for like eighty years!'

'That's different. I have to go; I'm late for my rounds.'

I went into the rec room to check the residents. Mrs Munroe, one of the more able residents, was grumpily knitting a baby jumper. 'My granddaughter's having her fourth. What's the matter with the girl? I keep telling her, it's not the fifties, get on that pill!'

'Pills? Is it pill time?' Miss Cole perked up. We wanted to keep an eye on that; last year she'd had back surgery and grown a little too fond of the painkillers. We had to do an intervention for her, like on TV.

'Almost, Miss Cole. Wait your turn.'

She pouted, sinking back in her chair, and I moved on to check on Mrs O'Reilly. She was crying again. 'Oh dear, what is it?'

'I ... ' She stretched out her trembling hands towards the TV, where Bob and Jill from Solihull were trying to auction off an antique fire-iron for £200. 'I just ... ' She began to sob. It's very hard sometimes, to watch the residents when they get to this stage. They can't even form speech any more, or work out what it is they need, so they just cry, like babies, desperate and wordless.

I stroked her forehead, the skull shining through the wispy grey hair. 'It's OK. Shhh. You're safe here.' I made a mental note to call her children and ask them to visit at the weekend. When the residents go like this, the end is often quick.

Next up was Mr Morrison – *Call me Terry* – and I skirted him warily. He tapped the crossword puzzle he was doing. 'Here's a question for you, lass. Capital of Mongolia?'

'I don't know, Mr Morrison,' I lied, removing his lunch dishes.

He chuckled. 'Call me Terry. Course you do, young Eve, you know everything. I think it's Beijing. Isn't it?'

I gritted my teeth. 'I wouldn't know.' He's certainly worked out how to push my buttons. From the day he came to Sunnyside for a temporary stay, still spry although slowed down by a broken hip, he'd noticed my memory but, far from being scared of it, had latched on to me as the answer to his pub quiz team's ambitions to win the local league.

As I moved away I mouthed to myself, *Ulan Bator.* The capital of Mongolia is Ulan Bator, which means Red Hero. It's the second most polluted city in the world. I imagined dusty streets, monks in orange robes. A place I will never go, just like most of them.

I was standing there, musing about the Mongolian steppes while scanning the room for anyone in distress, when I caught sight of our newest resident. He was now dressed in some of the clothes from our donations bin, which more accurately should be called the Death Bin, since that's how we acquire the majority of the items. He had on baggy khaki slacks that had once belonged to Mr Smith (I had checked the pockets for any remnants of Satanism), and, strangely, a jumper with kittens chasing a ball of wool, that had been knitted by former resident Mrs Coleman for the granddaughter she thought she had, when in fact her only son had died in 1976, of meningitis. One of the kittens was cross-eyed, and stared out at me as if I'd personally upset it. All the same I confirmed to myself that the new resident was, in fact, the most handsome man I had ever seen.

I fought to find my tongue. 'How are you, Adam? Settling in?'

'Oh, yes, everyone's very kind.' He sighed, and I saw he was struggling more than he wanted to show. 'I'm sorry. I'm trying to put on a brave face, but I just – I can't remember *anything*. I don't know who I am, my name, if I like custard creams or not . . . nothing.'

'It must be so hard.' Again, the itch to help him, to solve the mystery. 'I bet we can work out the custard cream thing, though. There's some on that plate there. Give them a sniff.'

Adam lifted the plate to his nose. 'Oh! Right, it seems I don't like custard creams.'

'Great! So that's one thing sorted.'

Adam took something out of the pocket of his khakis, a small notebook with the logo of an incontinence-product company on it (Magda gets them free), and wrote down a few words with a stubby pencil that said *Whipsnade Zoo*, which I knew Mrs Kadzinsky's grandchildren had bought for her to do Sudokus with. Mrs Kadzinsky had died three years ago, so technically I wasn't sure who the pencil belonged to now. Perhaps it too had come from the Death Bin, aka the box of found things. The opposite of Adam, who was a missing thing, although not to us.

'What are you writing?' *Stop it, Eve. You weren't going to get involved.*

'I'm trying to build a memory. From scratch – not very easy!' He was so sweet and earnest, his face creased with worry, that I just felt awful for him.

'It's a good idea to write things down. It's one of the techniques that help.' As soon as I said it, I could have kicked myself.

Adam was staring at me, like a dog trying to figure out what its owner is saying. 'Eve, I heard some of the residents say that you're – you have a special way to remember things.'

Oh dear. 'Hmm, that's strange.' I started to clear some dishes from the sideboard behind him.

'I was hoping maybe you could help me. This is just so hard. I have no reference for anything. I don't know if I even like cats, or if this jumper is something I would have hated.' He glanced down at the knitted kittens on his chest, doubtful. 'I keep thinking, do I have a life somewhere I need to get back to? A family missing me? A job I'm meant to be at, people who rely on me? What if they're looking for me, wondering where I am? Eve, it's – it's frightening.'

He had little lines around his eyes that made them crinkle, but right now they looked sad, full of worry and the same terror I saw in the eyes of the older residents. *I don't know who I am.* And in that moment I made up my mind. If there was any danger in taking on this case, it would only be to me, and I would have to learn to handle it. 'All right, Adam. I'll help you.'

He was now looking at me like a dog when its owner produces bacon. 'Eve! Can you really do that?'

'I think so.' *I think so* is a thing people say to decorate their sentences, because it's considered Poor Social Etiquette to blow your own trumpet, but Adam was very confused and needed firm answers. Besides, it was only the truth. 'Of course I can,' I amended. 'If anyone can bring your memory back, it's me.'

After they told me what had happened, I didn't understand for a long time. I would look for my mother in strange places – under the kitchen sink, in the boot of the car. She had to be somewhere, didn't she? The lady who was taking care of me – I think she was a friend of my mother's; Auntie Jane who wasn't really an auntie – told me she wasn't there. *She's gone away, Eve.* I didn't get it. *But* where *has she gone? Where?* After a while, I found I couldn't remember things about her any more. Her smell. The sound her hair made against my cheek. The exact colour of her eyes. All of her was just ... gone. And I have never been able to find her again since.

EVE

The first step in my method was to ask questions. This wasn't easy, because Adam had the attention span of a golden retriever puppy. 'Do you remember anything, anything at all?' I began. We were in a quiet corner of the rec room, or as quiet as it ever gets in here with the TV blaring out the search of Monica and Jeffrey from Aylesbury for a semi in Murcia (seventh-largest city in Spain, known as the orchard of Europe), as well as various residents talking to themselves, singing, muttering or even crying. Julie and Anthony were passing out biscuits, and soothing outbreaks of weeping or sudden rage with the television (I didn't blame the residents, daytime TV could make you feel like you had something wrong with your brain even if you didn't).

In answer to my question, Adam said, 'You're Eve Mahoney, aged thirty-four. Tuesday is custard and sponge day. Magda lost her glasses this morning, but they were on top of her head the whole time. I can look at my notebook if you want more?' His brow furrowed.

'That's great, but I meant before. Do you remember anything before you came here? Even the tiniest flash can help me.'

He gazed at me so intently, little frowns puckering his forehead and making the injury there glow red. It was hard to look at him, because he really was so handsome. His green eyes had flecks of hazel and gold in them. His dark hair flopped over his forehead, little strands of silver in it, and even though he smelled of the cheap soap we use here, that cleans you by basically sand-blasting off layers of skin cells, his own smell underneath was something like toffee and grass. 'I remember the police finding me. It was dark and windy, and there were cars zooming past. I was scared and I just knew – I had to run.'

'What about just before that? I know it's frightening.' Sometimes, if you start from a memory and work back, you can fill in what came before. Context memory, it's called.

He frowned harder. 'The car. I remember – driving too fast, and I was afraid, and I didn't quite know what was happening – I couldn't quite remember my name.'

So we'd established he was in a car before running on the motorway. 'That's great. Anything else?'

'When the car stopped, I got out at the lights and ran. I don't know why. I was scared. Bleeding. I had no shoes on. I ran and ran until . . . I don't know. The police found me, I think.'

'Good. Really good. And before that?'

More frowning. 'I'm sorry. It's like . . . a sort of fog comes down. I don't know.'

'Why did you run? Was someone after you?'

'I don't know. I just had to. And then the police station. Then I was in hospital for a few days, doing all these tests. The food there was SO bad. Much worse than here. But I don't know my real name. I'm so sorry.' And he really did look sorry.

'It's not your fault.' I held up a little plastic bag with his possessions in, which Raheem had brought round, taking the opportunity to steal five of Julie's homemade caramel shortbreads. I suspected the police were relieved to give the items back. Officially, they were still investigating Adam's case, but I didn't know what they could do if no one reported him missing.

My eyes were drawn to the ring, the weight of it in my hand, the sparkle of it in the light. It must be a woman he'd bought it for. Maybe he was going to propose to her the day he'd gone missing. How could he forget something like that? But there was no recognition in his eyes as he scanned the objects. 'Those were mine?'

'They were in your pockets, yes.'

From my experience of memory hunting, the easiest place to start should have been the dry-cleaning ticket, or whatever it was. If it had the name of a business on it, we could go there and ask who it was left the jacket or trousers or whatever, and maybe after a small quibble about data protection they'd tell us the name of the customer and perhaps even their phone number. But it wasn't going to be so easy. There was no name on the blue square of ticket, just a number and a scribbled date from two weeks ago. Perhaps it wasn't even a dry-cleaner's but a cobbler or a key-cutter or the kind of old-fashioned shop where they repair clocks and antique umbrella-stands. I gazed at it, frustrated. I imagined the police would have already tried following up on it, but again, you couldn't take it for granted these days. If no obvious crime had been committed, they might not bother.

'Does this mean anything to you?' I held the ticket out using a pair of Julie's eyebrow tweezers, even though of course the police would have already done what they could with fingerprinting.

He stared at it like someone trying to be helpful, with no sign of recognition. 'I'm sorry, no.' He massaged his temples, frowning. 'I try but I just . . . I can't.'

I sighed. The ticket wasn't going to be of much use. I decided instead to start with the ring. Clearly Adam's memory wasn't at a point where it would come back, not yet, and so I let him go. *Diagnosis Murder* was starting soon in the TV room, and all hell would break loose if anyone talked over that.

A lot of residents pass through Sunnyside Independent Living Centre. Sometimes they live here for years, sometimes they arrive and immediately something goes out in them, like a light on a dimmer switch, and a few days later, we go in and find them cold in bed. This sounds sad, I know, but you really do get used to it. We all die. And you know, there are worse things than dying in a warm comfortable bed, with people around you, having just finished off a cup of milky tea and a bourbon biscuit.

So because some of them aren't here for that long, I do get closer to some residents than others. Mrs Gillespie was one of those.

'Oi, girl. GIRL!'

When I say close, I don't mean we get on. I mean I have to spend a large proportion of my time hovering near her chair, because she never shuts up complaining for more than one second.

'What is it, Mrs Gillespie?' I forced on a big smile, as if my mind wasn't 90 per cent occupied with Adam, who was outside walking around the small patch of slug-eaten roses we call the garden. He'd had a headache all afternoon, likely a side effect of his injury, and I knew that, no matter the risks, I had to try to help him. After all, if the police were right about how he'd come to be on the M25, at this very moment, a hitman or a drug dealer could be drawing up outside Sunnyside, intent on wiping him out for ever (Magda had made me watch a show called *Breaking Bad* and it had warped my thinking somewhat).

'I don't like these biscuits,' said Mrs Gillespie, beckoning me over with an imperious gesture.

I looked at the ones she had on her plate. A jammy dodger, a custard cream (invented in 1908 and voted Britain's favourite biscuit in 2007, which I for one find very surprising) and a pink wafer. 'That seems like a good selection to me, Mrs G.'

'Don't call me that! And don't be ridiculous. I want a chocolate one. Everyone else has a chocolate one.'

I went back to the biscuit tin, which lives on the sideboard next to the stereo, but the only ones left were the Nice ones and the digestives. I always feel sorry for them, left to last, like children no one wants to adopt. 'I'm sorry, there aren't any.'

She fixed me with a death stare. 'My son is paying a LOT of money for me to be here, and I should think the VERY LEAST you can do would be to provide me with chocolate on my biscuits.'

I wanted to say that he wasn't paying a lot – in fact, we were the cheapest home in the county – but I could imagine it was very frustrating to be old and not able to move around much, and be denied the small pleasure of chocolate on your biscuit. I promised her I'd make sure she got first pick of the next box, and she nodded grumpily. 'See that you do.'

I sat down beside her on the little stool I use for talking to the residents. 'So, Mrs Gillespie, how are you settling in?' She'd been with us for around two months now, coming in after she'd found herself at the library in her nightdress, under the impression it was Sainsbury's and loudly asking why there wasn't any asparagus. Her son, who lived overseas, had not visited her in all that time.

'Oh, this is a terrible place. The walls are paper-thin! Always someone muttering or shouting or singing all the words to "Don't Rain on My Parade" (written by Bob Merrill and Julie Styne for the 1964 musical *Funny Girl*).'

'That's Ms Jerman, she used to sing in the West End.'

'If I wished to hear a cabaret performance I would buy a TICKET!'

My smile glazed over. 'Is there anything we can do to make you more comfortable? Apart from the biscuits and the walls, that is.'

She sighed. 'I would be so much happier if you'd find Graham.'

In my head I leafed through Mrs Gillespie's file, which I had memorised. Graham? Was that her husband's name? No, it said in black and white that her husband's name was Arthur. He'd died in 1984. 'Who's Graham? Was he a friend of yours?'

In reply she just looked past me, at something that wasn't there. This is common in the residents, staring at something in the past. I've always wondered: if it's not there, and I can't see it but if they can, is that something like a ghost? Is that all ghosts are, memories not everyone can see? 'Graham's been gone for such a long time. I do miss him.'

Another spark of interest. Graham must have been some long-lost lover! This is also common. The way dementia works is that the memories sort of peel away like an onion, and you go further and further back into your past. Graham could be someone from eighty years ago.

Feeling sad for her, I patted her wrinkled hand and she withdrew it in deep umbrage. 'If I wanted to be manhandled I'd go to a MASSAGE PARLOUR.'

'Sorry, sorry. I'd love to help you find Graham, Mrs Gillespie.'

'You would?' She looked suspicious. 'I told my son and he didn't want to know.'

I nodded. 'That's pretty standard.' It can be upsetting to learn that your mother or father has been secretly in love all these years, not with your other parent, but with someone they'd met once at a dance in Scarborough in 1953. That this other person lingered in their minds, while you and your mother or father were entirely sloughed away. 'Can you describe Graham to me?'

Her grouchy expression softened. 'Oh, he has the loveliest green eyes you've ever seen. Mesmerising, they are. And all that black shiny hair. Beautiful.'

'He does sound handsome. And, Mrs Gillespie, I'm sorry to ask this, but, to the best of your knowledge, is Graham – living?'

Another death stare. 'Of course he is. He's only young!' That made it tricky. How young did she mean? In her head, were she and Graham both twenty? Had she fallen for a much younger man? Had Graham died decades ago? This is always the problem when trying to find the memories of the residents. Often, the person they most want to see again has been gone for years. Some of the residents believe they'll see their loved ones again after they die – and Charity is always telling them they will, while pressing earnest pamphlets on them – but I don't know. It seems to me that Heaven and Hell are both in the fathomless space between our ears. I've seen residents fall into black holes, emerging after what seems like seconds, but to them it's suddenly a different century. I've been trapped inside my own brain, the vast warehouse of lost days I lug around with me everywhere. I don't think we need to invent more than we already have to deal with, either bad or good.

I went back to Graham. 'Great. And can you tell me anything else about him? Where did you meet?'

She began to fidget, a sign of agitation or distress in dementia.
'In London, silly girl. He came from Birmingham originally.
He had five brothers and sisters – maybe he went off to see one
of them. I do miss him so!'

I told her the same thing I'd told Adam. 'Not to worry, Mrs
G. I'll help you.'

My second new client in less than a week – I was going to be
busy. That was good. It was the empty space, the quiet time,
that I had to watch out for, because that was when my memories would swoop in and fill it up.

RACHEL

Spring cleaning! Love getting my KonMari on.

The old Rachel, before all this happened, a massive six days ago, might have Instagrammed this moment, the piles of clothes lifted out of the chest of drawers, the storage boxes pulled from under the bed. Old Rachel liked to document the details of her life, everything hashtagged and soft-filtered. But she wouldn't be putting anything about this online. Because she wasn't spring-cleaning – she was looking for clues. She imagined Instagramming the truth – *Hashtag my husband has left me! Hashtag or maybe I killed him!* It was so ridiculous she almost laughed, catching sight of her frazzled face in the mirror, her hair straggly and full of dust, her nails chipped. She looked like a crazy person, and indeed felt like one too. She wished there was someone to talk to, ask for advice, but she could hardly call her mother, and her brother was in Australia and anyway she hadn't spoken to him beyond the odd WhatsApp for two years. Her former friends – Maura from university, Jen from her old PR firm, Ilana from Bikram yoga – had all seemed to melt away when she moved out of London, wrapped up in her sudden all-consuming love for Simon, and then their home, their child. Their life.

Maybe if she had a job it would be easier to distract herself from the constant panic, but she hadn't worked since Hannah was a baby, a fact that still surprised her when she reminded herself. *I don't have a job! I'm a non-working mother!* She had of course planned to go back to work in the glass-filled PR office near Soho, with the Nespresso machine and games area and nights out that didn't end until someone puked. But Hannah had been a small and sickly baby, rushed to hospital four times before her first birthday, suffering with croup, colic, endless fevers. After another late night pacing the living room with a red, screaming child, Rachel had blurted to Simon that she had to quit. And here she was, doing all the cooking and housework and childcare. Shopping for and preparing organic, low-sugar and low-salt food for Hannah, making a packed lunch that would pass not only the rigorous nutritional standards of the school and the other mums, but also the competitive lunchbox-comparison Hannah and her friends engaged in – *Mummy, Zara had her carrots cut into the shape of Olaf from* Frozen, *why can't you do that?* Keeping the house clean and tidy, to the level of an uninhabited show home. Not for the first time, Rachel wondered where her old self had gone. Missing, presumed gentrified. Gone as completely as Simon had.

'What are you doing, Mummy?' Hannah stood in the doorway, hands on hips. She was such a sturdy little person, passionate about animals and the environment, fierce about recycling.

'Oh! Just tidying.' Rachel was on her knees, feeling underneath the chest of drawers in her and Simon's bedroom. It seemed like a good place to hide something, but maybe she'd just watched too many Nordic crime dramas. On a TV show, sinister music would start to swell right about now, and she'd pull out a burner phone or an incriminating picture or a terrifying photo shrine to another woman, with the eyes scratched out. So far all she'd found was a lot of dust and several happily settled-down spiders.

It was so ridiculous. Most likely he'd just left her, and absolutely no one would be surprised by that. Things hadn't been good between them, not for a long time, and at least half the parents at Hannah's school had already split up, the mothers reinventing themselves as cupcake bakers or yoga teachers, the fathers taking up Iron Man and getting trendy new haircuts. For perhaps the millionth time that week, Rachel dissected the message she'd seen flash up on Simon's phone that night. If only she could get into the phone to check it again, scour it for clues. Like who the hell that girl was.

Hannah was still standing there, watching her get up from kneeling, a process that took at least five times longer than it had pre-child. 'Mummy, I thought we were going to have fun while Daddy's away. I didn't mean *clean*.'

'All right, darling, if you say so. What shall we do instead?'

'I'll make a list,' said Hannah, who was a very organised seven-year-old.

'Great!' Rachel pasted on a smile until her daughter left, her feet thundering down the stairs. She hadn't found anything in her search to explain Simon's continued absence, his total silence, how he was coping without his phone and bank cards. Which meant either he had a separate life she knew nothing about or he was hurt, injured somehow. He didn't need his phone, because he couldn't use it anyway. The part of her mind spewing doom and gloom whispered, *And it's your fault.* It was stupid, thinking like that. But all the same she couldn't shake the dread that curdled in her stomach.

Churning with anxiety, she began to tidy away the socks

she'd pulled out of his drawers. Every pair had cost at least twelve pounds. As a child, she wouldn't have known it was possible to get socks that didn't come in five-pack sets from the supermarket.

'Mummy.' Hannah was back. 'I was looking in the scrap-paper drawer and I found this. Daddy always says not to draw on things like this, so you better take it.'

'Oh, OK, darling.'

After Hannah popped back out again, tramping down the stairs like a herd of Highland Cattle, Rachel turned over the sheet of A4, slightly crumpled. If they got anything in the post that was only printed on one side, they usually shoved it into a kitchen drawer so Hannah could scribble on the back. All part of their middle-class, recycling, low-carbon-output drive, conveniently ignoring the fact they flew on two foreign holidays a year. *Hashtag helping the planet!* This piece of paper had the logo of Simon's company on it. It was a letter. She began to read, ignoring a growing ache in her stomach that told her she wasn't going to like what it said.

Dear Simon, I'm sorry to have to tell you . . .

EVE

The ring from Adam's pocket looked beautiful to me: a large sparkling diamond with two smaller ones on either side, all on a silvery band I assumed was platinum (atomic number 78, from the Spanish for 'little silver'). This is the next part of my method – looking for clues. I've learned over time that every memory leaves a trace. There will always be something, a small item, a scrap of paper, a photograph. When I held the ring up to the light, in an airport plastic bag I'd stolen from Magda (she keeps a stash of them in case she's ever in a place that charges for them), it sparkled and shot light right through me. I felt it burning in my pocket all the way on the bus, and I did worry someone might knock me down and run away with it. The world outside Sunnyside always makes me feel this way, my heart racing, my eyes darting around for a place to hide. As if someone will see what I am. *Oh, there she is. A freak.* But I had to do it, for Adam.

There are quite a few jewellery shops in town. The rich bankers and lawyers who work in London need them to buy engagement rings and 'push presents' and 'I'm sorry I worked all night again' gifts for their stay-at-home wives. But I didn't go into any of the shiny shops on the high street, their windows sparkling with diamonds, sapphires, emeralds (did you know, all diamonds are at least three billion years old? One of the very few memories I have before the age of six is of my mother washing my hair over the kitchen sink, saying it was a good way to clean her engagement ring, a small chip of diamond, and . . .)

No, I didn't have time for that. I nipped the memory in the bud before it could spread, bloom and blossom into an immersive film playing inside my head. Avoiding the big shops, I went down a side alley, past a computer repair shop and a hair salon, and I pushed open the tiny green-painted door to Spitz and Sons. It's so old that the current Mr Spitz, my friend (seventy-something, born in Latvia, cries when he listens to Beethoven), is the great-grandson of the original. He told me once his great-grandfather escaped a pogrom with emeralds sewn into his trousers, and even if it's not true, I've learned that sometimes it's best to let people hold on to the stories that glint and shine, if the facts are dull and colourless.

'Mr Spitz, hello!'

Mr Spitz is a small man with a goblin-like white beard. He looked up from his bench through those magnifying things jewellers wear. 'Oh, is the girl from the home.'

'Eve, yes.' When I was younger I'd get offended that people forgot my name, until I realised it's normal for most people not to remember you if they've met you only once, or even two or three or more times. It's me who's strange, always remembering.

'You have something for me.' Even though I never buy anything from Mr Spitz – maybe one day! – he's something of a detective himself, and he likes to help me. Over the years I've taken a lot of jewellery in for the residents, to get valued or identified. It's one of the few things they hang on to, from the torrent of objects they've owned in their lives. A locket put around their neck as a child, by a long-dead parent. A wedding ring engraved with the name of a spouse they can't remember.

38

A brooch they carried with them when they fled their home country. Mr Spitz can tell just by looking where something was made and when, and sometimes even link it to a part of the world. A few times that's helped me recover a memory, like the name of a village where someone grew up, or what their mother was called, or even the year they got married. It makes me sick to think of people losing these things. The things that make you who you are.

I handed him the diamond ring, relieved that I got it this far without being mugged. It crossed my mind for a second that other women my age might hope for one of these, dream and pray for it as the solution to all their problems. Maybe there was a woman out there who'd been waiting for this one, and had no idea how close she'd got. Perhaps by doing this, I'd bring her and Adam back together. I found it hard to believe someone like him could be single.

Mr Spitz frowned, then peered through his little magnifying glass. 'Eva, what is this?' He sounded cross so I explained about Adam, the items he'd had in his pocket, about the police giving them back. He did a little laugh-sigh. 'Eva, the police would not give back if they were real diamonds!'

'They aren't?'

'Rhinestones, plated band.' He made a noise like *tchuh* and I felt bad.

'Oh.' I stared at the ring. 'You mean – it's not worth anything?'

'Maybe one, two hundred pounds at most.' He was scowling, as if he didn't even want to touch it.

'It looks real to me,' I ventured, bracing myself to be told off again.

'Is a good fake. Maybe for someone who does not know the

real thing.' He seemed to take pity on me. 'Next time you have real diamonds, Eva, bring them to me!'

'So . . . there's no way to trace where it came from?'

He shrugged. 'Is cheap, common thing. You can buy in any high-street place.' Mr Spitz has a deep contempt for the high street. 'No hallmark, no stamps, nothing that could trace.' (Did you know that all precious metals in the UK have to be assayed and hallmarked before they can be sold?)

My heart sank. I'd imagined it to be a one-of-a-kind ring, made specially by an in-demand jeweller who would immediately tell us the name of the person who'd bought it, i.e. Adam's true identity.

To cheer me up, Mr Spitz let me try on a diamond tiara he had in his collection, which lived in a dusty green velvet box, glittering with fierce hidden fire. 'Here, Eva.' He placed it on my head. His hands were so gentle and deft, though twisted with arthritis. I looked at myself in the mirror. A short woman in her thirties, dressed in jeans and a plain sweatshirt, like a teenage boy might wear. Fair hair scraped back. No make-up, no other jewellery. The holes in my ears, which a girl in one of the care homes (Jade, scratched her arms at night until they bled, was one of six children all split up in foster care) had pierced for me with a hot sewing needle, have long since healed, but the bumps are still there. All memories leave traces, scars. The diamonds on my head shimmered, adding warmth to my pale pinched face. Magda says I don't eat enough, that I go hungry all day fussing round the residents, then fill up on starchy junk food. Julie says I should make more of myself, wear nicer clothes, do my hair, go out and meet people. Maybe they're right.

'Thank you,' I said, taking the tiara off as gently as I could. Its metal frame was cool and heavy, the diamonds rough against my skin. He'd told me it once belonged to a Russian countess, who'd fled to England during the revolution, everything she'd salvaged carried in one tiny evening bag. I wanted to believe it was true.

As I waited for the bus back to the home, shivering in the still-cold air, I wondered why Adam would have a ring in his pocket, a woman's ring, that was pretending to be better than it was. This case just kept getting stranger and stranger.

I had to dash back after my jewellery shop trip, because today was going to be a sad-ish day at Sunnyside. Sad isn't quite the right word for the feeling. There isn't really a word for it at all, though there should be. You see, our residents are often very old, and usually they've lived full lives, and by the time they get to us they're very tired and worn. Sometimes, the idea of dying isn't that terrible to them.

Our most recent death, Mrs Kilmartin, was one like that. She was a Scottish lady of ninety-two, and she'd lived through the Second World War, when she worked in a telegraph station that helped break the Enigma Code. She had four children and had followed her husband around the world in the army. Last week, I was tucking her in to bed with a (probably substandard) biscuit and a cup of tea, when I asked if she needed anything. She took off her glasses and said, 'Och, hen, I need to be out of here.'

I was confused. 'Of Sunnyside?' Running away is a symptom of dementia – our residents try to escape more often than hard-bitten criminals in Alcatraz. We had to ban the showing of *The*

Shawshank Redemption in the rec room; it was giving them ideas.

'All of it. Life. The world. It's a piece of shite, isn't it, dearie?'

'Well – not entirely.' I was starting to get a bit worried. The residents often said things like this, or asked us to slip them a few extra pills or even 'just hold a pillow over my head, love', and I sympathised, but Magda had given us all a stern talking-to about how this kind of thing can land you in prison, even if they've begged you for help. I don't think I could stand it in prison. If I don't keep busy sorting out other people's memories, mine might engulf me. Anyway, I didn't need to worry, because Mrs Kilmartin had such a strong will I think she actually ordered her heart to stop, and the next day we found her dead, her arms neatly folded over her tartan blanket, a smile on her face.

Today, her family were coming to get her possessions. She didn't have a lot – a few clothes, a collection of *Midsomer Murder* DVDs, some Agatha Christie books. We used to talk about the solutions and see if we worked it out. I love that I hardly ever do – it's a rare pleasure for me not to know the answer to a question. I made it back to Sunnyside and raced up the stairs to the recently vacated room Mrs Kilmartin had lived in. Someone else was moving into it tomorrow – there was always a new supply of people starting to lose their grip on the world (someone develops Alzheimer's every three minutes in the UK).

As her daughter (Kitty, sixty-ish with flicky ash-blonde hair and a gilet) was packing some bobbled jumpers into a small suitcase, she was sniffling. 'Poor Mum. She wasn't ready to go.'

Eagerly, I said, 'Oh no, she was totally ready! She told me it was all a pile of shite, the world and that.'

I thought this would please Kitty, that her mother had been

ready to die, but she gave me a funny look. 'I know that's not true; my Fraser's getting married in July and she wanted so much to live for that!'

'Oh, is Fraser the one who failed his exams and didn't get into law school?' I can't help remembering things like this, but I think she complained, because later on Magda came and gave me her special talk about Telling the Truth to Families, and When We Should Not Do This. Sometimes, I'm so overwhelmed by facts that I forget lying is also an option.

I had once helped Mrs Kilmartin remember the name of a village she'd been to as a child on holiday, which had a sweetshop that sold the best butterballs she'd ever had in her life. The name, we had eventually worked out through extensive trawling of maps of Scotland, was Dunknockton, and the sweetshop had closed down in 1965 and was now a Londis. Still, she was glad to remember it finally, and I tracked down an old-fashioned sweetshop on the internet and got some butterballs sent to her, which made her happy. So although she had died, and her memories were now gone with her, one more person knew about Dunknockton and the butterballs, and I felt that made it all worthwhile. I only hoped I could help Adam in the same way.

When Kitty had stomped out on to the landing with a box in her hands, muttering about what kind of place was this anyway, I took a last look around the room. There's always something left behind, and sure enough, there it was – a shiny silver butterball wrapper, wedged between the bedside table and the wall. Careful that no one could see me, I fished it out, a wisp of foil paper. It was rubbish, really, but in the Museum, it would be a little part of Mrs Kilmartin left behind. When I went out into the corridor, Anthony was lurking there, so quiet that I jumped.

'Sorry,' he said, pushing back his jet-black hair (I think he dyes it). 'I was going to clean the room, if you're finished.'

'Oh, um, yes, of course, go on in.' I hid the sweet wrapper behind my back, like an idiot, and for a moment we just looked at each other, neither of us saying anything. Anthony seemed puzzled. Then I walked off. *Eve, you're so weird.* I didn't know if I would ever leave that behind.

Ah darling, your poor mam. She's with the angels now. A lady who was apparently my grandma, Nana Mahoney, hugged me to her huge bosoms, which were soft and smelled like biscuits. I was still trying to puzzle everything. My mother was not coming back – she was somewhere else, apparently with the angels. And since she was gone, I had to find another place to live. Auntie Jane tried to explain that she couldn't keep me; she was a nurse and worked strange hours, plus she only had a tiny flat with a bed in the living room. And Nana Mahoney lived far away in Ireland, and she was too old to have me. I didn't understand one thing. *Nana, if Mummy is gone, why can't I live with Daddy? Where is Daddy?*

Nana's eyes skipped over me. *Ah, pet, don't be asking questions like that.* I was cross. Whenever I asked about my dad, people's faces changed, and they would start talking about something else, like potato waffles or *Sesame Street*, instead of telling me the truth. I hated it.

EVE

'No! No! You're torturing me! I'm calling Boutros Boutros-Ghali!' Mrs O'Reilly was rigid in her bed, like a dog trying not to be given a bath. Charity was holding one arm, I was on another, but it still wasn't enough.

'Isn't it amazing she knows the name of the former secretary-general of the UN, but not that she gets this shot once a week?' I winced as her foot, complete with jagged yellow toenails like knives, slashed at me. Mrs O'Reilly, formerly a mild-mannered woman who loved *Strictly Come Dancing* and baking bread, had been turned by fear, by confusion, by this terrible disease, into a dangerous ninja.

'There now,' muttered Charity, as between us we restrained the old woman. 'Quietly, my darling. It will make you feel better.' She slipped the needle into Mrs O'Reilly's upper arm, which drew a howl of pain.

'You're monsters! What do you *want* from me? I keep telling you I don't *know* anything!'

Charity pressed cotton wool to the puncture wound, then taped it over with expert hands. 'She getting worse, you know.'

'I know.' As we released Mrs O'Reilly, weeping and shaking, I saw finger-bruises on her fragile skin and my heart sank. When we couldn't keep people here any more, it was hard to know what the next step was. We were almost relieved when a resident moved out to the hospice across town. It was a quiet, comfortable place, which the relatives liked so much better than hospital. People could live out their final days there in dignity, at least.

Charity was packing up her needle kit. 'You read that pamphlet I gave you?'

'Yes,' I lied. 'Lots to think about.' Charity is very kind, and when she found out how I'd grown up, she took it upon herself to give me the religious education I'd missed. She's always inviting me to her church, or to pot-luck dinners or prayer groups or film showings (this is not as fun as it sounds, as they're always about God), and sometimes when I'm alone in my flat at evenings or weekends it's tempting to go, but I don't think I could pretend to believe. With my memory, it's hard to forget all the times that prayers don't come true.

Charity zipped up her kit. 'I think all finished now. How about a cup of tea, my darling?'

'Oh, thank you, but I better get off home. Lots to do!' It was true. As well as cleaning up after dinner and handing out enough pills to kill a stableful of horses, I had cases to crack.

Generally, my evenings aren't that exciting. Sometimes Julie or Sharice, Charity's daughter who comes in to do physio (twenty-three, five foot eleven, pretends to Charity she goes to church every week when really she gets her nails done), ask me out with them, to the kind of bars where the music is so loud you have to shout and they have all these confusing combinations of brightly coloured drinks, four for ten pounds or five for six pounds or whatever, and sometimes it doesn't make mathematical sense and that hurts my head. I usually say no. They put their heads to one side and say, *But Eve, don't you get lonely? Don't you want to meet someone?*

46

The truth is it's too hard letting a new person in, the flood of information about them, the way they like their tea, the names of their siblings, their opinions on immigration or avocados or *Game of Thrones*. I have to find space for all that in my head, because I will never forget any of it. It's not as if I haven't given it a shot – over the years I've gone out with a few people, but no matter how hard I tried not to betray my weird memory, I couldn't hold it in for ever. There was Ebe, a friend of Charity's son, and Peter, who comes to do the gardening in the summer months, and way back in the last care home, a boy called Charlie who had shaved lines into both of his eyebrows (at the time this was the height of cool). Every time it was the same – *how do you remember that? Are you stalking me or something?* And: *You're such a weirdo, Eve.* Imagine if you remembered every single row, every slight, every nasty word or time they were late or forgot your birthday. You can see how hard that would make relationships, even friendships. Forgetting seems to go hand in hand with forgiveness.

I live in the little flat in the grounds of Sunnyside. Magda said I could after I'd been here two years, and I was so happy to be out of the hostel I'd been staying in. There, if I left something down, a book or a toothbrush or a jumper, it was either gone or moved when I came back and I hated that. Before heading over there, I checked on the residents and trouble-shot issues as best I could, like Miss Cole becoming convinced Tom Jones was hiding in her curtains (hallucinations are a symptom of late-stage dementia) or Terry in just shorts in the corridor, flirting shamelessly with an unimpressed Mrs Munroe. I said good-night to Julie, who was prepping breakfast already, listened to her complain about the poor quality of the margarine Magda

47

orders, which is all we can afford on our current fee scheme, and then to Magda, who never seems to go home, and to Anthony, who is usually on night duty. I think he sort of wishes he could be a vampire – I once caught him googling fangs on the internet.

When I got to the flat and locked the door, I added a few little things to the Museum, and made sure the other items weren't dusty or cobwebbed. Mrs Kilmartin's sweet wrapper, Mrs Kadzinsky's pencil, which I swiped after Adam had finished with it.

I made a baked potato, plain food like they taught us in the last care home, and while I ate I watched my quiz shows. I record them on the box Magda got for me. *Pointless*, *Millionaire*, *Eggheads*, *Only Connect*, I watch them all. People sometimes assume, when they hear about my memory, that I have all the facts and figures of the world at my fingertips. But it doesn't work like that. For me to remember a fact, I have to tap into the day I learned it, and that's easier said than done. Because once I do, it's like fishing in a raging river, and I can easily be sucked in and drown. So I test myself, allowing small flashes of memory at safe moments, in the hope it can be discharged, like electricity.

Then, I took out the striped notebook I keep at my bedside table, and made some notes on my ongoing investigations. I had to find Graham, based on the scant knowledge that he had green eyes and had come from Birmingham, and then just the small matter of figuring out who Adam was, and where he'd come from, and return him to his life. I had explained to him what I'd found out about the ring, but he just shook his head, as puzzled as I was.

I must admit, part of me had been daydreaming about how nice it would be if I located the long-lost love of Mrs Gillespie's life and brought him to see her. I imagined her grouchy pinched face lighting up with joy, how she'd rise from her seat, newly mobile. Maybe he'd say something like, *Nobody puts Mrs Gillespie in a corner*, and then they'd dance, even though Mrs G hasn't been able to walk properly for five years. In my head, Graham had a grey beard and hair, but was fit and strong, for some reason wearing a lumberjack shirt.

The first step was to contact the family. I had found the son's number in her folder, and called him on the mobile Magda got for me, having worked out that if the time difference was three hours, he'd probably be finished work and maybe relaxing on a terrace with some camels in the distance. (Having never left the UK, I don't have much sense of what other countries are like.) I know that Dubai is home to one in every four cranes in the world, but I have no idea what it smells or sounds like, or what it feels like to have hot desert wind on your face. Probably I never will. The phone rang quite a few times, and when James Gillespie picked up, I could hear loud music in the background. He sounded cross. 'Hello?'

'Hello, Mr Gillespie, can I call you James?'

'Who is this? If it's about PPI, I'm not interested.'

'My name is Eve; I'm calling from your mother's nursing home.' My work often means I need to ring people up, but it never gets easier, reminding myself not to say something weird or repeat things back to them verbatim or anything like that.

'Wait a minute.' I heard him breathing and walking away – it sounded like he was in a bar – and then it was quieter. 'What is it? Is there a problem?'

'No, everything's fine. I'm helping your mother with some of her memories, you see. Finding them, and putting them in the right place.'

He made a sort of sighing noise. 'And?'

'Have you ever heard her mention a Graham?'

'I don't think so. Why?'

'Well, she … ' I thought how to phrase it tactfully. 'I'm sure she loved your father very much, James, but it seems that Graham is someone who was once very important to her. She can't quite remember when she last saw him, or who he is, and I wanted to try to trace him for her.'

'You're saying he's, what, some kind of old boyfriend?'

'Maybe. She'd just … like to know where he is.'

'This is very strange. I don't know a Graham. And frankly I'm not sure it would help my mother to be dragging up the past.' He sounded even more cross now. This was sometimes an unfortunate side effect of my work too. 'Is this really part of your job?'

'She's asked for him a lot. She said – she could be happy, if only we could find him.'

There was a pause as he took this in, and I pictured him, this man I had never met, somewhere with a star-studded desert sky, maybe wearing a linen suit. Nearby, someone shouted: 'Come on, Jimbo, it's your round!' Which wasn't something I had imagined a person saying in Dubai.

'As long as you don't upset her.'

'I won't.' Though really I couldn't promise that. Mrs Gillespie was remarkably easy to upset.

'There's quite a lot of old stuff at her flat – I haven't got round to clearing it or putting it on the market. If you promised not to break anything, you could take a look.'

'Oh could I? Thank you, James, thank you!' A real break-through on the case. I'd be able to approach her things in my own manner, follow my own methods. Admittedly, I would have to leave Sunnyside to do it, but that couldn't he helped.

'A friend of mine has a spare key. I'll put you in touch. But you should know, there's nothing of value there, and I'll send my friend over to check it's all been safely locked up again.'

I didn't like the way he said it – it brought up a memory, a nasty one – so I quickly said, 'Thank you, you have our number,' and hung up on him, cutting the connection all the way to Dubai. I hadn't even had a chance to ask about the camels.

I hope you're not touching that, young lady.

N-no. Sorry. I moved away from the table of small objects. I was shivering, rain dripping from my thin tracksuit top and on to the floor of the shop. It was an expensive shop, selling things like candles and cushions and signs and other things I could not even begin to imagine what to do with. I had come in to shelter, having nowhere else to go on that freezing, wet night. I had stepped off a Megabus in this town and I'd no clue what to do next. That's the problem with running. You have to stop at some point.

The lady who ran the shop – I remember her silk scarf and her neat grey hair and the way she looked at me – came and stood beside me. *I think you should leave. Before I call the police.*

Two cases. Two memories to find. As I fell asleep, I found I was turning Adam's case over in my mind, and thinking about the crease right between his eyebrows, and wishing I could do something to ease it.

RACHEL

Walking to school this morning. So important to get out in the fresh air!

'Bye darling. Be careful, OK?'

Hannah struggled away. 'Mummy, I'll be late and get a sad face in my book.'

'OK. Off you go.' Anxiety making her shoulders rigid, Rachel watched Hannah stride across the school playground. Since everything happened, it had been harder and harder to let her out of her sight. Not least because, without Hannah's merry chatter, the thoughts in her head threatened to overwhelm her.

'Rachel!' Oh God. The last person she needed to see.

On the night of the incident, Hannah had gone to stay with her friend Jago Hewson-Taylor, a feral little boy whose mother Janine was the kind of person who'd bring over homemade loaves because she 'was at a loose end', so had spent the day baking. This on top of having four children and being active in the PTA and the board of governors and the local Neighbourhood Watch. Rachel had always felt that Janine's life was deliberately constructed to annoy her, from her neat stud earrings to her pouffey shoulder-length hair. She prayed Janine wouldn't ask any awkward questions – she wasn't ready to explain the disaster-zone her life had become. 'Hi, Janine. Just running off to ... '

'Did you get my message about the bake sale? We've all decided to do homemade things this year.'

Oh God. 'Sure, sure, no problem. I have to ... '

'Oh, and Charlie was wondering if Simon's OK?'

Rachel's heart swooped and dropped. 'Of course, why?'

'They were supposed to play squash last night, but Simon didn't show up. Charlie waited for twenty minutes!'

Oh God, oh God. 'I'm sorry, yes, Simon had to go away for work. He must have forgotten.'

Janine had a penetrating gaze, and Rachel realised how difficult it was going to be to hide what had happened. 'A last-minute thing?'

'That's right. Things are just crazy at his office.' Another lie, another step on the road to deception, crime, the dark side. 'I'm sorry, Janine, I have to run.' She fled.

Back home, Rachel stared again at the piece of paper Hannah had found. It was just a letter. One page of printed A4, with the logo of Simon's company, Braithwaite Capital, at the top. She'd never been entirely sure what they did – stockbroking of some kind, moving virtual money around into different pots. What did it mean? From what she could gather – the second page of it was missing – Simon would not be receiving his end-of-year bonus at work. Was it just him, or everyone at the firm? Were they broke now? Would they have to take Hannah out of school? What if she went to the supermarket and her debit card stopped working? So many years since she'd said those particular prayers, to the gods of the overdraft, that magic would happen and the card machine make a happy beep of relief, otherwise you wouldn't eat that night. She'd almost forgotten that some people lived their whole lives that way, shielded for years by her own good job, then Simon's stratospheric one, by living in a four-bedroom detached house with a garage and Jacuzzi setting on the bathtub. Now the old whispered worries were back – *Rachel, you got complacent. The money's gone. There'll be a knock on the door and it's someone coming to take the TV . . .*

The letter said *as discussed.* The whole firm could have been in trouble, which would explain all the late nights, the phone calls Simon shut himself away in the bathroom to take, emerging with his hair sticking up from where he'd run his hands through it. Why hadn't she asked him, *How's work? How are our finances?* Why had she got into the habit of not listening when he talked about his job, not sitting him down and demanding the truth? Not that he was ever home, these days. Some nights she would fall asleep and wake up without him there, and only know he'd been home by the vague impression in the mattress beside her, now turned cold. How stupid could you get, to rely entirely on another person for all your income, and not just that, to feed your child? To take it for granted that the cash would just keep coming, even though she knew better than anyone it didn't work that way? Idiot. When she thought about how foolish she'd been, she wanted to bash her head off the wall. Except even the paint had cost £75 a tin.

It hadn't always been like this. Once, Rachel was a very different person. Independent, solvent, cynical about marriage. The first time she met Simon, she'd felt like a child going downstairs on Christmas morning. But a child of, say, eight, who might have started to hear rumours from friends that Santa wasn't real. That maybe everything was a lie. Only to wake before dawn and run downstairs and see the presents, the sooty footprints on the hearth, the reindeers' carrots nibbled on, and know that it was all true after all. That magic was real.

When Rachel met Simon, she was thirty-two and had all but given up on finding the guy. Not the 'one' – she was long past believing in the one. But 'a' one, who would make her feel the way songs and films suggested was possible. She met him on a summer's day, which back then, a decade ago, still felt like a gift, but a conditional one that might disappear at any moment. Rachel had woken up in her own lovely, neat flat – cleaned by her cleaner, dirtied by no one but herself. She'd seen the sun on her expensive shutter blinds and realised that she had to make the most of the day. Some hurried texting and calling then ensued, and she managed to whip up a small group of friends to go to a beer garden. Putting together the vision in her head, laughing with friends over a Pimm's, big sunglasses on. Rachel had noticed that she increasingly thought of her life in terms of how it would look on social media, and she didn't like it, but didn't know how to stop.

We have Dan's friend visiting, texted her friend Maura. *We'll bring him along.* Rachel had even felt a slight annoyance at this – a stranger might upset the carefully calibrated band of friends, and maybe get in the way of the laughing over Pimm's. But she quickly put that aside, mocked herself for being such a control freak, and dressed in a striped yellow and white dress with a wide-brimmed hat, her sunglasses, white wedge sandals. As she set off to the pub, which was within walking distance of her flat in Angel, she felt at peace with the world. A woman in her thirties, with a job in PR that involved owning pretty dresses and drinking champagne and one time meeting Liam Neeson, as well as a nice flat, lovely friends, great accessories and over a thousand Facebook friends who would see what a nice time she was having. It was one of those days when heat overcomes the habitual mutual distrust of Londoners, and people were smiling at each other, saying hello, everything opening and blossoming like a flower. A policeman tipped his hat to her as she passed. Rachel could remember feeling intensely happy during that short walk.

She saw him before she knew who he was, and understood with a deep certainty that this was Dan's friend, and within two seconds her brain was berating her for not having met him before. He was at the bar, ordering a round of beers and white wine, clutching crisp packets in his strong even teeth. His white shirt was rolled up to show tanned, gold-flecked arms and an expensive watch. His dark hair flopped over his forehead. And when he turned to look at her, the green of his eyes stopped her in her tracks, and she dropped her impractical sunhat to the floor. Never taking his eyes off her, he set down the drinks and snacks, bent to lift it.

'Thank you,' she stammered. 'I'm Rachel.'

'I know,' was all he said, and that was it, she'd found a harbour from the storms of dating in London. And there was a wedding a year later, with flowers tied to rustic pews and a ceilidh and a cake made of cheese, and then Hannah, just eighteen months after that, and their jobs both went well, money practically being flung at them by eager bosses, and they bought first one lovely house, then a bigger lovely one, and life was good. It was Instagram Pinterest MySpace-profile-pic good, except in real life.

Until it wasn't. Until she learned that the storm hadn't passed, it had turned around and was heading right for her, only this time she'd taken off her lifejacket, and this time Hannah was in the boat with her too. The past two years of moving further and further apart. Not laying eyes on him sometimes from one end of the week to another. A single mother, virtually. And now Simon might be in trouble at work.

The phone was ringing. Rachel snapped back to the present, feeling the same crash of alarm as she did when she woke up in the morning. It could be him. It could be the police. It could be the FBI, explaining that her husband was a secret agent, although what would the FBI be doing in England? She answered, hearing the shake in her voice. 'Hello?' Nothing. She could hear someone breathing. 'Hello, who is this?'

It went dead. With shaking hands, she hit 1471 – number withheld. She told herself to calm down, be sensible. It was nothing. Just a wrong number, probably, or a sales call from overseas that hadn't connected, but it shook her, on top of the letter. She headed into the kitchen, telling herself she needed wine. People were asking questions. She couldn't stay like this for ever, suspended in inaction. She had to do something. Starting with ringing the number she'd seen on Simon's phone that night. She found herself standing in front of the bread bin, shoving slice after slice into her mouth, barely bothered to put the butter on first. *Hashtag carb attack! Hashtag off the wagon!*

Silently, she told her old self to shut up.

EVE

'Hello, Eve.'

'Hi, Adam. How are you?' I'd just seen him helping Mrs Munroe, patiently explaining the plot of a *Murder, She Wrote* episode that was on TV. *No, he did it. Yes, him with the hat!* Now, he had followed me into the front hallway where I was putting on my coat.

He forced a smile. 'Oh, not so bad. Everyone here is so nice. Even though I can't remember World War Two or even the sixties, they're still kind. It's hard to make friends when you can't remember who you are.'

I wanted to tell him the opposite was true as well. 'I'm sorry it's so hard for you.' It was a setback that my usual memory techniques had so far yielded nothing, but I was determined to keep trying. 'Well, I'll see you later.'

I was buttoning my coat, and had started to walk to the front door, but he followed me, as if we were attached by a small piece of string. 'Where are you going?'

'I have an ... errand. A mission.'

He seemed to perk up at this. 'Like in *Columbo*!' They show pretty much nothing but old-time detective series on the TV in the rec room, so I suppose it's really Sunnyside's fault that the residents see mysteries everywhere. 'Can I come with you, please, Eve? It's just – I don't want to be ungrateful, everyone is so kind here, but they're a little ... older than me?'

'Well, yes.' By about fifty years, in some cases.

'I'd just love to speak to someone who can remember what I said two minutes ago. I mean, who am I to talk? I don't even know my own name. But ... you get it?' I knew what he meant. Unlike most of the residents, Adam was perfectly lucid, he just couldn't remember anything before being found running down the motorway. I thought about it. Usually I worked alone, and I didn't know how I felt about someone watching me do my memory techniques. He might find me too weird. On the other hand, he was currently dressed in what I was pretty sure was a woman's blouse from the Death Bin, so he wasn't in a position to judge.

Before Sunnyside, Mrs Gillespie had lived in a small and poky flat in a tower block in the Elephant and Castle area of London. Adam and I took the train there, and then a bus from the train station. The area seemed to be in the process of being ripped up and put back together. Adam stared at everything, as if searching through his memory banks. 'What is this place?'

I told him.

'Why Elephant?'

'It was the name of an inn that used to be near there, which might have come from the phrase the Infanta of Castille – you know, Catherine of Aragon when she came to marry Prince Arthur, Henry VIII's older brother who died.' I reeled it off, unthinking, and found him staring at me. My stomach sank. I had forgotten Theresa's number-one rule – *just pretend to be normal, Eve, for the love of God.*

But Adam looked impressed. 'That's amazing! I know I'm not a good example, because I can't remember anything, but can people normally do that, just pull up facts and figures out of their brains?'

'Well – no. My memory is a bit – it sort of works better than most people's.' I blushed. I had hoped to keep this under wraps for a bit longer.

'Why is that?'

I squirmed as we got off the bus, struggling down the stairs. 'I don't know. I think it started when I was little. Something happened. A thing – a bad thing. After that I could remember everything.' Before that day, I couldn't remember much, despite years of trying. Just flashes of childhood things – birthdays, a trip to the zoo. As far as I know, this is how everyone else's memory is all the time.

'Everything?' said Adam, sounding awed.

'Yes.' It was the truth, although it sounded like an exaggeration. 'I remember everything that's happened since I was six.'

'You can just – pull up past days, whenever you like? What you had for breakfast, what you watched on TV?'

'If I concentrate.' But it was more than that. It wasn't just a fun party game where you could tell people what you ate for dinner on 27 March 1999 (nothing, as it happens), it was also remembering the look on people's faces when they shouted at you, it was hearing again the exact words they used when they told you why you weren't wanted. It was feeling pain, as if it was happening to you all over again. It was the waxy sheen on the face of someone dead. It was broken glass in your hair, the sound of someone screaming. I pushed the thoughts away before the memories could break through the hole in the dam, flooding me like an abandoned village. 'Come on, help me find this building.'

Elephant and Castle was quite confusing, with lots of tunnels going under the road that smelled like the rec room (wee, mostly). Adam trotted along beside me, helpfully peering at all the signs, and eventually we found the block Mrs Gillespie had lived in. I wondered why her son, who seemed quite rich, hadn't moved her to somewhere nicer. The tower block looked like it was going to close down soon because of all the redevelopment, and lots of the windows were boarded up. Some kids sat on the steps, their hoods up.

We went up in the lift (more rec-room smell) and found the right number for the flat. I didn't even have to check the paper I'd written it down on. I'd seen it once, so that meant it was lodged in my brain for ever. It's kind of exhausting sometimes. I think of my brain as a huge warehouse full of facts, only sometimes it takes a while to rifle through it. You need a good filing system to stay on top of things, as I always try to tell Magda about the office and she always ignores in favour of keeping resident notes in piles like 'annoying relatives', 'incontinence sufferers', 'involuntary flashers', etc.

I used the little silver key I'd got from James Gillespie's friend, a nice man called Steve with a shaved head and muscles, who'd dropped it off at the home. It hung on a keyring of a little black cat. I wondered about that. Who had chosen it and why? Where had it come from? A Christmas present from James to his mum, which she'd treasured all these years? I tried to stop myself going off down the rabbit holes of the memories of every little object I come across. We were here to find something specific. I just didn't know what it was yet.

Inside the flat smelled musty, like old talc and sweat. Adam wrinkled up his nose. 'This reminds me of . . . Oh.' He stood in the hallway, frowning. 'I don't know what it reminds me of.'

Smell is the most powerful way to trigger memory, they say.

It happens to me a lot. I'll catch a whiff of, say, peppermint, and my brain-filers will run through the stacks to find the memory of being four and offered a Polo by my lovely granddad, who died the following year, more's the pity. 'Come on,' I said briskly, trying to stop the tidal wave of memories. 'Let's have a look for anything that mentions a Graham.'

I'd done this kind of work before, of course – usually the residents' children are too busy and stressed to look for items themselves, and they think I seem trustworthy so they often let me have a rummage in their houses. I've poked about in so many old people's bedrooms that I can sometimes smell Anaïs Anaïs in my sleep. There are certain places people keep things – underwear drawers, for example, or in old biscuit tins under the bed. I instructed Adam to look for tins of Family Circle or Peek Freans, while I hunted in Mrs G's unmentionables drawer, as Magda calls them. Her small bedroom was sad somehow. A single bed, a blue striped duvet pulled flat, a book left on the nightstand. A Catherine Cookson. I wondered had she finished reading it, if she had forgotten the story already.

'Find anything?' Adam's voice was louder and nearer than I expected, and I jumped.

'Not yet! You?'

'There's a biscuit tin, just like you said! Gosh, you are good.'

I couldn't help but feel a small tinge of pride at that.

The first foster home was all right, though the washing powder they used smelled funny. Not like home. The bedspread was blue stripes, like for a boy, and I had to share my room with two other girls – Natalie aged eight, who pinched me when no one was looking, and Jenny, the foster parents' own daughter.

She was eleven and hated having us there. I didn't really blame her. The first night Theresa brought me there, Anne, the foster mum, took me to meet the other girls. She said, *This is Eve, her mummy and daddy died, so we have to be nice to her.* I didn't know how to explain that this wasn't true. Not entirely, anyway.

EVE

Adam and I sat at Mrs Gillespie's little melamine table to open the tin. I had a strange moment of imagining we lived together. Of course, we'd decorate the flat more nicely than this. Some of those little wooden signs that say things like Bless This Mess, or Prosecco Time! Jars of herbs and spices. A pinny that Adam would wear as he cooked me dinner. I caught myself – why was I thinking like this? I already knew that wasn't an option for someone like me. Perhaps because Adam was so restful to be around – a blank slate, with no memories of his own to overwhelm me. He didn't know the facts of his life, so I couldn't know them either.

'Are we waiting for a reason?' Adam's voice was hushed and respectful.

'Er, no.' The lid had once been sealed with old, yellowed Sellotape, like the skin on the bottom of feet, but it had been broken at some point. Inside were what I'd expected – black-and-white photographs. I recognised a young Mrs Gillespie, wearing a print dress, with her hair in a silk scarf. She was beautiful, her dark eyes snapping like they still did. The pictures helpfully had writing on the back, which was something people did in the olden days and which I greatly appreciated. But they all said *Elsie and Arthur* or *Elsie and Jimmy* (that must be James, since Mrs G only had one child) or *Elsie, Jimmy and Arthur.* Arthur looked like a stiff, stuffy man, with a bristling moustache. In every picture, even one on the beach, he wore a suit and tie. There was no mention of a Graham anywhere.

'No luck?' said Adam. He was leaning very close to me, his tanned hand on the table, flecked with golden hairs. I wondered when he'd been in the sun. What was it like, to have no idea who you were, where you'd been, what you'd done? Not for the first time, I suspected it might be peaceful. My brain felt so full sometimes, as heavy as a hundred filing cabinets.

'Not yet. But we won't give up so easily.'

We did a sweep of the whole flat and found little of interest. Some of James's old toy soldiers, a very old packet of Dunhills hidden on top of a wardrobe, and in the unmentionables drawer, a small box of jewellery. That was also a good place to look for clues, but I couldn't see anything except for costume stuff – a tourist pin from Margate, a Miraculous Medal, a copper bracelet and a strange collar thing with rhinestones. Unless that was a clue Mrs G had secretly been part of the BDSM scene and Graham was her 'dom'. I'd seen stranger things (at least 20 per cent of the population is into BDSM, rising to 36 per cent in America, unsurprisingly). When you don't know what's in your memory any more, you don't know how to hide your secrets. Things you've kept locked up for fifty years suddenly pour out, much to the embarrassment of the families.

'I'm sorry, Eve. We didn't find anything.' Adam looked disappointed.

'That's OK. It's not easy – if it was, everyone would do it.' I'd heard that line on a detective show once. 'We just have to think sideways. If we take some of these items back with us, maybe it will trigger Mrs Gillespie's memory and she'll know who Graham is.'

'Would that work for me too?'

'It might. But we don't know where you live to go through your house.' And no one had reported him missing still, and that was strange. Why? Was there some conspiracy? Was Adam a spy, living deep undercover? Had he been on holiday, or somehow wandered on to a train and ended up in Bishopsdean, so people were looking for him in the wrong place? But why then did he have no shoes on? It didn't make sense.

I saw that he was looking sad, and had collapsed down on to Mrs G's old chintzy sofa. 'Are you OK? Do you have another headache?' They'd said his head injury might hurt from time to time.

He ran his hands over his face. 'I don't know. I'm trying to be positive, but all I can think is I must have things like this somewhere – photographs, knick-knacks – a history. I must have a life. Why can't I remember it?'

'You will,' I said, hoping I sounded more confident than I felt. His was indeed one of the toughest cases I'd ever come across.

'I don't know. It's been over a week now and there's just nothing. Like someone . . . clicked and deleted all my memory files.'

Hadn't I wished for that, over the years? That I could simply delete the bad memories, pretend they'd never happened? Something made me put my hand out, hesitantly, and touch his shoulder. Under the borrowed shirt it was solid and warm, the shape of the bone curving under my fingers. 'I promise I'll do everything I can to help.'

He smiled sadly. 'I know you will. Thank you.'

After that, we headed back to the home. In an effort to bring Mrs G back to herself, the objects we had selected were the packet of cigarettes (empty, as Sunnyside was a Strictly No-Smoking environment); a snow globe with a miniature Eiffel

Tower inside it; a toy soldier, the paint on his wooden face almost worn away and some photos from the biscuit tin. One was of Mrs G holding a baby James in a garden in the sun, smiling and squinting, dated 1965, surrounded by a group of female friends (not Graham, obviously, but they might know who he was). These small objects were all we had to recover her memories and let her live out her final days without being robbed of the only thing we can really take out of the world. The people we remember, and the people who remember us.

RACHEL

Mysterious number! Shall I call it, Instagram??

Rachel stared at the phone number, the one she'd seen pop up on Simon's phone screen that night and scribbled down on the edge of the local paper, thinking she might need it. Proof, maybe, that she wasn't going mad. That there had been a text, and a girl, and surely that was connected to the fact Simon was now missing.

What did it mean anyway, missing? Just because one person didn't know where they were, it didn't mean they were lost or hurt. And hadn't she often had no idea where Simon was? All those nights sitting alone in front of Netflix, refilling her wine glass in dribs and drabs, telling herself it was just one, then just two, then just a tiny top-up, then might as well just finish off the bottle. *Hashtag rude not to. Hashtag Mummy's little helper.* He was 'at work', but was he really in the office until ten every night? Or he was 'with clients', which explained why he slipped into bed smelling of beer, and sometimes, cheap perfume. And there was nothing she could do about it. Withhold sex? They hadn't done that in months anyway. Nag constantly? He'd only stay out longer. Tell him to leave? He was the one with the money, and besides, who would she be then? A single mother. A woman in her forties with no husband and no job, with a child at a very expensive private school. The struts of her life would collapse around her ears, and the thought was utterly terrifying. So she'd done nothing.

Until that day. Rachel had picked Hannah up from school, but she'd had to park up the street from their house, as someone was blocking her drive. She'd thought it was the people next door, who had suddenly bought 'run-arounds' for each of their teenage children, who were blocking the road. She'd been fuming about it as she walked down the street, Hannah chattering beside her about the class hamster (there was nothing like parking to throw middle-class English people into murderous rages). As she'd approached the house, she'd seen that the door was open. For a second she'd panicked – she'd forgotten to lock it! But no, Simon was there on the front step, and it was his car in the drive, along with an unfamiliar Mini. He was never home during the day. And with him was a young woman, no more than twenty-five, with bouncy blonde hair and long legs in a shift dress. Rachel pulled Hannah up short.

As Hannah was distracted, Rachel saw the woman climb into the Mini – folding her long legs away – and Simon leaning in to say goodbye. Smiling. She hadn't seen him smile like that in years. As soon as the woman sped off, he got back into his own car and left too. She'd planned to confront him about it that night. But then everything else had happened.

So wasn't the most likely thing that Simon was with *her*? That Rachel had been ghosted by her own husband, like a teenager dumped after going too far behind the bike sheds? That might be true, except for Hannah. He loved Hannah, he really did, even if he wasn't home very much. He brought her a present from every trip, usually some form of Lego to add to her already cupboard-busting collection. He made her breakfast before he left for work, even if she wasn't up yet, leaving her cereal in the bowl ready for milk, with a note and a drawing, or

69

pancakes kept warm under tinfoil. She was fairly sure Hannah was why he'd not left her already. He wouldn't have just gone, not without a word. Would he? She had to find out.

It was time. Hannah was safely at school, would not overhear whatever Rachel and this girl might have to say to each other. And so, pulling together all that mother-bear courage you were supposed to develop once a baby had come thundering past your perineum, she went to the landline and dialled. Maybe the girl would answer if it was a strange number. Or maybe she wouldn't. Rachel remembered being shocked when a temporary receptionist at work, a 'millennial' in her twenties, had fished her ringing phone from her bag, looking at it with curiosity, as if it hadn't been designed for that function, and simply hit reject.

'What if it's important?' Rachel had said.

The girl had shrugged. 'They'll find me.' Rachel had felt a thousand years old. This girl, Simon's girl, she was a millennial too. You heard of it, twenty-something women with forty-something men, and the unfairness, the sheer biological imbalance of it, made Rachel want to cry and stamp her feet. It was 2018. It wasn't supposed to be like this any more!

Shaking, she listened to it ring. No answer. Relief began to creep in. Maybe, as Simon had claimed that night, it was all nothing, she had the wrong end of the stick. Of course, he hadn't much time to explain himself before … the incident. Thinking about that made her feel sick.

She was about to hang up when the line clicked, and Rachel's heart stopped.

'Hello?' A woman's voice.

She forgot for a second how to speak. 'Hello.'

'Who is this, please?'

'Um – my name is Rachel. I – I got your number from Simon's phone. I'm his wife.' This was the point where the girl would hang up, Rachel was sure. She should have lied about who she was. This was stupid. Of course the girl wouldn't want to talk to her, why on earth would she?

But she didn't hang up.

The girl on the other end of the phone said, 'Mrs Kempner—'

'It's just Rachel.'

'Right. I don't think we should be talking about this over the phone.'

'What's your name?' Amazing to think she didn't even know! He wouldn't tell her when she asked. She'd imagined something sexy and young like Zoe or Chloe. This girl had been in her house, doing God knows what with her husband.

The girl paused. 'Jess.' *Jess.* That was a young name, wasn't it? Just how young was she?

'I saw you at the house, you know.' Her voice wavered. 'And I saw your message.'

'What?'

'On his phone, from you. About – whether he was going to tell me or not.' The image flashed through her mind again, forcing bile into her throat. In the kitchen that night, the dish-washer open ready to be stacked. Noticing that Simon had left his phone on the side, picking it up when it buzzed. Had she known, even then? Had a prick of suspicion caused her to glance at it? There was a message from an unknown number up on the screen, asking, *Have you told her yet?*

And then Simon had come back in, saying, 'Have you seen my . . . ', trailing off as he saw her with the phone in her hand,

71

and suddenly all the rage of the past ten years had come up in her, and she'd screamed, and . . .

She swallowed. She wasn't ready to relive that memory yet.

'It isn't what you think, Rachel. But I can't tell you more. Now I'm sorry, but I have to get off the phone.'

'But wait! What's going on?'

'You should ask Simon. It's up to him to tell you.'

'But I can't!' Too late, the girl – *Jess* – had hung up. She'd said to ask Simon. Meaning he wasn't with her? Meaning his girlfriend also had no idea where he was?

EVE

Mrs Gillespie stared intently at the objects I'd put in front of her on a cushioned tray (very useful, I have one myself for crosswords). 'What is this muck?'

'It's from your house, Mrs G.'

'And what were you doing in my house? ROBBING it, no doubt!'

'I got the key from Jimmy.'

Her brow wrinkled. 'Jimmy?'

Oh dear. It always hurt my stomach when the residents started to forget their children. It was so cruel somehow. 'Your son, Mrs G.'

She gave a stare that was no less terrifying for being framed by white eyebrows and huge clear-framed glasses. 'I know the name of my son, girl! He's not been Jimmy for years. Insisted on James as soon as he went to big school, didn't he?'

'OK, James then. I found a few of these things and I thought they might spark a memory. Of where to find Graham, perhaps.'

'How will a load of old junk help find my Graham?' But she looked at the objects all the same, begrudgingly. She sifted through the photos, then the cigarette packet, the snow globe, the toy soldier. That last one she picked up in her arthritic hand. 'That was his. James's. When he was ever so little.'

'Do you speak to him much, Mrs G?'

She set it down again, its worn face turned to the tray. 'Never

73

comes near me. Always too busy. And the time difference is too hard, he says.'

I made a mental note to see if I could get her on Skype. 'And none of these people are Graham?' I fanned out the photos I'd found, double-checking.

She looked at me like I was crazy. 'Of course not! That's my brother. Our Eric.' She touched the picture lightly, a young man in a suit and boater, with a sweet open face. 'He were killed in the war, bless him. I can hardly recall him now. Isn't that funny? All those years we spent every minute together, and now he's just . . . in the wind.'

'And your dad was Eric too.'

'Aye. Miners' lung got him.' God, things were grim in the past.

'Who are these people, Mrs G?' I showed her the picture of her with James as a baby, smiling in the group of women. Three of them plus her, in a garden somewhere, on a long-gone summer's day.

She peered at it. 'Oh! It's my pals from nursing school. Betty, Janet and Cathy.'

My heart beat faster. This could be a breakthrough! 'You don't remember their surnames?'

Her eyes went glassy, but then she dredged it up from the depths of her memory. 'Janet were wed at the time. Janet Marks, she was. And Betty, she died in 1975. Cancer. Cathy – she never wed. Cathy Gilmore.'

I was scribbling the names down excitedly. These women might know who Graham was. Maybe a friend or a cousin or . . . I tried to think how to say it delicately. 'Was Graham someone you knew before Mr Gillespie – before you met Arthur?'

74

'Don't be daft. I knew Arthur Gillespie since I were a lass of five. Next-door neighbours, we were.'

'This was in Leeds? Did you ever move away, do something else for a few years? You might have been separated?'

She nodded. 'Went off nursing for a while.'

I was finally getting somewhere! 'Great, so maybe, Mrs G, could you possibly have met Graham then?' That was it, I was sure. A long-lost love. No pictures of them together because maybe she'd already been engaged to Arthur. A forbidden memory, a long-ago fling. Perhaps she hadn't spoken his name out loud for sixty years, only to have it uncovered by the archaeology of dementia.

Mrs Gillespie frowned, and snapped her head around, and I could see that I'd lost her, that she'd become untethered in time again. 'What's happening?' She peered at the objects on her tray as if she'd never seen them before. 'Load of old rubbish. Get this away.' With one shaky hand she swept them to the floor. 'And I still don't have chocolate on my biscuit! I'm going to get my son, he'll call the police on you, girl! The POLICE, I tell you.'

I sighed and bent down to rescue the items. The little toy soldier, weak with age, had bashed his hat against the side of her chair and chipped a little more of the paint away. I was sure James wouldn't remember playing with these – he probably played with very expensive toys nowadays – and Mrs Gillespie didn't really remember either. That part of her brain was gone, crumbling into the sea like those houses built on cliffs. So what was the point in keeping the soldier, caring for it? What was the point of trying to help, when Mrs G was so grumpy and confused and angry? All the same, I found I couldn't stop, and slipped the soldier into my pocket to add to the Museum later on.

Eve, you can't take all that rubbish with you, said Theresa, looking at my bulging suitcase. It was a small plastic one from the market, with a picture on it that was meant to be Beauty and the Beast, but where the Beast looked like an angry cat.

It's my toys! I had packed only my best things, the raggedy doll with the soft ribbon on her dress, the teddy bear with one eye, the children's encyclopaedia with all the important information about everything from Egyptian mummies to dinosaurs. And of course, the last ever Lego house, though at the time I didn't know it was the last. The thought of being without my things, leaving behind these worn and cheap objects, made me panic. My nana in Ireland had died suddenly, solving the question of whether or not I was going to live with her. Instead, I was going into something called foster care, with people I had never met. Theresa was taking me there.

There won't be space, Eve. I'm sorry.

Holding back tears, I got down and started unpacking my case. They still hadn't let me see Daddy. They wouldn't tell me, but I knew something terrible must have happened to him too.

EVE

The next day, Julie and I were loading sheets into Sunnyside's huge washing machine, the one I could sleep inside (but I wouldn't because at least one child dies this way every year), when Magda came in. Today was a three-pen hair day, I could see. 'Eve,' she said, before immediately getting distracted. 'Is that the premium washing powder?'

'Um, I don't know. I just used what was here.'

Magda pursed her lips. 'Do they think I'm made of money? We should switch back to the cheaper brand.'

'But remember Mrs Willis had that problem with allergies, and we had to change the dressings on her legs all the time?'

'Oh dear, you're right. Maybe we need the even better kind? That Gwyneth sells posh washing powder, hypo-allergiwhatsit.' Typical Magda, switching from frugal to even more generous in a heartbeat.

'I think this is fine,' I said, before she spent the entire annual budget on Goop (valued at $250 million, did you know?). 'What did you want me for?'

'Oh yes. It was about our new resident.'

My heart began to beat and I leaned over to shove some sheets into the washer. I use gloves for this, of course – you wouldn't want to know what's on some of them. But despite that I do enjoy it as a task, especially when they come out all clean and sweet-smelling. I wished I could do that with some of my memories, spin them in a gigantic washer until they were fresh and nice and white again. 'What about him?'

'How's he getting on? You've been spending time with him?'

'A bit. He's just – he's lonely, I think. Everyone here is so much older.' All the same, Adam had settled into Sunnyside surprisingly well. He was much in demand for lifting and moving things, changing the channel on the TV and reading aloud bits of the newspaper, seeing as he still had the use of his limbs, eyes and ears.

Julie, who'd been shamelessly listening in, said, 'You like him, dontcha, Eve?'

'No! Well, I mean, of course I *like* him. He's a nice person.'

She wagged a gloved finger at me. 'You gotta treat him mean to keep him keen. Don't keep running round after him like you are.'

I hid my hot face in the washer. 'It's not like that! He's a resident. I'm just helping him.'

'Not made any progress, though?' said Magda.

'These things take time,' I said vaguely, reaching for another sheet.

Sometimes, I forget how sharp Magda is under all that scattiness. She and Julie exchanged a significant look, but she didn't say anything more on the subject. Instead she said, 'The police are having no luck either – not a trace of him anywhere. They want him to go back to the neurologists, in case that helps. Same ones he was in with after they found him, in London. Will you take him?' Magda has always been very supportive of my memory detective work. She's seen how many of the residents have been able to remember things, and how happy it makes them at least for a while, even if we're fighting a losing battle against dementia. It's very hard to watch people come in here, year after year, and slowly shed bits of themselves, as if they are flaking away to nothing while we watch, helpless, with only tea and biscuits to stem their decline.

I looked down at the grubby sheets in my gloved hands and thought about spending another whole day with Adam, and I felt the way I used to as a kid when I woke up in the summer, no school, and saw a square of sunlight on the carpet through my thin curtains. Before everything that happened, in the time I have hardly any memory of, the time I would most wish to remember.

But then again, I'd have to go to hospital. That thought made my breath rattle in my lungs, and I wanted to lean against the washer for support. Magda, sharp as ever, spotted it. 'Someone else can do it, if you don't want to, lovie.'

'No, I'll go,' I said quickly. I would just deal with the hospital when I got there. It would be worth it, after all, to have a day with Adam. For investigative purposes, you understand.

Magda paused. 'There's another thing. You sometimes take the residents places, don't you, to try to help them – somewhere they used to go a lot, their old house, something like that?' It was one of my techniques, activating what's called location-specific memory.

'Yeah, but I don't know where Adam lives.'

'I was thinking of where he was found. If we brought him back there, it might trigger something, what do you think?'

'But . . . it was on the M25.'

'I know, lovie.' And I understood what she was saying, and I shrank back in myself.

Julie was nodding. 'Good idea, Mags. My Uncle John, right,

he went doolally and buried my mum's good pearl necklace in the garden, and he'd no idea where he put it till we took him back there and walked him round it.'

It wasn't much that Magda was asking of me. Go to a hospital, drive in a car. Not much for a normal person, anyway. If only I could forget, if only painful memories eventually faded, instead of staying with me for ever, pin-sharp as the day they happened.

'Don't you want to try everything to help him?' she prompted, and I knew she was right. I would have to do it.

'I won't be able to stop, you know,' warned Magda, as she barrelled down the M25. 'It's illegal, apparently, even if you've dropped your mascara on the floor. Trust me, I should know.'

I clung to the handle on the side of the door, wincing, doing my best to take measured breaths. In the back seat, I could see Adam grimacing as Magda veered from lane to lane. 'You put your mascara on while driving?' I panted.

'Well, not if I've dropped it I don't, no. This must be near the place.'

Studies have shown that we remember things better if we go back to the place where we formed the memories. It technically wasn't possible for Adam, since he'd been running down the central reservation of the M25 and, as Magda said, in an uncharacteristic moment of rule-following, we weren't allowed to stop there, but driving past it might help.

As we approached the place, I squinted all around me for clues on the featureless stretch of motorway. 'There's a service station not far off. Maybe you ran from there? Ring any bells – Little Chef, WH Smith?' (Did you know, the first ever Little Chef was in Reading?)

Adam shook his head. Magda had slowed to a crawl now, and the cars behind us were beeping violently. She didn't seem to hear them. 'If he got out of a car, how did it stop? Must have been at a junction, right? And it must have stopped, because he wasn't injured apart from his head.'

I thought about it. If you jumped from a moving car – on a motorway, at least – you would surely be killed or badly injured. Adam had the head injury, consistent with being hit by an object of some kind, but no damage to his legs or hands. Hands were what got most hurt when you fell – the residents were always covered in painful scrapes and cuts. Maybe Magda was right, he'd got out of a stopped car.

I scanned the road signs ahead. 'There's a junction there. Pull off!'

Magda took me at my word, swerving suddenly across three lanes – Adam shut his eyes and I saw my life flash before mine, and it was a lot, because I remember all of it – and swung the car off on to a slip road. It led to the service station I'd mentioned, and also to several smaller villages. I read out the names. 'Little Sudbury. Cherry Heath. Rawlington. Any of those ring bells?'

Adam frowned. 'Maybe. Say them again?'

I did what he asked, from memory of course, as Magda drove on past the service station. 'Anything?' Adam peered out at the landscape, a bland town outskirts with a huge Tesco, a recycling plant and some nondescript houses.

'I don't know. It looks like somewhere I've been, maybe.' His forehead was creased with effort. 'I'm sorry, Eve. I don't – there's maybe a tiny something but I can't remember. It looks like so many places, doesn't it?'

I didn't blame him – there was nothing here to remember,

nothing of any interest. 'We'll try something else,' I promised him, then was promptly thrown forward as Magda suddenly started reversing down the road, because she'd just remembered Tesco had an offer on Ben & Jerry's Cherry Garcia.

RACHEL

Me and this one on a spontaneous daytrip – hashtag seize the day!

'Mummy, when you said we could take it easy while Daddy's away, I thought you meant we'd go to Legoland or something. You said we could, remember?'

Had she actually agreed to it? Rachel couldn't afford to be absent-minded around Hannah, or before she knew it they'd be on their way to buy a pedigree puppy or give all her designer shoes away to a charity for saving tree-frogs.

'We can talk about that later. I just need to pop in somewhere, OK?'

In the back of the car, from her child seat, Hannah stared out at her, mutinous. Today Rachel had dressed her in a striped Breton top and jeans, her curly hair haloed around her head. Rachel's heart ached. So many things she had done to keep her one child safe – private school, car seats, immunisations, yogurts that claimed to boost gut flora – and all of it would be lost, swilled down the sink like dishwater, through the actions of one crazy second. *Rachel – don't.* The look on his face changing from weary hostility, defensiveness, to actual fear. The incident. She pushed the thought away – just an accident, surely not that bad, not the reason he'd been missing for over a week now.

'Where are you going anyway? This isn't a place we go.' Hannah had her arms folded, looking out at the parade of downmarket shops they were parked near, unimpressed.

'It is now. I just have to check something.'

'You aren't supposed to leave me here. Someone could steal me or I could die in the hot car.'

'It's March, darling.' There was still unmelted snow on the ground. Hannah had a point, though – was Rachel going to take her in with her? What if there was a nasty scene? If this went on much longer, it would be Easter and she'd need child-care – she began to run through the school mums in her head, wondering who was the least awful.

'Who are you going to see?'

'No one you know.'

'I know everyone.'

Oh, the arrogance of seven-year-olds. As if Rachel had never had a life, as if those thirty-odd years before Hannah arrived were nothing. The worst part was she might be right. But Rachel couldn't say, *I'm going to confront your father's girlfriend.* 'Please, Han. We can get milkshakes after.'

The eyes narrowed even further. 'They're full of sugar.'

Rachel's temper flared. 'You're right. Full of sugar. Let's drive straight home instead and eat carrot sticks, OK?'

A pause. 'I didn't say I didn't *like* them.'

Rachel felt a pathetic moment of triumph. 'Come on. You can wait in the corridor or something.' Assuming there even was a corridor. She had no idea where she was going.

'I can't wait in a *corridor*!'

'Oh, Hannah, come on, you're seven years old, not Kim Kardashian.'

Nerves jangling, she turned her attention back to the matter in hand. After some extensive googling, she'd learned that the phone number on Simon's mobile had been linked to an address on this street, in a small parade of shops edging into Bishopsdean. She knew this kind of thing rarely ended well, but she had to try.

She walked along, Hannah beside her radiating disapproval. 'This place smells funny.'

'God, you're so *spoiled*.' It was out before she realised. Hannah pouted. Rachel pleaded. 'Come on, love, please. Five minutes.'

Number 47 was a hair salon, and on the other side was a fried chicken shop. The smell made Rachel both hungry and nauseous. Number 49 was a single door between the nail bar and a phone-unlocking shop. She almost let herself have a snide thought – *He's really slumming it* – and then she pushed the door, before she could lose her nerve. It opened without anyone speaking from the intercom, and she went up, her weak legs buckling on the dirty stairs. At the top might be Jess, the woman her husband was most likely sleeping with. Who he might have left her for.

She'd expected another door when she got up there, a flat maybe, but instead found a small reception area with chairs and out-of-date free magazines. A dying pot plant. 'Wait here, please,' she instructed Hannah, who scowled at the cheap padded seats like Maggie Smith in *Downton Abbey*. The rest of the room was taken up with three desks holding old computers. One was empty, and a middle-aged man sat at another, talking into the phone so quietly she could barely hear. 'No. I do see. Yes. No.' The address she'd found was an office. A sign on the wall said the company was called Wise Buy, and its logo appeared to be some kind of owl (tawny? Snowy? *Oh, shut up, Rachel, it doesn't matter*), but she couldn't tell what sort of business it was. Something like an estate agent, maybe, but not that.

At the other desk was a young woman, maybe twenty-five, with long blonde hair and lacquered nails. Her clothes were neat but cheap, from Jane Norman or Dorothy Perkins or some brand that would be too unforgiving on Rachel's forty-ish body. It was her – the girl Rachel had seen at her house. She had risen to her feet, in sky-high heels. 'Hello, can I help you? Are you Tim's four o'clock?' Tim was presumably the man on the phone.

'No – I'm looking for Jess.' Rachel kept her voice low, conscious of Hannah just metres away.

'I'm Jess.' A polite frown. 'What was it concerning?'

'I – I'm Rachel. We spoke on the phone. Simon's wife.' She felt so stupid saying it, like someone in a cheesy melodrama.

Understanding dawned, along with a little confusion and some slight annoyance. 'I see. Rachel, I'm sorry you came all this way, but I can't discuss client matters with anyone else. Even a spouse. It's the law, you see.' *Client.* This, coupled with the lack of visceral fear under the girl's heavy make-up, made Rachel suddenly understand that Simon had been telling the truth that night, that terrible night when she'd screamed at him – *Who is this?* – and he'd said, *No, no, it's not what you think.* She saw now that she had indeed failed to grasp the right end of the stick. So what was going on? Her eye was caught by a leaflet on a small coffee table beside Hannah, next to the dying pot plant. Equity release scheme. Remortgage products. A cold feeling began to creep its way up from the base of Rachel's spine.

EVE

I was making slow progress in my cases, though I had at least tracked down Mrs G's old friends, or at least found addresses for people with the same names, and sent off letters. A lot of older people aren't online, so this is the only way to contact them. I just had to hope it would yield some clue about Graham. Finding most people is easy – as well as social media, which people will happily fill with every secret detail of their lives, there's publicly accessible electoral records, marriage certificates, death certificates. If I didn't work here, I sometimes imagine I could help the police with missing persons cases. I felt they could use the help – they seemed nowhere near finding Adam's identity, and the last time Raheem came round, he only had time to stuff four of Julie's homemade granola bars into his uniform pocket then rush off, muttering something about a murder case over in Ramsgate. I suppose that had to take precedence over a found person we couldn't identify, who nobody seemed to be missing, but all the same, Adam couldn't stay here for ever. Could he?

'Take a good look,' I urged.

Adam squinted hard at the cheap, already leaking pen he'd had in his pocket when he was found. I had done my best to find the logo on it, a sort of vaguely owl-shaped bird, but since I couldn't Google-image search, nothing came up, and there was no text printed on it, which I found odd. He shook his head. 'I'm sorry. It does look vaguely familiar, but without the words . . . it's like a pub quiz clue or something.' He rubbed his temples, as if it was bringing on a headache.

I sighed, putting the pen away. We were out the back of Sunnyside, on 'the terrace', as Magda calls it. In the brochure they'd made it look like the kind of place you might sip lemonade under striped umbrellas while laughing about your yacht, but in March, this particular endless cold March, everything in the flower beds was brown and dead and the pigeons who lived in the plane trees (Latin name *Platanus x hispanica*) had spattered the flagstones with white poop. Inside, in the rec room, I could see Anthony handing out the mid-morning biscuits. I hoped Mrs G would at least get one with chocolate on, otherwise there would be uproar.

Adam and I sat at a picnic bench, shivering against the cold. 'Eve,' he said hesitantly. 'Earlier in the car – you didn't like it, did you?'

I dipped my head. 'When I was younger I . . . there was an accident. I try not to go in cars if I can.' I had never learned to drive, pretending I cared about the environment too much, and I get the bus everywhere instead of cabs.

Adam hadn't finished asking questions. 'Why do you live here, Eve? You're young. You're . . . ' He waved a hand at me. 'You're pretty.'

Immediately, a full-body blush ran through me and I couldn't look at him.

'I just meant . . . do you like it here? You don't want to . . . get out and about more?' So even the man with the brain injury (probably) had noticed I rarely left Sunnyside.

'I get out,' I said defensively. 'I go into town.'

'On errands. For other people.'

I was very uncomfortable now. I wanted to tell him I had all kinds of exciting hobbies, but watching quiz shows and maintaining the Museum probably didn't count as such. Besides, I wasn't ready to tell anyone about the Museum. 'I'm fine, Adam. I like it here.' How could I explain that I wasn't like other people? I couldn't just go out and meet someone, make friends, fall in love – I wasn't *normal*.

'Doesn't it make you sad, though? One of the residents – Mr Chu – he thought I was his son earlier.' That didn't make any sense, because Mr Chu's son is Chinese, but dementia is rarely logical. 'He was – he cried. Asked why I didn't visit.' Oh dear. I knew for a fact Brian Chu had visited just last week, along with his wife and daughter Lily (seventeen, has a tragus piercing, plays tuba in a marching band). 'It's just so hard to see them, all these people ... ' He waved a hand towards the rec room. 'The way they go downhill, day by day. How can you stand it?'

'I just ... try to help them, as best I can.' And in truth, I sometimes envied them, in a horrible, shameful way. As terrible and frightening as dementia was, at least they had also lost the bad memories of their past, the pain and suffering, the dark days. I could never do that. 'It happens to so many people, there's no point in not facing it. None of us knows if or when it'll be us.'

Adam was nodding sadly. 'I guess I'm getting a taste of it early. Eve, do you think I'll ever remember who I am?'

'I hope so. We could try something else, if you're up for it?'

'What's your idea?' His eyes lit up with hope. It was still alive in him, despite each day that went by without his memory coming back.

I took the striped pebble from the little plastic bag I kept the five pocket objects in. 'Do you trust me?'

Reconstruction can be a good tool to help people remember. We now know that memory isn't stored in just one place in the brain, because there's a thing called procedural memory, the memory of how to do tasks and processes, that isn't affected by dementia. This explained why Adam still knew how to tie his laces and how Parliament worked, even though he didn't know his own name.

I felt a bit silly, but visualisation had worked before, like when Mr Maginty couldn't remember the name of his childhood dog. We'd pretended we were calling the dog in, and suddenly this frail old man, sitting in a wheelchair in the garden, had yelled out, 'Patch! Dinner!' and held out his shaking hands as if expecting a long-dead collie to come running up and lick them. (Lassie was a type of collie too, did you know?)

'Close your eyes,' I said to Adam, and when he did, I took the chance to gaze at him for a second. He was growing a proper beard now, silver and black, and his eyelashes cast long shadows on his cheeks. They were also filling out, as Julie stuffed him daily with something like five times the recommended calorie intake. 'Imagine the moment you found this pebble. Probably you bent down. Picked it up off the ground. A park, maybe, or a beach? Can you hear anything?'

For a while he said nothing, and I was sure it wouldn't work. Then: 'Waves,' he muttered. 'Yes, I remember waves. I remember! They were crashing, so loud. I was cold. And I was feeling . . . afraid. Guilty.' He opened his eyes, frowning. 'I think I did something bad, Eve.'

My heart was hammering. 'But this is good! The first memory

you've had!' He still looked sad. 'Hey, I'm sure you didn't really do something bad. You couldn't.'

'But I feel it. Here.' He put a hand on his chest, as if he had heartburn. 'Eve, I'm afraid. What if I find out who I am and it's not good? The police said it was strange I had no ID or phone on me; that no one's come to look for me yet. What if I'm wrapped up in something dodgy?'

I took Adam's hand again and squeezed his cold fingers. 'What's the alternative? You can't stay here for ever. You're young. You must have a life out there.' As I said it, I forced myself to face the facts I already knew – a man his age, with a woman's ring in his pocket, was likely married or in a relationship. He wasn't mine to keep here, as much as I'd started to rely on his presence, to look forward to coming into the rec room in the morning and seeing his face. 'Come on, Adam. Help me find your life for you.' Though I knew that, as soon as I did, he'd likely be gone from mine.

'Isn't it beautiful! I mean, look at it!'

'I know, it's nice, but maybe we should sit down now?'

Adam was glued to the window as the train went into London Bridge, goggling at the sweep of the city in front of us. I suppose it was nice, the skyscrapers sticking up in their distinctive shapes – I liked The Gherkin best, it was round and comfortable somehow – the pink-tipped clouds on the horizon, the churches and buildings and the river glinting grey in the distance. For me it was always overwhelming, coming into the city. Every street, every corner, it was overlaid with memories like a dance-floor stamped with feet. Not just my own memories. Think of the history somewhere like the riverbank – literally millions of people have passed there over the years, loving, living, dying. It drowns me, sometimes.

Adam sat, reluctantly. 'It's just so much.'

'I know. But you must have seen this before?' If Adam lived within a radius of our care home in a commuter town, he likely took the train into town every day for work. I imagined him in some kind of office job, wearing a suit, talking on a mobile. Or perhaps he'd been an artist, with a studio somewhere, or a musician or an actor. I wondered if it was exciting, to not know who you'd been, or just frightening.

He frowned. 'I suppose. But it's all new. Fresh eyes, you know?'

It was true. Through him, I found myself looking at it too. Instead of feeling scared and overwhelmed by all the people – even in the quiet middle of the day it was thronged – their memories, their worries and their loves, I tried to see the beauty in it. The glimpse of someone's laundry, drying in a top-floor flat. The red buses crossing the river. The round dome of St Paul's, which had barely survived the Blitz (29 December 1940). It was beautiful. And not just because I was seeing it by the side of a handsome, kind, open-hearted man, with green eyes the colour of pond weed (but in a nice way, you know) and dark hair glinting silver. Although, I have to admit, that was part of it.

'Where did you grow up, Eve?' Adam asked, breaking in on my thoughts.

'Oh! All over the place, really.' I felt my walls go up again, as I groped for the safe phrases, the way I'd learned to describe my childhood.

'Did you have a parent in the army or something?'

'No, I . . . my mum died when I was young.' The broken glass in my hair, the crunch of it under my feet as I tried to stand up. *Mummy?* The waxy stillness of her face.

'I'm sorry. And your dad?'

'I ... ' *Daddy. What's the matter, Daddy?* 'I didn't really know him.' I stared out the window, willing him to stop talking.

Adam sighed. 'I said the wrong thing again, didn't I? I'm sorry. It's just I have so few memories, I'm curious to know everything I can find out. I won't ask you again.' He took out the notebook and scribbled something in it. I could only imagine what my entry looked like. *Eve, right weirdo. Can't go in cars or meet new people. Can't forget. Not a single thing, no matter how much she tries.*

EVE

When we stepped into the hospital, I went quiet, hunching my shoulders in my coat. Adam noticed. 'What's the matter, Eve?'

'Nothing.'

'I can see you've sort of . . . put up armour.'

How to explain? 'When I was younger I . . . I had to spend time in hospital. After the . . . when my mother died.' *I put my foot down, in its pale pink sandal, my favourite. There's something sticky on the road. I lift my foot up again and it's red, all red.*

He nodded. 'Hospitals make me feel funny too. I was in here for a few days when they found me. Everyone else had visitors, families, and I was just . . . all alone in my bed, no idea who I was, no one coming to look for me.' He sighed. 'It was so lonely, Eve. Not even knowing who it is you're missing.'

'I'm sorry. That must have been awful.' *Blood, that's what it is on the road. I'm old enough to know it's blood. I say,* Mummy? *It's so quiet. Why is it so quiet?*

The memories were too much, lapping around my neck. 'Come on, let's go.' I rushed him to the lift. If I kept busy, maybe they wouldn't find me.

'Adam! My man.' Adam's doctors were young, both in their twenties. The man, who was Asian and a bit scruffy, high-fived him when he came in. The woman, who was white and blonde and had the kind of neat bun that hair never seems to

94

escape from, just smiled. I stood there awkwardly until Adam smoothed the situation over.

'This is my friend Eve, who's looking after me.'

I mumbled something and sat down on a plastic chair at the side. It was all freaking me out – the white walls, the blue plastic curtains, and above all the big brain scanner on the other side of a glass wall. Adam was going to go into that. My breathing was already funny and I could feel myself being sucked into the whirlpool, the memories closing over my head. *Daddy? What's the matter, Daddy? It's me. It's Eve.*

'Eve? Are you OK?' Adam had noticed my strange expression and clammy breathing.

'I'm fine. I just – I don't like hospitals.'

The doctor – he'd said to call him Praj, not even Dr anything (Bengali background, semi-addicted to Twixes, supports West Ham) – smiled. 'That's pretty common, you know. Maybe if we talk you through what's happening, it would help? We're just going to put Adam into the MRI, and we'll use it to look at the part of his brain that controls memory. When he was last in with us, we couldn't see any obvious damage that would explain the amnesia, so we need to look again.'

'The hippocampus,' I muttered, before I could help myself. Both doctors looked surprised.

'Eve's got an amazing memory,' said Adam proudly, as I was cursing myself.

'Oh, no, not really, I just like medical shows,' I lied.

'She's being modest! Honest, she can remember anything. The capital of any country. What day of the week it was on June the first 1997. She never forgets!' *Oh shut up, Adam, shut up!*

But it was too late. This was what I'd been afraid of. I should have trusted that instinct. I should have been more careful.

The doctors exchanged looks. 'Is that true, Eve?' said the female one (Zoe was her name, though I got the feeling she'd have rather been called Dr Something, brought up in Hertfordshire, never ate carbs, had a phone cover with unicorns on it).

'Um, no, I don't know.'

She wouldn't let it drop. 'You have superior autobiographical memory – hyperthymestic syndrome?'

I thought about pretending I didn't know what that meant, but realised it was no good. When you remember the exact truth of everything, lying is hard. Hyperthymestic, from the Greek from *excessive remembering*. Sounds about right. 'Yeah.'

'But this is amazing!' Praj was smiling widely, a real eye-smile too. 'When we're not busy here – like maybe seventeen minutes a day – Zoe, I mean Dr Evans, and I are part of a big study into dementia and memory loss. We're actually recruiting people with unusually good memories to try to find out what makes them tick.'

'Lots of people at Sunnyside have dementia,' said Adam, as if realising this for the first time. 'Eve! This could be how you solve your cases!'

'Cases?' Zoe frowned, hands in the pocket of her clean white coat.

'Eve's a memory detective.' Adam said it so proudly again, but I cringed at how stupid it sounded in this room with machines and charts.

'I just try to help the residents remember things, that's all.'

'And how do you do that?' she pressed.

'Oh, it's nothing. I just – collect up objects from their pasts. Things that could trigger memories. And I ask them questions, talk to their families, that sort of thing. Play them music sometimes.'

'Fascinating!' Praj exclaimed. 'That really fits with the work we've been doing on neural pathways. Did you know dementia patients can respond to music right up to the end, when they can't remember anything else? You wouldn't think about joining it, the study? It would just be a few quick scans, answering some questions ... '

I stood up fast. 'I'm sorry. No. Adam, I'll wait outside.' I didn't know what else to do. If I stayed in there any longer, I wouldn't be able to stop remembering the accident, and the hospital, and everything that happened after. And if I joined the study, more people might know how strange I was, my weird memory, the fact I couldn't forget. *Freak.*

'Get out of the way, gel!' An elderly man pushed me aside with his walking stick. I watched him struggle out through some double doors on to a terrace, and immediately light up a cigarette, leaning on his IV drip. The smell of the smoke was going to bring back some bad memories too, so I moved away, heading to the snack bar. So far I had no unpleasant associations with cakes or biscuits. If I did, I'm not sure life would be worth living.

I don't remember the accident itself. I must have been looking down, reading my picture book, although I couldn't read much at all yet. I remember looking at the word 'bunny', right before the world turned upside down. Suddenly I was lifted up and spun, and for a moment my stomach lurched, and out of the car window I saw the world fly by, slices of blue sky and green fields. Then the bang. Then we landed, and all the air was knocked out of my lungs and I had broken glass in my hair, sparkling in the sun. But somehow I was fine and I undid my belt and climbed out of the car, and I set my pink sandal down on the road.

And then. The hospital, the police, Theresa. All the rest of it, in that moment still to come. Sometimes I think about it – the last second before everything changed. Before I knew what had happened. When I was still a normal little girl, with two parents and a memory like everyone else.

RACHEL

Off on a secret assignation today! Channelling Raymond Chandler!

The sign on the door wasn't even a sign. It was a piece of paper, Sellotaped up a long time ago, so that bits of yellowing tape hung off like the gross bits on cooked eggs. *Mark Cooper, Private Investigator.* Rachel stood in the hallway for a moment – there wasn't even a chair, let alone a proper waiting area – thinking of how far her life had unravelled. Normally, it was rigidly controlled. She shopped, she cooked healthy food, she went to the gym and yoga and took part in the competitive school-gate chit-chat ('It's kind of embarrassing, really, the teacher said Morgan was years ahead of the rest of the class!'). She never allowed herself to eat carbs, or sugar, or to leave the house without make-up. All that had gone out the window the night it happened. She was back on the bread, she hadn't brushed her hair that morning, she'd let Hannah go to a play date at the Hewson-Taylors' with non-matching socks on, and here she was, about to go and talk to some seedy PI, like a femme fatale in a Raymond Chandler novel. *Hashtag secret assignment!* Simon had loved those, the clever wordplay and twisty plots and world-weariness of it all. He *loved* them. He still loved them. Was it a bad sign she was thinking of him in the past tense? *Don't think about that.* She was finally getting help, and things would be better from now on.

She wished she believed that.

She knocked, and after a moment a voice started to say, 'Come in,' before being choked in a storm of coughing. When she opened the door she understood why, because the place stank of cigarettes. 'Er, hello, I'm ... ' Oh God, what was the fake name she'd given on the phone? How did people manage to tell lies? The sheer admin involved was overwhelming. She'd found this place using the old-fashioned method of going through the Yellow Pages. Perhaps it was paranoid, but she knew that the police could check what you'd searched for, and googling 'private detective missing husband' was going to look a bit dodge.

The man behind the desk – private detective Mark Cooper – said, 'Jennifer?' Simon's sister's name, Jen of the holidays in Barbados and the horse-riding. She would never be in this situation.

'Right,' she said, not meeting his eyes. 'Jennifer.'

'Take a seat.' He had a broad Northern accent, Cumbria or somewhere like that, which despite herself she found comforting. He gestured to a broken plastic chair opposite his overflowing desk. She'd never seen such an untidy room. Small to begin with, it was crammed with dinged-up metal filing cabinets, Post-its on every surface, and bulging manila files stacked on the desk, threatening to fall down at any moment. She made a mental note to avoid deep breaths. The detective was untidy too, in a bally navy-blue fleece. He had wiry brown hair and a rumpled, weary face, as if he'd heard every trick in the book. 'Let me guess, it's your husband? You think he's having an affair.'

For a moment she wanted to cry, the seedy cliché of it all. 'I thought he was. But now I'm not so sure.'

'Oh?' A flicker of interest crossed his beaten-up face. He had a boxer's brow, and a thick stubborn nose, bushy eyebrows. All the same, it was a face you wanted to tell things to.

Rachel leaned in. 'The thing is ... '

'Careful!' He sprang forward to stop her. 'These files are stacked like a dry-stone wall. Move one a millimetre and we'll be buried.'

She sat back. 'All right. Here's the thing.' And she told him what she hadn't told anyone else since the terrible night everything had happened.

When she'd finished, he was watching her intently. 'I have to hand it to you. Takes a lot to surprise me, but you have.'

She was surprised herself to feel a flicker of something like pride, and pushed it away, embarrassed. She didn't even know this scruffy man in the untidiest office she'd ever seen. What did it matter what he thought of her? 'So you see my problem.'

'I'd say you have more than one.'

'I can't go to the police, after what ... happened. And he hasn't shown up on the news or anything yet. So where is he?'

He held up a strong, broad hand. She had a flashback to Simon's hands, the long fingers that had stretched idly over the baby grand she'd bought him as a fortieth birthday present. She still felt a thrill passing it every day in the dining room, that she lived in a house with a grand piano, her who'd once had to sit on the stairs to listen in to next door's TV. She tried to think when Simon had last played it; couldn't.

Mark Cooper said, 'Here are the options as I see them. One, he's dead, and his body is lying somewhere.'

She nodded, trying not to feel sick. She'd pictured that many times, him stiff and cold.

'He'll turn up one day. And if you didn't report him missing . . . Well, that's going to cause all manner of trouble for you.' She swallowed hard. Even though she knew all this, had spent days turning it over in her mind, it was difficult to hear it from a stranger. 'However, given the built-up nature of this area, I find that unlikely.' It was small comfort.

He held up another strong finger. 'Option two. He's fine but he's avoiding you. In essence, he has left you, maybe for another woman.' Again, she'd had this thought. She told herself to hold it together. 'However, that one is also unlikely, because people almost always want to get one over on the estranged spouse and take their belongings back. Especially if he was the main earner.'

Estranged spouse. Was that what she was now? 'OK,' she said, horribly afraid she might cry.

'The most likely option, therefore, is option three.'

'Which is?' Nothing good, she knew. There was no good way out of this.

'He's run off. Disappeared on purpose. Given the letter you found, it's highly likely he was having money problems. I'd say ninety per cent of the misper cases I do involve debt.'

'There were messages from a woman on his phone. That's why I – that's what caused the whole thing in the first place. I tracked her down.' She filled him in on Jess, so mysterious and cagey, who worked in another shabby office across town. What would Simon be doing in a place like that? As she spoke, the detective's shrewd brown eyes never left her face.

'And she wouldn't tell you how she knew him?'

'No. But she did say he was a client. The place she works – it's some kind of equity release firm.' Which meant – Simon was remortgaging the house? Could he even do that without her knowing?

He picked up a cigarette from a packet lodged underneath a carton of mini rolls, and tapped it on the desk. 'Did you have any money troubles that you know of, Jennifer?' From the way he said it, she could tell he knew it wasn't her real name.

'No, of course not. We – we're very comfortable.' The euphemism that meant wealth beyond the wildest dreams of her childhood. Four holidays a year, plus weekends in spa hotels whenever they found life a strain. Not one but two spare rooms, ready and waiting for visitors. Not that anyone came. Simon's parents were dead, Jennifer never left her stables, and Rachel hadn't invited her own family for many years, for various reasons.

'Let me guess. He handles all the money. You leave him to it?' He pointed the cigarette at her and, ashamed, she nodded.

'I haven't worked since we had our daughter.'

'The oldest story in the book. So you wouldn't necessarily know if the house was mortgaged to the hilt, creditors at the door, any of that?'

'Of course I would!' Would she, though? She thought of the dropped phone call, the letter from his work. When was the last time she'd opened a statement or checked their bank accounts? 'He has a really good job. He makes plenty of money.'

'Far as you know.' He tapped the cigarette a few more times, and to her relief, put it down unlit. 'Look, why don't you tell me your real name? I can't say Jennifer with a straight face.' She flushed. 'It's OK, at least half my clients sign up with a fake one.'

'Rachel,' she said reluctantly. It felt like a risk, like her life

103

was slowly sliding open so that everyone could see it, as if the bottom of her handbag had collapsed spilling tampons and lipstick into the street.

'OK, Rachel. I'll look into this for you. But I have to warn you, before we go any further, that you should most likely go to the police. I have to advise you of that, even if you choose not to. And also, you should know – you probably won't like what I find.'

She nodded. She knew they were past that, and at least if she found out the truth she could put aside the shame at being the duped woman, the clueless wife who woke up one day to find bailiffs removing the sofa.

Just like her mum.

'All right then.' He stubbed out his unlit cigarette in an ash tray, and saw her looking in surprise. 'Oh, I've given up. I just like to smell them, is all.'

'But isn't that harder? To have them to hand, and not smoke them?'

'Much harder.' He heaved himself to his feet, and she saw he was wearing cargo shorts over strong, hairy legs, even though there was ice on the ground outside. The kind of man who liked to be outdoors, who could fix engines and retune the Wi-Fi. Who wore fleeces and carried a compass. A sort of comfort settled over her, a sureness that this strange man was going to help her find a way out. 'I like to challenge myself,' he said, holding the door for her. 'It's complacency that will kill you, Rachel.'

When she got home, a grumbling Hannah and several shopping bags in tow, the phone was already ringing. Distracted, it didn't even occur to her it might be significant. 'Can you get that, Han-ban?'

Hannah ran across the room. 'Hello? I mean, Kempner residence?' Simon's mother, who'd died the year before, had taught her to answer the phone that way, and it made Rachel cringe, the posh ringing tones of her daughter's voice. It still surprised her that Hannah was growing up two or three social classes above her – Rachel remembered the first time she'd gone to stay at Simon's parents' house, her bewilderment with the array of social customs she'd never encountered, the number of forks on the table at dinner (which she had to call dinner and not tea). 'Hello?' Hannah held out the receiver. 'Mummy, I think someone's there but they aren't saying anything.'

Rachel was across the room in two seconds, the shopping bag dropped to the floor with no regard for the eggs inside. 'Who is this?' Silence. The faint sound of breath. Was she imagining it? Her heart hammered. 'Why are you calling? I warn you, I'll go to the police.' Did she imagine it or was there the tiniest snigger at that? As if whoever was on the other end knew she was lying, that she couldn't call the police. What did they want from her? The certainty lodged itself in her solar plexus – this was all connected. 'Simon?' she whispered, trying not to let Hannah hear. 'Is that you? Are you hurt? Please – tell me where you are.' Visions of him in a dungeon, his arms tied and mouth gagged.

The smallest hitch of a sigh, the breeze of a breath. Rachel ran cold all over, as the line went dead and she heard the dialling tone in her ear. 'Who was that?' Hannah stepped over the chaos of spilled shopping, turned on the TV.

'No one,' Rachel said firmly, trying to convince herself, as an apple rolled past her foot. 'It was no one. And no cartoons before dinner, you know the rules.'

EVE

Adam and I didn't speak much on the way home. I thought he was disappointed in me after what happened in the hospital, and it gave me a hot breathless feeling that was only partly to do with sitting on the tube (under tons of a clay-based soil that retains the heat). The smell of the old man's cigarette clung to my hair and jumper. How could I explain my horror – my absolute be-sick-in-my-mouth fear – that helping his doctors would make people look at me again? That if more people knew how weird I was, I'd never be able to live a normal life? Get close to anyone?

When we got back to Sunnyside, trudging up the gravel path past the roses, I immediately heard an uproar. The door flew open – I pulled Adam back –and Mr Evans (ninety-four, born in Cardiff, hates parsnips, loves Penguin bars and also actual penguins) bowled out. His shirt was on backwards and his face was wild. 'Get off me!' he was shrieking at Julie, who ran after him, panting, her long nails flashing. 'I don't belong here, I haven't done anything! Get off, you Nazi bastards!'

Oh dear. This happens quite a lot with our older guests – the Second World War does seem to loom rather large in their memories. Well, it would, I suppose. Magda followed him out, her hair absolutely bristling with pens. 'It's happened,' she whispered to me. 'His first Big Episode. Thinks he's in a POW camp in 1943.' The Big Episode is what we call the moment one of our early-stage dementia patients – managing fine, a little forgetful of names and details, but basically happy – slips over the edge of the lifeboat, ravaged by the waves of the full-blown disease. It comes to all of them in the end.

'Have you phoned his daughter?' I shouted. Mr Evans has one daughter, Mary, who lives in Brighton, and a son, Donald, who's up in Aberdeen on the rigs and therefore of limited use in an emergency.

'He doesn't remember her,' said Magda briskly. 'Thinks he's engaged to someone called Etty, when I know fine well his wife's name was Susan.' Indeed. I remembered he'd once told me that Etty had been his first love, who he met on leave in London during the war. I had helped him remember her name when he first moved in.

'Let me try.' I approached him, making myself small and smiling like you might to an angry dog. 'Mr Evans! Are you looking for Etty?' He turned on me, understanding dawning in his cloudy blue eyes. Just a pinprick of it, as if that name was all he could see in a choking fog.

'Etty? You know Etty?'

'She was ever so pretty, wasn't she?' I said. 'That auburn hair, and such a lovely smile.' I'd found a picture, back when we searched for her.

He smiled too, and Julie relaxed her grip on him. One of her false nails was bent and she wobbled it, scowling. He said, 'I only knew her one night. We danced till it was dawn! I said, "You're a girl in a million, and I need you to come back to once we've shoved Herr Hitler out of France."'

'That's right.' My voice was soothing, and I gently began to lead him inside. 'And you did shove him out, didn't you?'

'Did we?'

107

I tried to imagine being in 1943, not at all sure if D-Day was going to work or not, or if Hitler would stamp all over the troops and invade Britain and kill everyone. I thought of what I'd read about Churchill in 1944, smoking, standing on a roof looking out towards the Channel, not sure if he'd done the right thing in choosing 6 June for the attack, or if some small and uncontrollable thing like rain or cloud or a clear moon would derail the most important fight in our history. I have to remind myself about that all the time. That memory isn't now, and you aren't reliving it even when it feels like you are, but even so memory was once the present. You acted how you thought best at the time, with nothing to show you where your steps might lead.

He was calmer now. 'Well, I'm glad we stopped Hitler.'

'You certainly did. He shot himself, you know. In his bunker.'

'Hurray!'

It was so strange, seeing how delighted he was that Hitler was gone, that the war was over. 'How about a nice rest, Mr Evans? You've done a good job. I think you deserve one.'

'Well, all right.' I felt his arms go limp, all the confusion and anger draining from him, and I led him back inside to where Magda was waiting.

'Should I call Charity?' she whispered.

I shook my head. He would sleep now anyway. I guided him up the stairs, into his room.

'What about Etty?' Mr Evans asked, as I helped him into bed. 'Was she waiting for me? When I came back from kicking Hitler's arse?'

'She waited for you,' I said, smoothing the cover. 'Maybe you'll see her very soon.' It was the kind of thing Charity would say, and I didn't think I believed it, but who was I to judge? Maybe he would see her, somehow. Maybe some flash of us lives on, long after the meaty tangles of our brains have vanished into the earth.

'Well?' Magda was in the corridor, hands on her hips. 'I need to know what happened to Etty.'

I leaned against the ugly yellow wall of the corridor, suddenly exhausted. 'Etty lived in Bethnal Green,' I said. 'She worked in a munitions factory – her hands were always yellow from the chemicals. She met Mr Evans – Bert – when he was on leave, like he said. On the night of March the third 1943, she was hurrying home to get ready for her shift when the air-raid sirens went. She ran to the tube . . . '

'Oh no,' said Magda quietly.

'Yeah. She was killed in the disaster – everyone panicking and getting crushed. Her name's down there on the memorial.' Gone for over seventy years, and yet in Mr Evans' head she was as bright and shining, with her auburn hair and her smile, as she'd been all those years ago.

Downstairs in the rec room, Adam was helping settle Miss Cole, who had burst into tears over the incident. Mrs O'Reilly had already been put to bed. When he saw me, he straightened up. 'Eve, I saw how you helped him there. That was . . . '

'I'm sorry,' I blurted out. 'I'm sorry I said I wouldn't help the doctors. I just – I have reasons. I can't explain, but being in hospital, it just . . . '

He put his hand on my arm – warm, heavy. I didn't flinch. 'I know. I understand. It's just – it's so hard, hearing again that there's no physical reason for me to be like this. But I still can't remember! And if there's a way to help people going through

109

this, not able to remember their name or their family or if anyone loves them . . . But I respect that you can't face it.'

What else could I say? I thought of Adam and Mr Evans and Mrs O'Reilly and all the residents who had lost themselves. The pain it caused. The possibility that I could do something to help them, alleviate their suffering, bring them back to themselves. The hope that some answer might lie in my strange brain. I said, 'It's OK, Adam. I'll help.'

Why can't I see him, Theresa? Why, why? I didn't understand. I was being moved to yet another foster home, my third since my mother died. In this one, the bedspread was yellow with bumble bees on it. I knew they weren't real, but all the same I was slightly afraid they might sting me in the night.

Theresa was smoking as she drove the car. The smell of cigarettes is the smell of my childhood. Of moving on from another home. Of not being wanted. *Because, Eve. It would upset you.*

Is he dead too? Are you lying to me? It was all I could think of to explain why I hadn't seen my dad since the accident. He wasn't even at my mum's funeral, because he was still in hospital.

Theresa looked at me sideways. *You really want to see him.*

Yes!

She sighed, blowing out a long plume of smoke. *All right then. But don't say I didn't warn you, kid.*

EVE

In the middle of town, just near the arcade of shops with only two still open, behind the post office where the queue sometimes stretches out the door, is a small building with black iron bars on the windows. It's easy to miss, as it almost always seems to be shut. You might mistake it for a closed-down shop, one of the nice kind we used to have before the recession, that sold fancy cheese or coats for dogs. But what it really is is Bishopsdean's museum.

I know it seems crazy that somewhere like this could have a museum. Most of the town was destroyed in the Blitz, save for some sandstone buildings in the centre that date back to the 1800s, when it was briefly a fashionable spa town. But I love that. I love that people have taken the time to set up a museum for the world's most forgettable town, written up little cards and displayed a hotchpotch of items that remind us of something in the past. All museums are really just memories, gathered together and made solid. Did you know there are over 1,600 independent museums in Britain? In Bishopsdean, the museum is run by Sandra (sixty-eight, no children, was once crowned Miss Kent 1973). Adam and I were standing at the door at bang on midday, which is when she opens up, and I saw her coming to unbolt the door, wearing her special museum tabard. She paid to have it made herself, since the museum gets next to no funding.

'Eve, darling! How nice. I haven't seen you for a while.'

Sandra is a loud, posh, jolly sort of lady. There was a time when I popped in every time I had a day off. It was the only place I felt safe in town, somewhere old and musty where things weren't shiny and plastic and displayed under fluorescent lights. Well, that and the charity shops, of course, my other spiritual home (where you can actually buy people's memories and take them home with you). Usually, there's no one else there. Sometimes a mum with a buggy, sheltering from the rain. Sometimes a school group, the kids wearing matching backpacks and running amok amid the collection of antique snuffboxes.

'Sandra, this is my friend Adam.'

Sandra looked him over and gave me a wink, which made me blush. The older people get, the happier they seem to be saying their inside-head thoughts out loud. 'You're a treat for the eyes, aren't you? Where's Eve been hiding you, darling?'

Adam looked confused. 'I live at Sunnyside,' he said. 'Eve's helping me because I can't remember who I am.'

Sandra's well-plucked eyebrows shot up. I produced another of Magda's little airline bags from my pocket (she was going to go mad at me next time she took an EasyJet flight from some cheapo airport and found she had to fork out for more). Inside was the pebble, striped like a humbug and pleasingly heavy in my fist. 'We need your help, Sandra,' I said.

Ten minutes later, Sandra was off the phone. 'Dougie says he'll take a look. I'll stick it in an overnight envelope and we should know soon.'

Dougie was her friend who ran a geological museum up North. Apparently there is such a thing as the Small Museum Association, a collection of all the dedicated people, many of them unpaid volunteers, who run these little places. Some of them are only one room. Some of them are museums of pencils or steam engines or custard pies. Between them, there's nothing so small that they won't know about it, nothing too obscure to care about, to remember, to put in a case. Dougie was going to analyse the pebble and hopefully tell us what part of the country it came from.

'Thank you, Sandra. It's very kind of you.' Adam sipped tea from his museum-branded mug (I have ten of them, even though no one ever visits me for a hot drink).

'Not at all, dear. A bit of mystery brightens my day right up. But I'm surprised the police haven't put your picture on the news, darling? Isn't that what they do when someone's missing?'

Adam looked puzzled. 'But I'm not missing. I'm right here!'

Sandra laughed. 'Yes, darling, but I'm sure someone's searching for you. I mean, look at you!'

Adam blushed, but I knew she was right. It was only a matter of time before someone came to find him. And here I was, doing my best to help him remember, and speed that process up.

As we drank our tea and I pointed out the main exhibits to Adam – it didn't take long – Sandra was at the reception desk, sighing over some forms. 'Oh dear, I can't make head nor tail of this, it may as well be Ancient Greek. Although, as a matter of fact, I was rather good at Ancient Greek in prep school.'

'What is it?' I saw her staring at a thick wodge of stapled paper.

'Oh, a grant application, darling. Some council thing, funding for temporary exhibitions. I need to think of a good local theme, but what is there about this place that people would want to see? I've not got anything except "snuffboxes through the ages", and to be honest, they weren't popular in THAT many different ages.'

I sympathised. Nothing much of note had ever happened in Bishopsdean. 'What about the war – the people who went from here to fight?'

'Been done,' she said, shaking her head. 'Those so-and-sos over at Peak Hill did it last year.' Peak Hill is a National Trust property about ten miles away that Sandra hates with the fire of a thousand suns. They have a tea room and yearly concerts and one time Princess Anne visited (and did you know she's the only competitor in Olympic history who never had to prove what gender she was?).

I wandered over to the postcard dispenser. 'Adam, let's buy something for Magda.' I like to get something when I'm here, or put a little money in the donations box at least. Sandra says not to but I'm terrified that one day the place will shut down, and then where will I go?

The postcard-makers of Bishopsdean have their work cut out for them. Most of the town is what you might call pleasant, with some nice shops for the richer people, and pretty-ish parks where the flower beds have been made in the shape of things like cartwheels and sundials, but none of it is really what you'd deem noteworthy. They'd taken a few nice pictures of the pavilion and of some of the items in the museum. The snuffboxes, of course, and a hat the Prince Regent had left behind when he passed through here once on his way to Brighton. Adam rummaged among the cards, showing every sign of interest in the flower beds and hats and snuffboxes. I saw how hard he was trying to be upbeat, even about a trip to the world's most boring museum and getting a postcard and a hot drink. I saw how much he wanted to be back to himself, his life, and it made my heart ache, because I knew that his real life had no place for me in it.

We had just left the museum, and were waiting for the bus to take us back to Sunnyside, when I saw it. On the side of the bus approaching us, lumbering up the hill, was the familiar logo of a misshapen owl, and this time, some words alongside it: Wise Buy.

RACHEL

Got my glad rags on for a trip to the big smoke!

She'd dressed up for today. Not in the work clothes she would once have worn in London, leather skirts, silk blouses, heels so high she worried daily that she would fall over and plunge down the escalator of the tube. Instead, she was wearing expensive jeans, polished boots, a loose chiffon blouse in a deep turquoise shade. Jewellery. Plenty of make-up. She was dressed as a corporate wife, which, she now realised, was what she'd been for the past seven years. Rachel Anderson, that was someone else, a person who didn't really exist any more.

It was Mark's suggestion that she do this, while he went back to the place Jess worked to see if he could find out more than Rachel had. In the meantime, she would go to Simon's office and dig there. She put on a huge smile as she approached the reception desk of Braithwaite Capital, which was in one of the shiny new skyscrapers in the City. Outside, the tops plunged into the clouds like daggers.

Nasreen, that was the receptionist's name. Very pretty, with shiny dark hair and dark eyes. 'Hi, Nasreen! How are you? You probably don't remember me. I'm Rachel, Simon's wife. We met at the Christmas party!'

Nasreen was nodding. 'Of course. Hello, Mrs Kempner. Can I help you?'

'It's silly really. I was just coming into town when Simon

remembered he'd left a charger in his office. Something absolutely vital apparently, for his Xbox or whatnot.' She rolled her eyes. *Men. What are they like?* Nasreen's smile was uncertain. 'I just need to pop in for five seconds, if that's all right?'

'I thought you were on holiday?' The receptionist looked puzzled, her perfect eyebrows arched. 'According to our leave log he booked two weeks off.'

Holiday? This was the first she'd heard. Her heart began to pound again. 'Of course! I, er, we haven't gone away yet. I was coming into town anyway, so I said I'd swing by. Simon's up to his eyes building a treehouse for our daughter.' They came so easy, the lies. Perhaps because she'd pictured that for years, begged him to take time off so they could stay at home together. Imagined him in the garden, a mouth full of nails, how delighted Hannah would be to have a treehouse. But it never happened. He was always at work.

'It's just, I'm not supposed to let people in without an appointment.'

'Oh, I know, what are they like with their rules and regulations! I'll be two seconds.'

'Maybe if Simon could ring in . . . '

'He'll have his hands in Ronseal and that. I'd hate to have to come back; I have a *very* busy day ahead.' She looked at her watch, summoning all the middle-class passive-aggression she'd learned since she left Rotherham behind.

Nasreen was wavering. She reached for a button on the desk, and the automatic door slid back silently. 'Just a minute then.'

'Oh, thank you, you are sweet.'

She was poised to rush in, when Nasreen called after her, 'Actually, if you're not away, I believe Mr Braithwaite has sent a few email queries that could do with being answered. We understood Mr Kempner might be out of range of wifi.'

As if Simon would go anywhere without internet! She remembered him on their honeymoon in Bali, shifting his sunlounger around all day on the beach, trying to pick up a signal from the hotel. She was as bad, posting non-stop shots of her feet in flip-flops, cocktails in front of a Berocca-orange sky, the cyan blue of the sea. Really, Rachel wasn't even sure she *liked* the person she'd become in the last few years. 'Oh yes, I think he's maybe – I think his phone's been playing up. I'll tell him. Bye.'

This had been a mistake – they'd know now that Simon had been gone for a while and she hadn't reported it. They'd say that she'd been acting strangely, when the police spoke to them, as surely they eventually would. Heart pounding, Rachel made her way along a narrow corridor that smelled like the inside of a new car. Plastic. Sterile. A water cooler and a pot plant. Simon's office had his name on it, stencilled on the frosted class. *Simon Kempner, Asset Management.* She didn't have any idea what he did all day. Moved money around, invested it, and somehow it made him thousands. Millions, some years.

So Simon had taken time off work, which was why they hadn't missed him – but *before* any of this happened. Why? Again she imagined the body in the railway siding, cold on the morgue slab. A police officer somewhere, getting closer and closer to finding her. Her, dragged through the press. *Heartless yoga-killer, Rachel Kempner.* Maybe they'd even think of a name for the crime, like the Aga Murder. She was rubbish at yoga and didn't have an Aga, but that wouldn't matter, the media would love to tear down a middle-class woman like her. Her heart jumped up into her throat like an anxious bird. *Stop it.* It was far more likely that he'd left her.

His office was unlocked; she slipped inside and closed the door after her. The view was dizzying – the skyscrapers of Canary Wharf, so high that fog obscured the top floors, and the dull shine of the river below. What was she even looking for? She rattled the drawers of his desk. They were mostly empty, with paperclips and a stapler, a packet of protein bars she remembered buying for him when he confessed he didn't have time to eat lunch. A framed picture sat on his desk. The three of them on a beach in the south of England, smiling, jean legs rolled up, splashing in a dark blue sea. They looked so happy, it made her heart ache. You'd never guess Simon was missing, and their marriage was in such a bad state Rachel had no idea whether it was even deliberate or not.

Seized by panic, she pulled his tiny white keyboard towards her and a log-in screen appeared. What would his password be? Foolishly, she tried her own name. Nothing. Then Hannah's. Then the name of his childhood dog – Rusty. Long dead under the wheels of a milk cart. She'd seen this scene so many times on TV and they always managed to crack it. How could you guess a password out of millions of options? She couldn't be much longer or Nasreen would get suspicious. Then, her eye was caught again by the framed picture. The beach in a remote corner of the Kent coast. An unusual word. A flash of memory, Simon saying, *I use this place on all my passwords. It's so special. Plus, no one can spell it!* How trusting they'd been with each other back then. And now here she was, trying to hack her way in to all his secrets.

How did you spell it? She keyed in DUNGEVIN and,

119

suddenly, like a miracle, his screen lit up and she was in. But there was no time. She went to his emails and selected as many as she could, scrolling down, then forwarded them to Mark as arranged. There was a noise in the corridor. She had to get out of here.

She grabbed the charger she'd thought to bring in her bag – thinking like a criminal! – and legged it to Reception, where she smiled at a worried-looking Nasreen. 'Men! His version of "in the left desk drawer" turns out to mean "in the third drawer of the filing cabinet"! Anyway, got it now, thank you.' And she left, before anything else could be said. She was sure Nasreen would not say anything, as she'd bent the rules to let Rachel in. Now she just had to hope there was something in the emails, any clue that might explain where the hell her husband was.

EVE

I peered around the side of the tanning shop, feeling very much like a detective on a stake-out. Next door was the local branch of Wise Buy, the nearest of a chain of equity-release brokers that Adam perhaps had a connection to. There was always a chance he'd just picked the pen up, of course, stealing it like Magda always steals mine (179 times now and counting), but I really hoped not. Another dead end might plunge him into gloom. In fact, I hadn't told him I was coming here, in case it didn't work out. He was back at Sunnyside, helping Mr Chu with a vast jigsaw of some puppies playing with a basket of socks.

The office looked like a shabby place, on the first floor above a betting shop. I went up the stairs feeling a familiar nervousness in my stomach. Places like this kept records. Perhaps Adam's name and address would be in one of the computers. Suddenly not wanting to do it, I opened the door to the office.

When I did, I found a scene of low-level chaos. A middle-aged man in a badly fitting suit was wrestling with a printer that was spewing out reams of paper.

'Er ... hello,' I said timidly.

He glanced up, harassed. 'Sorry, sorry, are you a new client?'

'No. I wanted to enquire about an existing one.' I had thought a lot about how to explain what I was looking for. 'I'm trying to track down someone on your system.'

'What?' More paper flew out, landing on his shoes. 'Oh bugger. Look, it's not a good time. We've lost our admin girl and it turns out no one else knows how to work anything round here. I've had bailiffs at the wrong houses, fee records deleted, seventeen major data breaches, and it's only lunchtime.' *Bailiffs?* What kind of business was this?

'Would you just look at this picture for me?' I held out my phone, which I'd used to snap a picture of Adam in his kittens jumper, looking slightly bewildered in the rec room, but the man barely glanced at it.

'Sorry, doesn't ring any bells. Anyway, I couldn't give you his details if I knew them because . . . '

'Data protection, yes I know.' I sighed. The bane of my life. 'Would anyone else know if he's a client?'

'Only Jess, but she's quit. She was quite rude about it actually, said she didn't like the way we did business! And no, I don't have her details either.'

Of course not. My hopes of an easy solution had been dashed, but I found that, even though I had been professionally frustrated, I didn't feel all that bad about it. If I'd found Adam's name here, after all, he might have been back home within hours. Maybe I wasn't quite ready to say goodbye. Not that I was shirking my duties, of course not. It was just . . . taking longer than expected.

'You should try turning the printer off at the wall,' I advised the harassed man, but I have to say he didn't take my helpful advice all that well, retorting that obviously he had fudging thought of that already (he didn't say fudging exactly, of course).

Once a month, we have a small group of musicians who come to Sunnyside and play for the residents. I've looked into this, and I know that music has been proven to get through to even the most tangled, damaged brains. When dementia has blown through like a hurricane, taking with it names, faces, love, sadness, joy, the patients can still hear and recognise songs. They can even remember the words sometimes, and join in. The study I read said that maybe song lyrics and tunes are stored in a different part of the brain, like a squirrel hiding precious nuts all over the garden, to keep them safe.

'Morning, everyone! Who's ready for some singing!' Keith, the man who leads the music (fifty-eight, allergic to mushrooms, was once almost a member of Steeleye Span), has a straggly grey beard and usually wears a waistcoat with pin badges stuck all over it. He plays the guitar while his wife, Rosemary (sixty-three but says she's fifty-seven, has a son she never sees who lives in Belfast, loves asparagus), whose long grey hair matches his beard, plays the tambourine and sings. (Did you know the tambourine was invented in Ancient Egypt?) She likes to dress in flowy frocks and put flowers in her hair, even in the middle of winter. Sometimes they have a piano player too, Arjang (twenty, Iranian parents, secretly wishes he'd learned electric guitar instead of classical piano). He's a music student at the local university and dresses the complete opposite to Keith and Rosemary, in cool vintage T-shirts and jeans, his hair gelled up, and his phone never stops buzzing with messages from lovesick girls. But he knows all the old songs that the residents love, and when he puts his fingers on the keys, magic happens. The residents sit up straighter, their eyes clear, and some kind of spell, the evil magic of their disease, is broken. Just for the three minutes of the song, of course, but around here we take what we can get.

Today, no one really responded to Keith's welcome. Miss

123

Cole grumbled that she couldn't see the television, and Ms Jerman, the former West End star, looked affronted and pointed out that she only sang for a significant fee. Mrs Gillespie pointedly turned off her hearing aid, and Mrs O'Reilly burst into tears, as she does these days for everything from an unexpected biscuit to seeing Boris Johnson on the TV (she thinks he's a scarecrow come to life).

It was Adam who pulled it all together. 'I'd love to do some singing, Keith,' he said, in the primary-school tones of someone wrangling young children. Which this isn't all that different to. 'Who else would?'

I stepped forward, even though I hate nothing more than being the centre of attention. 'What shall we start with? How about "The White Cliffs of Dover", Arjang?' That one always goes down well, since so many of them lived through the war.

He began to play, and I watched the magic start. Mrs O'Reilly, who for weeks now has been sinking into a world of her own, jerked her head up. Terry, who loves a sing-song, began to tap out a rhythm on the edge of his chair. Mr Chu came in with the words too soon, his voice high and warbling. And soon we were all singing about the cliffs and the bluebirds and coming home again, and I looked over at Adam, singing his heart out, and thought how strange it was he should know the words to this old, old song, but the part of his brain that knew his name was all locked up.

Suddenly, as the music filled me up, my voice faltered, and tears pricked my eyes. I was going to lose him, like I'd lost my parents, though in a different way. Like I would lose each of the residents in this room, over the next few months or years. One by one they were all going to die, as if they were getting to their feet, standing out of their chairs, and quietly leaving the room, never to return. Only I would be left.

Because there were tears in my eyes, I wasn't really paying attention to what was going on. I hadn't realised Mrs O'Reilly was getting more and more upset. 'No,' she was saying. 'Not this one. He didn't come back. He DIDN'T COME BACK!' If I'd been paying attention, I would have known she meant her first husband, Jonny, who went to fight and was killed at D-Day, leaving her with a toddler and a baby on the way. A man she hadn't seen in over seventy years, but who she mourned now as sharply as then. She got to her shaky feet and approached the piano.

'That's right,' Rosemary called, writhing with her tambourine. 'Join in! Dance around if you feel like it!'

But Mrs O'Reilly wasn't planning to dance. She marched up to Arjang – I saw him frown in confusion – and before we could stop her she had slammed the lid of the piano shut on his fingers, with all the strength that a dementia patient could muster.

'Oh my God. Oh, Arjang, your poor fingers!' I exclaimed over him.

'It's all right.' But he was pale, cradling them to himself. They looked white, and red at the ends. This was not good.

'It's not all right; you have piano exams next week! We need to get you to hospital.' Hurried arrangements were made. I couldn't drive, and anyway, someone had to stay with the residents, so Magda loaded him into her car, muttering about lawsuits. Arjang was by then the colour of milk – I really hoped his fingers weren't broken.

Mrs O'Reilly was weeping, aware that she'd done something

125

wrong but not what. 'He didn't come home,' she was sobbing. 'It was a lie. A lie!'

Charity, who luckily was in today, led her off, no doubt to be sedated. 'I know, I know, my dear. Not your fault. Let's go and have a nice rest.'

What now? The singing session was in disarray, Rosemary was crying, Keith looked shell-shocked, and several more residents were also crying or out of their chairs, wandering in confusion.

'What a SHAMBLES,' said Mrs G loudly. 'What do we pay for, in this place?'

'We need someone else to play the piano,' I hissed to Adam.

A strange look crossed his face, as if his body was moving of its own accord. He sat down on the stool, pulled it up to the piano. Stretched out his long fingers over the keys. 'Let me just try something,' he said. And under his hands, notes began to sound. I tried to make out the tune. Something jolly, that made me want to sing. 'She'll Be Coming Round the Mountain' (which some say is actually a slave song, about the Underground Railroad). And the magic began again. People sat down. They smiled. The tears stopped. Hands began to clap, feet to tap.

Mrs Burke, who could not remember her own children, giggled loudly and said, 'We sang this in summer camp, down in Bognor, it was. Billy knew all the words!' Mr Chu was clapping his hands, singing along in what sounded like the Chinese version of the song. Ms Jerman had joined in, hitting the high notes. Everyone suddenly looked happy, smiling. They were singing the lyrics, humming if they couldn't remember them, joining in the 'aye-aye-yippies'. And I had discovered a new fact, something I hadn't known before. A clue, maybe. Adam,

126

whoever he was, and wherever he'd come from, could play the piano.

Eve, your turn please.

I stared down at the xylophone in front of me. This school – the fifth I had attended in the last three years – had music lessons every week. What I didn't realise was that everyone else had been studying it for months now, and could already tap out the opening bars of 'Für Elise'.

Eve? We're waiting.

Without saying anything, I got up and ran out of the room, followed by a sudden murmur of laughter, like rain falling on the roof.

I was in foster care from age six to seventeen, plus three stints in care homes, the kind of place where kids cried all night and banged their heads against the walls. No one really hurt me, not exactly. It was just so lonely. Not having anyone to care for me specially, knowing that even the kind ones often did it for the weekly cheques, understanding that your time there was limited to the day they got sick of you, or you talked back, or they just didn't like your face. As I walked out of the classroom that day, I knew that my time in my current home was limited, and that pretty soon I would be moving on again.

EVE

Adam was smiling. 'This place is amazing!'

I pasted on a smile too. It was so busy in the toy shop, so many kids and parents running around, shrieking with happiness. I felt like a porch light, battered by moths, only the moths were other people's memories and hopes and desires. The kids wanted train sets and dolls and teddies. The parents wanted their kids to be happy, or at least to be quiet for ten minutes. They wanted to buy something that made their love concrete, a symbol of all their care and attention for this kid. I'd never been taken to a place like this (Hamleys toy store, founded over 250 years ago as Noah's Ark) when I was young, and it too overwhelmed me.

After my trip to Wise Buy, I had badgered Raheem to investigate it further – the police would be able to get into the client files, or track down the girl who'd left and maybe she would recognise Simon's picture. Raheem (his face stuffed with fruit loaf) had promised to follow up, right after he'd dealt with the massive human-trafficking case that had just come in (twenty people in the back of a supermarket lorry at Dover) and solved the one or two outstanding stabbings on his beat. It seemed no one but me had the time to find who Adam was. And did I even really want to? I thought of my sudden tears during the music session, my revelation that he would leave me, perhaps sooner, perhaps later, but sometime.

Tracking down the source of his Lego brick, it turned out, had been much easier than I'd thought, which was typical seeing as I'd left it to last. That was everything now – the ring, which was fake; the ticket, which told us nothing; the pebble, which Sandra's friend Dougie was still analysing; the pen, which had told us Adam maybe went to a possibly dodgy equity release firm (or maybe just stole a pen off someone else), and now the Lego. I'd taken it into the one remaining toyshop in Bishopsdean – a tiny little place filled with expensive wooden toys that the local mothers buy for each other's kids on their birthdays. The lady who works there, Amanda (thirty-eight, also a part-time Pilates instructor, does the buttons on her cardigan up wrong), had been very helpful. I don't think she has many customers now there's online shopping and that.

She was able to tell me that there was a Lego expert in London, in one of the big famous toy stores. If anyone could identify the brick in Adam's pocket, he could. I'd thanked her and bought a little wooden spinning top on my way out. I didn't know any children to give it to, but I could add it to the toy box at Sunnyside, which we keep for the residents' grandkids (or kids, in the case of Mr Jackson, whose third wife was forty years his junior). Now Adam and I were in London again. I'd told Magda I was taking him on another fact-finding mission, and she'd just raised her eyebrows.

I found myself being defensive. 'I have leave left over.'

Magda stared at me over her glasses, her eyes wise and kind. 'I know you do, petal. You have nothing but leave, seeing as you've hardly left this place in seventeen years. But do you think it's wise?'

'I'm just trying to help him remember!'

'That's not what I mean, lovie. Be careful, yeah? You're . . . not like other women your age.'

She'd meant I was weird. Vulnerable. *A freak.* I'd turned away, choosing not to hear. And now we were in the toy store, and he was so happy, and my heart was lying in the pit of my stomach like a squeezed-out teabag. Magda was right. I'd been fooling myself, thinking Adam and I were friends, or even a bit more than that. He was just a resident, and he only spent time with me because he'd lost his real life. 'Why don't you go and explore?' I said. 'I'll talk to the Lego man.'

'Are you sure?'

'Of course. It might take a long time; your head will start hurting.' Also, I had a feeling that, whatever the Lego man knew, if anything, it might be something I'd want to mull over before telling Adam. The visit to Wise Buy had made me uneasy – it didn't seem like a nice place – and then there was the fake ring, and Adam's own feeling that he might have done something bad. Who knew what would be next? So I left him happily browsing in the *Game of Thrones* merchandise, and I took the escalator up to the Lego section.

Even I couldn't help but smile when I got up there. It was magical. There were people built out of bricks, and houses, and islands, and pirate ships, and castles. Everything was yellow and green and red, bold primary colours filling my eyes. I went up to the assistant, who wore a little earpiece, like a bouncer at a club. 'Hello, is Darren here please?'

'Over there.' I looked where she pointed, then looked again. That couldn't be right. I could only see a small child.

'Are you . . . ?'

'That's him. Youngest Lego expert in the world. Legally he can only work a few hours a week, but we can't get him to go home.'

'How ... ?'

'Fourteen. Older than he looks, but not by much.'

Thoroughly wrong-footed, I made my way over to the dark corner where the person I'd taken for a child was hunched over a stack of bricks. His hands moved quickly, pressing them together into a shape I couldn't see yet. 'Hi, Darren? I'm Eve. Amanda sent me?'

He looked up, his fingers still feeling for bricks and putting them together as if of their own accord. Something about the motion, the deftness of his touch, triggered a memory in me. A landslide in my brain. Lego. Bricks. A little house. I did my best to stamp on it. 'Oh yeah. You want a piece identifying.'

It seemed a stupid question to ask – how could one little bit of plastic stand out from the rest? – but I took out my airline security bag all the same and held it up. He stopped with his own project, setting it down gently on a nearby bench, and held the brick up to his eyes. I could see him mouthing something to himself. Then he said, 'Easy. This is from a limited edition Enchanted Castle set.'

'How can you tell?'

He shrugged. 'Colour. Size. Easy when you know what to look for.'

'And did many of these get sold?'

'Nope. Goes for a grand, this set.'

I gasped. 'Do you have one here? Can I see it?'

He gestured over to the display, which held a huge, beautiful fairy-tale castle. It had everything: turrets, a moat, a forest, a witch, a Lego princess in a tower. A Lego dragon. A part of me throbbed inside, thinking how much I would have loved this as a kid. How I might have pestered for it. *Daddy, please can I have it?* 'It's amazing. All made from Lego?'

He gave me a look as if I was daft. 'Course.'

'Darren, you wouldn't happen to know if anyone bought one of these sets, would you? Like in the last few weeks?' Although I knew it could have been longer than that. The piece could have been in Simon's house for years, and one morning he'd just stepped on it in his bare feet and irritated, put it in his pocket.

Did this mean Adam had kids? I didn't want to think about that.

Darren turned the brick over in his hands inside the bag, his eyes faraway. 'There was a fella came in a few times to look at it, but he didn't buy it.'

'Why not?'

'Too expensive. Asked if he could buy a little bit of it instead – he wanted it for his daughter, sort of like a present, I think. Like a promise that one day, when he had cash, he'd buy her the whole castle. Sort of weird.' But Darren seemed to have a live-and-let-live approach to strangeness, as well he might, I thought, watching him pick up the Lego again and snap pieces into place, all without looking at it.

'So you sold him one brick of it? Is that unusual?'

'Not meant to do it, really. Only meant to sell sets, like. But they always send spares with the big kits, so I just gave him one, like. One brick, s'all.' Suddenly he became animated. 'That's what it's about, ya know? Lego. Not the sets and look-ing good and pretty and being finished. It's about the *bricks*. Every little bit. It all matters. If it wasn't for the little things, there would be no big things. You see?' I nodded, as his words hit home. Wasn't that what I did too, collected up the little

132

things to try to build a whole? The snow globes, the postcards, the costume jewellery, the old pictures. The items no one else would miss. Each tiny piece making up a life, trying to cling on to them against the non-stop forward motion of time, of forgetting.

Darren's head jerked suddenly. 'That's him there! The fella!' I turned to look, but I already knew that it would be Adam coming towards us. (I didn't know he'd be wearing a helmet and carrying a replica sword, but still.)

'I don't understand,' said Adam. We were making our way home on the train, full of weary late commuters, coffee on their breath and bags under their eyes. Had he once been like that too? 'I went in but I just got one brick?'

'I think it was meant to be symbolic. To show you'd buy the whole set one day, for your . . . '

He stared at the faded pattern on the seat. 'I have a daughter. Maybe.'

Darren hadn't known anything else. He didn't know Adam's real name, or the daughter's name or how old she was, but if she liked Lego I guessed she must be under ten. I'd been right. He had a family. Most likely he also had a wife. But Adam was looking dejected. 'What's the matter?'

'It's just – I'd been imagining all these cool things about myself. Like I'm a spy or a concert pianist or a life-saving doctor. But I guess I'm just an ordinary guy who goes to dingy offices and steals the cheap pens, does some shopping, has a normal life.' He sighed. 'At least when you don't know who you are, you can be anyone. And everything we've found out so far – the ring, the dodgy firm, it makes me feel . . . I have this

133

terrible sense I might have *done* something. Like . . . I might not be a very good person.'

I knew that feeling. It comes with the territory of not being able to forget anything – which means you have a live twenty-four-hour showing of all your worst moments and greatest mistakes. I looked at him. Today he was wearing ill-fitting jeans from the Death Box and a sweatshirt that said *Drama Queen*, which Julie had picked up in a local charity shop. All the same he looked perfect, to me. His hair, ungelled, sprung up in all directions, and he hadn't shaved since he came to us. 'Do you – do you think maybe you don't *want* to remember who you are?'

'Maybe not.' He bit his lip, which only highlighted the line of his jaw. 'I'm not doing this on purpose, Eve, I swear. I know Praj and Zoe said they couldn't find a physical reason why I don't know who I am. But maybe – maybe my brain is trying to protect me from the truth?'

I envied that. Mine had never protected me from anything; instead, it let me live all the bad things over and over again, as if they were happening for the first time. 'So what, we should stop looking?' I imagined that for a moment. Adam, living at Sunnyside for ever, in his little room upstairs. Me, across the garden in my flat. Maybe he'd come to visit, drink tea from one of my many mugs, play against me at *Only Connect*. Say, *Good one, Eve*, whenever I got something right. But it wasn't possible. I knew that.

His eyes darkened. 'I think we have to keep on looking, don't we? Even if what we find out isn't what I'd like to hear. Because, Eve – I probably have a family out there somewhere. I owe it to them to get home.'

So why weren't they looking for him? 'Adam, I – it might be

time to go back to the police.' It was hard to force the words out of my mouth, they felt so heavy. 'It would be a good idea to put you on the news, I think.'

He looked glum too. 'Because they might recognise me. My – family.'

'Right. They must be worried sick.'

'But they haven't filed a report. We don't know. I could be divorced, estranged from them, or maybe I've never even met her. My – the child. Or it could be a niece or something, maybe the Lego guy had it wrong. I just don't know.'

Not knowing is such a relief sometimes. You can kid yourself everything is fine, that the unknown questions all have good answers. You can suffocate yourself in the cotton wool of pretending. But you can't keep it up for ever. 'Adam,' I said gently. 'It's not even your name. You don't belong at Sunnyside. You have a life out there, somewhere.'

His face twisted and for a moment I thought he might cry. 'Then why aren't they trying to find me? Don't they care?'

'Maybe they are trying. There's so much we don't know. But if you have a daughter, a young daughter ... ' My heart broke as I said it, and, all in a rush, I realised I was going to tell him my story. Some of it, at least. 'When I was six, I lost my parents. My mum. My dad. He used to buy me little things – Lego. A knock-off Barbie from the market. We didn't have much money – he worked in a supermarket – but he loved me.' I remembered that feeling, which I've never had since. Of being truly loved. The way I'd climb on his lap when he came in from stacking shelves, tired in his uniform, smelling of cold and petrol. He was older than my mother, with grey in his hair, but he always had a smile for me. *How's my little Magnus?*

He called me that because I asked so many questions, like the man on TV in the show with the big chair. *Maybe if you look in my pocket, you'll find something for you.* And in his work fleece there'd be some small thing, an orange or a packet of Smarties, and once a Lego set, a small pirate boat with two figures. I had treasured it. He'd shown me how to shape the bricks into something more than themselves, building sturdy little houses and cars and spaceships.

I remember so little about my parents. I have tried so hard, over the years, to bring them back, to conjure the pattern of my mother's favourite dress or the sound of my father's laugh. And haven't I wished, time and time again, that my unusual memory had worked before the accident, so I could summon up all those days with them, snuggled on the sofa watching *Rainbow*, or lifted on to Dad's shoulders to touch the trees? But I can't. I only have ordinary memories from before, leached of colour, clung on to like dandelion seeds. Almost thirty years ago now. They are gone, lost for ever.

Adam was staring at me, his green eyes horrified. 'Eve, I'm so sorry.'

'So you see, you can't stay like this. Your little girl, she needs you. I'd give anything to see my parents again. Anything.' I meant, but could not explain, to see my dad the way he was *before*. Not ... after.

'God, Eve, I'm so sorry. You're right. When we get home, we'll call Raheem.'

I put my hand over his, trying to remember every bit of him before he went. Before I lost him too and he existed only in my mind, archived away in one of the vast warehouses inside my head. I might have a perfect recall of memories, but they were still only shadows of the real, living breathing things. The ridge of his knuckles. The stray grey hair in his left eyebrow. His smell of grass and lemons. We sat like that all the way back to Bishopsdean.

RACHEL

Trip out of town today, yay!

Hannah was complaining again. 'But, Mum, I'm too old for soft play!'

'You're seven! How can you be too old for anything?' Just last week, she'd loved soft play, now she was too old for it? Rachel stared at her daughter, as if seeing her grow up before her eyes. Maybe that was why she took so many Instagram pictures. To try to fix Hannah as she was, the week she'd decided avocado was her favourite thing on earth, only to declare the day after it was 'pond slime'. The constantly changing little girl beside her.

Hannah just gave her a look. 'I need something more stimulating than bouncing around in a ball pit.' Rachel sighed. When had she even learned a word like 'stimulating'? The whole point of meeting at this out-of-town shopping centre, driving all the way here on the M20, was so that Hannah could be occupied while she spoke to Mark, so Rachel didn't have to worry about who was looking after her, if she was safe and happy, if she'd picked up on what was happening. Plus, no one she knew would ever shop here, with its TK Maxx and fluorescent-lit food courtyard. She'd been avoiding her mummy friends, such as they were, since the incident happened, posting nothing on social media, ignoring the group WhatsApps about yoga classes and coffee mornings. If it all

138

settled down, she would say they'd gone on a family digital detox. The school mums were very big on those, although they posted so much about how it had gone it sort of defeated the purpose.

'Fine. What else do you want to do that will get you out of the way for an hour, but so I don't have to worry about you getting kidnapped?'

Immediately Hannah said, 'There's a Lego demonstration at the toyshop. It's just over there, look.'

'Fine. Stay where I can see you.'

'And can I have some money to buy more? It's important to support local business, you always say.'

'*Fine.*' Rachel forked over ten pounds, unsure whether to be proud or worried. She watched her daughter trek forcefully across the crowded shopping centre to the toyshop opposite the food court. 'Don't talk to strangers!' she shouted, aware that Hannah would pull her up on this, saying everyone was a stranger until she'd met them. Then she saw Mark coming towards her and her heart dipped and swooped, and the skinny cappuccino she'd been drinking threatened to come back up all over her Seven jeans. What would he say? He'd found something out, she knew that much by his email. But what?

He came over, and without greeting her or saying anything, sat down at the table, which had been improperly wiped and was smeared with other people's crumbs and coffee. This was definitely not a place to record on Instagram. 'Thanks for meeting me here,' she said.

'That's OK. It's near where my daughter does judo.'

He had a daughter? It was strange to think of him as a real person, not just a symbol of how far her life had fallen. 'Oh, how old is she?' Rachel was aware she was putting off hearing the truth.

'Thirteen.' Then he said, 'I'm divorced.'

Why had he told her that? 'Sorry to hear that. Um . . . did you want a drink?' She said it to fill the silence, or rather the silence between them, which was battling against the roars and screams from the nearby soft play area. Across the food court, she could see Hannah's blonde curls bobbing in the toy shop window.

'Nah, I have a thermos in the car,' he said. 'Do you want to know what I've found out?'

No. No, please don't tell me, let me live in blissful ignorance for one more day. 'Of course.'

He put his large hands on the table, and she wished he'd got a drink, anything to diffuse the awkward intensity between them. 'OK. The woman, Jess Morris. As you found out, she worked until recently as an admin assistant for a slightly dodgy firm. From a bit of digging on her social media, a word or two with a chatty friend, I don't think they were having an affair – it was strictly professional.' She nodded. Was she pleased about that? Or did it mean something worse was going on? 'I managed to speak to her.'

'How? She wouldn't tell me anything.'

He shrugged. 'I'm persuasive. I showed her the picture, and it was definitely your husband. But then he disappeared, didn't sign the forms, so it never went through.'

'He was trying to remortgage our house?' That might explain the 'have you told her yet' message. And an equity release firm probably went to your house, didn't they, to value it and take photos.

'Looks that way.'

Rachel was astonished by this news, struggling to take it in, but the detective seemed to find it almost mundane. Perhaps his life was a high-stakes array of liars, cheats and fraudsters.

'But . . . why would he do it?'

Mark sat back. 'Isn't it obvious? He was planning to take the money and do a runner.'

At that exact moment, just as Rachel was gaping at him, Hannah came running up, breathless. 'Mummy, they have a special deal for buy one set, get one half price, can I have another five pounds please? Mummy. *Mummy!*'

Her daughter's voice was coming as if from a long way away. Rachel thought she might faint, something she had never done before. The left side of her body was drooping. 'Who are you?' she heard Hannah say to Mark. Two people who never should have met, in the normal run of things. Too late to do anything about it.

'I'm a colleague of your mum's,' he said.

'But she doesn't have a job,' Hannah frowned.

'She used to, though, didn't she? We're just having a catch-up. You better run and get that deal, sounds like a good one.' She was aware of him taking out a roll of notes with an elastic band, and handing Hannah a fiver. Who carried rolls of cash in their pockets? 'Off you go, missy. I'm going to buy your mum a pastry.'

He was back in a minute with something sugary, iced in thick white icing, and one for him too. The kind of bun she used to eat as a kid, as a treat after school on Fridays, but

141

hadn't touched in thirty years. Five hundred calories at least, she reckoned. 'I can't ... '

'Eat a bit. You've had a shock, sugar will help.'

She picked it up and chewed, swallowed, as he ate his own in two bites. A thick paste of icing filled her mouth. She tried to focus. 'I'm sorry. I'll pay you back for everything, of course.' She began to look around for her bag, her purse, but her brain seemed to be frozen, stuck on buffering.

'Rachel, I know this is hard to hear.' She looked up – his eyes were kind.

'I just don't understand. How could he mortgage the house without me knowing?'

'Are you definitely on the deeds?'

'Of course I'm ... ' She thought about it, the time eight years ago when they'd bought the place, when, three months' pregnant, all her focus was on not throwing up in the estate agent's car. Had she actually signed anything? Had he been planning this even then? She met Mark's eyes. 'It's possible I'm not.' God, how stupid could you get?

'My guess is he needed cash badly and couldn't tell you about it. The emails from his office – did you read them?'

She shook her head. 'There wasn't time.' And if she was honest, she hadn't wanted to. It felt like lifting a stone and looking underneath.

'Well, the firm's in trouble, that much is clear. He wasn't getting his bonus, you knew that, so he borrowed money, tried to remortgage the house, maybe even went to some loan companies.' She thought of the silent phone calls. Did bailiffs do that?

Rachel was stunned. Her life, which she'd always thought

so solid and settled, boring almost, was built on quicksand. But the remortgage hadn't gone through, so he must still need money. Where the hell was he? She wasn't sure which would be worse, to know she'd injured him and he was lying hurt somewhere, or if he'd simply left her and Hannah, and gone off.

Rachel found herself picking up the iced bun, and cramming the whole thing in her mouth, suddenly desperate to feel full, to feel like her old self, in the days when she'd been Rachel Anderson, a promising PR exec with her own flat, a good job, a lively social life. To the person she'd been before she'd ever met Simon Kempner.

Rachel drove home, Hannah in the back prattling happily about her Lego session and how she was going to be an engineer when she grew up. 'That's great, darling.'

'Who was that man, Mummy?'

'Oh, he was just – someone I used to work with.'

'Is he helping to find Daddy?'

Startled, Rachel looked at her daughter in the rear-view mirror. How did she know that? 'What?' Of course Hannah had noticed something was going on. Stupid to think otherwise.

'Where is Daddy?'

'Um, he's, well, he's working away.'

Hannah's eyes were sharp in the rear-view mirror. 'But Mummy, he always calls me when he's away. We FaceTime sometimes, before you wake up.'

'He . . . I think maybe his phone is broken, darling.'

'He left his phone behind. It's in the kitchen drawer with

the batteries and light bulbs.' Oh God. Her hiding place had not been that effective after all. Rachel concentrated on driving in a straight line. What could she say? *He's left us? He lied to us? And I – I did something to him too?*

But Hannah was suddenly distracted as they pulled into their street. Rachel had always loved the street. Each house was distinct, all at least a four-bed, freshly painted and gardened. Like a woman who never went out without a full face of make-up and carefully chosen clothes. Like Rachel used to be. 'Mummy, look, there's a man!'

Rachel glanced at her own house, and her heart failed. A man was on the steps, peering in through the stained glass on either side of the door. Her first thought was, *Simon*, but she knew it wasn't him. Too big, too muscly, held himself all wrong. The man wore a black T-shirt and jeans, and nothing else, though it was still freezing outside. Shaved head, tattoos. He turned at the sound of the car and looked right at her, and she saw he was chewing gum. She parked, erratically, on the street. 'Stay here,' she instructed Hannah. Throwing open the car door, she called, 'Can I help you?'

The man regarded her for a moment. When he spoke, he had an accent, she thought maybe Eastern Europe. 'I'm looking for Mr Smith?'

'Oh, there's no one here by that name. What address do you have?'

He didn't answer. His eyes flicked from her to the expensive car, Hannah in the back. Calmly, he said, 'I think maybe I have wrong house. Sorry to be bothering you.' And he sauntered off to his own car, a black Hyundai to match his clothes.

Hannah was curious when Rachel went to get her out of the car. 'What was he doing, Mummy?'

'Nothing. He was at the wrong house.' She told herself that's all it was, that this was nothing to do with the dropped phone call she'd had, or the continued fact that her husband was missing, and, as she was finding out, had a whole other life she'd known nothing about.

EVE

We got back to Sunnyside around six. It was the 6467th time I'd gone up those stairs and into the hallway with its smell of soup. Every day for the past seventeen years, since I'd shown up here a strange, withdrawn teenager, an orphan, running from foster care and looking for whatever unskilled work I could find. And soon, Adam would leave and I'd still be here, climbing the same steps each day. Dishing out the biscuits, making sure the distribution of bourbons was fair. Reminding the old folk what my name was, only for them to forget overnight and ask me again the next day, and the next. I'd liked it at first, being invisible, being forgotten. But something had changed in me. I didn't want to always be the one who did the remembering. It was the least you could ask for, wasn't it? It was why I kept the small objects that made up my Museum, to make sure at least one person remembered every resident who passed through our doors. I wanted that for myself, too. I wanted to be remembered, like any normal person could hope for, and not just for the things that made me different. For the things that made me the same.

'You've had a phone call,' Magda said, greeting me in the hallway. I could only count two pens in her hair, so deduced that the day had been event-free. 'Actually, two phone calls. What am I, your secretary?'

'Who was it?'

She consulted the scrawled notes on her hand. I keep trying

to get her to use a notepad, but I may as well whistle into the wind. 'Someone called Dougie? From – I might have got this wrong – The Rock and Pebble Museum?'

'No, that sounds right. Who else?'

Magda looked at her other hand, the nails painted in chipped pink varnish (shade name: In the Pink, rrp £5.99). 'A woman called Colette. Says she's the daughter of Janet Marks?'

My heart, which had been dragging somewhere in the region of my knees, lifted slightly. A lead on the pebble from Adam's pocket – maybe we'd learn something that would prove it was all a mix-up, Adam didn't have a family after all! He wasn't married! He hadn't done a bad thing! And Janet Marks, Mrs Gillespie's old friend, that could be another lead on Graham. Perhaps things would be all right after all. 'Magda? I need you to do something for me.'

'Of course. After all, I am your assistant. Oh no, wait! You're mine!'

She was joking. I thought. I glanced into the rec room, where Adam was chatting with Terry about the day's crossword, patiently helping him remember the word for 'awning'. The imminent loss seemed to ring inside me, a clear and heavy bell. 'Do you have a number for Raheem? I think – I think it's time we got Adam back where he came from. We can't keep him here for ever while the police get round to finding him, five years from now. I think they should put him on the news.'

Magda said nothing, just pressed her inky hand on my shoulder, and went to get Julie. I went into the office, where Magda had scrawled the phone numbers on the back of some important medical reports. Putting off dealing with Adam's case for as long as possible, I dialled the one for Colette first. When she picked up she sounded harassed, like a mum with too much to do. I could hear a child in the background, loudly complaining that someone called Bella had taken her My Little Pony and it wasn't fair. 'Yes?'

I explained who I was, that I'd found a picture of her mother among Mrs Gillespie's things, and her voice softened. 'Oh yes. Mum and Jean were great friends, back in the day. Until the falling-out.'

'The falling-out?'

'All right, Violet, I'll be there in a minute! She didn't say? It was sad really. They were both after the same man, and in the end he didn't marry either of them! Such a waste of a friendship.'

My heart began to beat – tick, tick, tick, like the timer on a bomb. 'Colette – you don't by any chance know his name, do you, the man?' Graham. It had to be Graham.

She paused, and I could almost hear her trying to think. 'I'm sorry. It's gone. But if you'd like to come and visit Mum, she might remember. She lives here with me, in Cardiff. Or I could bring her to you, so she can see Jean again. I know she'd love to heal the rift, after all this time. Bella, I'm warning you, put that down.'

It was perfect. I was going to reunite Mrs G, not only with Graham – I was sure the mystery man was him – but also with her old friend. I promised to call Colette back soon with a plan, and excitedly hung up. I'd almost forgotten about the second call, and my heart sank down again as I recalled that I was maybe one step closer to sending Adam back where he belonged. I punched in the number and, after a few rings, a gruff-voiced man with a strong Welsh accent answered. 'Ello?'

I explained who I was.

'Oh right, the young lady with the pebble!' He sounded excited. I wondered what the Rock and Pebble Museum was like, and resolved to visit it one day. 'Now then, love, this is quite a find. It's a very rare basalt with seams of cobalt!' Normally I'd have been pleased to learn something I didn't know, a new fact for my head, but today I couldn't feel any joy at that. 'Thing about this is, it's only found in two locations in the UK.' He then went into a complicated explanation about erosion and tide tables, during which all I could think was, *Adam, Adam, Adam.* Even though he was in the next room, I had a violent longing to run in there and press my head into his chest, breathe him in while I still could.

'Where are those locations?' I asked, trying to concentrate.

I could hear flicking, as if Dougie was looking through a map or a book or something. 'One's far away. On the isle of Harris.' My heart sank – we'd never be able to get there to check it out. 'And the other's down near you, in Kent. A place called Dungevin Beach.'

My mother died when I was six. A short phrase, when you say it out loud. What it means is, I can barely remember her. In the pictures I have of her – grainy shots from the early eighties – she has fair hair, like me, and a wide laughing smile. She wears jeans and a sweatshirt with an embroidered peacock on the front. I don't remember the sound of her voice saying my name, or the feel of her arms around me as she buckled me into the back of the car on that last day. I don't remember exactly what she looked like after the crash, nothing but a vague impression of a cold waxy face. I don't remember if I saw my dad in the wreck, if he could talk, if he knew what had happened. I know, because Theresa told me, that it was half an hour before anyone came to help us on the isolated road. I know the blood never came out of my pink sandals. I know it took her ten minutes to die.

EVE

Adam stared at the pictures on the screen. 'It looks beautiful.'
We were in Magda's office, looking at the computer.

Dark blue water, white sand, cliffs running down to a narrow
strip of beach and then the water, deepening to navy. Dungevin
Beach could have been in the Mediterranean, not Kent. 'You
don't remember being there?'

He shook his head in that slow, pained way I'd come to recognise that showed he was combing through his memory banks
and coming up with nothing. 'I don't know. Maybe. I must have
been there recently, right?'

'You had the stone in your pocket. I guess that's not something you'd carry around for months?' Once the trousers went
in the wash it would have to come out. But who knew? We
were just guessing, as with everything. Raheem had come to
speak to Simon, and they were going to film a live interview
tomorrow evening for the local news, who were quite excited
at having a real-life story that didn't involve another parking
dispute or someone complaining about potholes on the A21.
Probably then someone would see it and come to collect him.
His wife, most likely. His daughter. I couldn't keep him from
them any longer.

'Eve.' Adam reached out and covered my hand with his large,
warm one. 'I want to say to you ... the idea of going home, of
finding myself, it should be a good one. But, you see ... since
I've been here with you ... '

151

I found myself pushing the chair away from Magda's rubbish-heap of a desk. 'I'm tired, Adam. I'm going to bed.'

Across the lawn. Check the Museum for dust, realising again how big the collection had become. What had started as a harmless hobby, small tokens to remember each resident, had somehow spiralled. I was becoming like those hoarder people on TV, only it was outside in my flat as well as inside in my brain. Turning away from it, sick of myself, my stupidity, my endless parade of bad memories.

A noise made me jump, almost knocking over a cheap lighter I'd swiped from the room of Mr Delacourt, a French resident we'd once had, who'd given me macarons he ordered in from Paris, the prettiest shades of green and pink and yellow. What was it? I heard it again.

Someone was knocking on my door. I froze for a moment. No one ever came here. Even if Magda needed me for something, she would ring rather than struggle across the grass in her high heels. 'Hello?' I called.

'Eve, it's me. Can I come in?'

Adam was outside my door.

RACHEL

An unexpected visitor – glad I cleaned up first lol

'I already looked everywhere,' said Rachel, watching Mark on his knees, with his hand up to the elbow feeling around her kitchen-sink U-bend. When she'd told him about the man at the house, he'd asked if he could search the place, look for more evidence. It felt strange having him there, too intimate. As if he would see the real her, the one she hid from the world, and find her wanting.

'You won't know where. Trust me, people hide things in places you wouldn't even think to look.' He withdrew his hand, holding a bottle of eco-friendly washing-up liquid, which cost £10 a go. 'What's this?'

'Um . . . it's supposed to be less chemicals. Better for kids.'

He raised his eyebrows. 'There's always something nowadays, isn't there?'

Rachel was still trying to process the evidence from Simon's work computer. Obviously, he was in money trouble – she already knew that. But that wouldn't be enough to make him disappear, would it? If he wasn't getting his bonus, they'd just rein in their spending. Maybe take Hannah out of school, at the very worst. It wasn't enough to make him secretly remortgage the house and run away. Was it?

She thought of the man on the doorstep, the wrong numbers on the landline. Clearly, the situation was worse than an unpaid bonus. 'I'll look upstairs,' she told Mark, leaving him to pull the kitchen apart. Carefully, to avoid startling Hannah, who was glued to some YouTube idiot in the living room, she went upstairs to the bedroom. It was tidy, the covers pulled smooth, the surfaces clean and clutter-free. You'd think the people who lived here had their lives together. In happier times, she might have taken a picture of her feet in socks, artfully arranged with a book and a cup of tea on a small bamboo tray. *Hashtag cosy night in!* She wouldn't even have read the book; she'd have spent the evening scrolling through her phone instead. Appearances, that was what mattered. To anyone who looked, they were a happy, stylish couple, with a beautiful, clever daughter in a top school. Perfect. Except it was all lies, rotten and crumbling.

She began to dismantle it. There had to be something, some trace of Simon's secret life. Under the mattress. Under the bed, the few inches of space down there (again, she found more dust than she was happy with, made a mental note to hoover when all of this was over, if it ever was over). The wardrobe. The top shelf with little-worn clothes and hats and shoes, ski gear, summer outfits, snorkels. Inside all his suits. She even lifted up the corners of the carpet, feeling a bit stupid, like a woman on TV again, sinister music ringing in her head. Of course there was nothing, no hidden panel or wonky floorboard. He wouldn't hide anything in Hannah's room, she was sure of that, and not in the living room either. Rachel, a compulsive tidier, would have found it in days. Where, then? She stood for a moment. Of course. There was one place she never went, Simon's sole responsibility. The shed.

She left the bedroom, then shot back, slightly ashamed of

herself, to smooth down the cover of the bed and close the drawers. The urge to make things look OK, it died hard.

When she went downstairs, she found Mark flat on his stomach, looking at the bottom of the kitchen table. 'Um . . . I have an idea.'

He pushed himself out, like a mechanic under a car. 'Show me.'

'Just getting something from outside!' she called to Hannah, who didn't even reply. She unlocked the back door and they went out into the dark garden. On second thoughts, she locked the door behind them. Hannah had to be kept safe. Rachel's heart went cold when she thought of how lax she'd been, letting her go to the toy shop by herself, when strange men were calling at the house, turning up on her doorstep. 'It's just over here,' she whispered to Mark, not sure why she was being quiet. She led him across the lawn to the shed, wishing she'd put on shoes. The key was under a flower pot nearby and she scrabbled around for it, thinking of bugs. A single light bulb hung inside, and it smelled of cut grass and wood stain and earth. A smell that reminded her of her dad, and now of Simon, too, and overwhelming sadness seemed to crush her. Why so many lies? How many families were going around, smiling for the cameras, telling each other nothing about what was really going on?

Mark looked around him. The place was full of random pot plants, half-empty paint cans, bits of lawnmower, abandoned furniture. In the corner was a music box, something they'd bought for Hannah as a baby. Simon had taken it out here to fix when it had broken years ago, then never done it. She'd forgotten about it, as had Hannah, who had more toys than she knew

155

what to do with. 'In there?' he suggested, and suddenly Rachel knew, she just knew, they would find something. And, when she opened the lid – a faint chime from the sad ballerina – there it was. A Nokia phone, and a charger, neatly rolled up.

A phone. Just a small, innocuous bit of plastic. It sat on the kitchen table like a scorpion.

She would have laughed at the way her life was descending into a second-rate thriller, had she not been so scared. Should she even be in the house? Did she need to take Hannah and run – but run where? Her own pride had seen to it that she'd nowhere to go.

She reached out for it – holding it gingerly, as if it was dirty or might burn her. She'd half-expected it would be dead, but the batteries on those old phones lasted for weeks. The small green screen glowed, revealing Simon's secret shame.

There was no code on this phone, it was so old. To start with it was boring stuff. Requests for money, reminders about debt payment plans. Then they turned nastier. *This is a warning. Further action will be taken if you fail to make repayments.* There was mention of bailiffs 'gaining entry', a phrase that brought back horrible memories. She swallowed, glancing up to check they'd locked the back door after them.

In the 'sent' folder were Simon's replies. These messages were punctuated correctly – typical Simon, not letting fear for his life get in the way of being grammatical. *OK, I'm getting it. It's just hard. Give me more time.*

Then, she held her breath, seeing a message with the date that was burnt into her brain. Monday, 5 March. The night everything had changed. *I can't do this. Please. You have to stop.*

Were those the words of a man about to run?

Mark said, 'OK. I think it's time to go to the police now.'

'No!' The word was instinctive. 'I can't.'

Mark exhaled hard. 'You realise Simon could be in danger?'

Of course she realised that. The tone of the messages on the phone had become nastier and nastier, ending with a not-even-veiled threat about knowing where they lived.

'Rachel, it's too late now for everything to be fine – you know that, don't you?' He looked at her, exasperated.

Angrily, she shot back, 'Of course I know that. He's going to turn up sometime ... ' *Dead or alive,* a voice whispered. 'And if I've not even searched for him, how's that going to look?'

'Listen to me. I have some friends on the force still; we could explain the whole situation, that these loan sharks or whoever they are might be after Simon. Anyway, even if you did hurt him, you didn't mean to ... '

She slammed her hand on to the table with surprising force, making the sugar bowl jump. 'Are you mad? They might arrest me, and who would take care of Hannah?'

'You said it was an accident, what happened.'

'How can I prove it?' She had no idea what state Simon was in, whether the people behind the messages had caught up with him or what. Her best hope had been that he would turn up somewhere, safe and sound, maybe with a slight bruise on his temple, and then the police wouldn't have to know anything about it. But as the days went by, if he wasn't OK, well, she looked more and guilty.

'You can trust them. They're not out to get you.' His voice was gentle, his large capable hands on the table. She saw a fleck of white paint on one and imagined him touching up a wall, screwing shelves into place.

'No,' she said again, her voice wavering. 'I can't. It's a hard line, Mark.' It was maybe the first time she'd said his name.

He said hers back. It felt like putting cards on the table. 'Rachel, I can't work this case if you're putting yourself in danger. I'd lose my licence, for a start. And you could go to prison, and I can't watch that. I just can't.'

She could have asked why, told him to go on, but she knew that both of them had reached their limits in this conversation. They had walked right up to the things that were left to say, on either side of the brick wall of it, but neither could cross it. Not while this was going on. 'So – you can't help me any more?'

'Not if you carry on with this. You could be in a lot of danger. The police can protect you.'

She thought of that Christmas morning long ago, her mother on the phone in a panic, calling the local police station. Hearing the laughter down the phone, and then later, when her father tried to stop them taking the TV, the bailiffs had called the police for back-up and this time they'd actually come, and they'd taken her dad to the station. On Christmas Day. 'I don't know if I believe that,' she said.

'Then we can't work together.'

'OK.' The coffee she'd made them was bitter in her mouth. She had an urge to fill it up with sugar, pour a sweet silty mixture down her throat, trying to drown out the pain.

'Rachel.' He hesitated. 'Please. I'm begging you. Just come to the station and report Simon missing.'

It was what she'd been afraid of all along – admitting what she'd done, owning up and perhaps being arrested on the spot. Saying goodbye to Hannah. Maybe even going to prison. But on the other hand, what choice was there? Carry on like this alone, without even Mark to help her? Flee her home, and go where exactly? Live in fear for the rest of her life?

She sighed. 'Can it wait till the morning, at least?' The thought of waking Hannah up, dragging her from bed, trying to explain what was happening, was too exhausting. She paused. She knew he lived quite a way away. 'You could ... if you like, we have a spare room.' In fact they had two, a fact that now struck her as ridiculous.

Mark hesitated. 'If you don't mind.'

Rachel thought of going to sleep under the same roof as him, divided just by a wall. Hearing him walk around, clear his throat, brush his teeth. 'Of course I don't mind,' she said, but really, she didn't quite know what she felt about it.

EVE

'So you see, it's just a way to remember them. Not weird. Not like a serial killer or anything.' The more I tried to explain the Museum, the stranger it sounded. Adam was sitting in my arm-chair, and I was cross-legged on the floor. It had never occurred to me before to get a second chair. He was staring at my collection, spread out over most of the flat.

OK, this may sound a little odd, but bear with me. I work somewhere where forgetting is part of everyday life. Our residents forget their children, their parents, their own names. Eventually there is nothing left of them, just a body, empty as a sheet folded away in the linen cupboard. So what I do is try to hold on to bits of them. Just a small object that reminds me of each one, that I can look at and think about who they were, their little quirks, their likes and dislikes, now that they're gone.

My collection has been built up over all the years I've been here – almost twenty now – so it spills over the Ikea shelves I bought for the purpose, on to the TV and the shelves in my room. There's a linen handkerchief (from Professor Catesby, a very proper Classics scholar we once had) and a hairclip in the shape of a dog (Miss Da Costa, who hated having her hair in her eyes), and next to that, Mrs Kadzinsky's pencil. It was only a stubby little thing, with someone's teeth marks eating into the zoo logo, but it reminded me of her and her puzzles, the way that as her dementia progressed she went from doing *The Times* one in half an hour, to barely being able to complete word searches in the children's comic one of the residents' grandkids left behind. So many objects, representing so many residents who had come into my life and gone again, as quietly as someone shutting a door.

'It's silly,' I said. God, he must think I was a total freak. This was why I didn't have guests – I shouldn't have let him in the door. 'Please, say something?'

'I think it's ... lovely,' Adam said finally, filling me with relief. 'It's not silly, Eve. Will you put something from me in it, when I go?'

An awkward silence. 'I suppose so.' Not that Adam had anything of his own here. Just the clothes he'd been found wearing, which he'd brought with him from hospital in a plastic bag, and nothing else, not even a pair of shoes.

He frowned. 'I don't like to think of it. Just being a piece in your museum. Not seeing you again.'

I looked down at the pattern on my carpet. There were sixteen squares lengthways, ten and a half widthways. The size of my world for the past seventeen years. 'Me neither,' I said quietly. 'But you have to go back to your life.'

'Couldn't you be part of my life?'

I tried to imagine it. How would I fit in, a weirdo like me, with the way I pictured his world? A wife, a daughter, an office job. Maybe another kid or two. The gym, barbecues in summer, dinner parties. Try as I might, I could see no place for myself there. Anyway, how would it be when he came back to himself, became a person with history, exes, problems, sadness? Who had strong opinions on things from biscuits to politics? An entire life's worth of baggage and memories for me to absorb. Would I be able to cope with that? 'I don't know, Adam.'

'Oh.'

Silence ticked away between us, counting down the seconds we had left together.

'We should go to Dungevin.' I thought I'd misheard him for a moment. 'We should go,' he repeated. 'The beach. The one with the pebbles.'

'But – it's miles away!'

'It's only two hours by train. We could be there tonight, I checked on Magda's computer. See the beach in the morning, have a cream tea. Then come back for the news interview.' His eyes met mine, steady. 'Eve – this could be the last time.'

I stared at the Museum, not sure I could speak. I knew what he meant. A trip just for us. The last adventure we'd go on, him and me. Then he'd go back to his life and I'd stay in this one, such as it was. I heard myself say, 'I'll pack a bag.'

'This is crazy!' Adam and I ran through Bishopsdean station, huffing, lugging our overnight bags and carriers from M&S. We'd spent too long choosing our train picnic, and now the 20.52 to Dungevin was leaving in five minutes.

I shouted, 'I've never done anything like this! Just gone some-where on a whim!' I hadn't even told Magda we were going, not sure if I was allowed to take a resident off-site overnight, or if it was some terrible safeguarding failure. We'd just left, and I had even braved a taxi to take us to the station. I hoped she wouldn't be worried – I needed this time alone with Adam, before I said goodbye.

'Me either! At least, I think not!' He laughed as we ran. 'I don't even know if I'm impulsive or not!'

We found our coach, and clambered on, dragging all our

162

things to the table seat I'd booked. People looked up as we entered, and for a second I saw us as they must. A man and a woman, laughing, breathless, laden with wine and crisps and little rolls of cheese and ham that cost four pounds fifty for ten. We must have looked like a couple, on our way for a romantic mini-break by the coast. I was determined to enjoy each moment of being with him, instead of being sad because they were the last.

Two hours later, we pulled up at Dungevin station. The time had passed in a flash, eating crisps, playing Scrabble (originally named Lexico, then Criss-Cross Words, did you know?) on the travel set I'd borrowed from Sunnyside, making up stories for the houses we passed. Here and there the tracks ran right along the sea, and I imagined we could just get off and stay here for ever, much the way I'd ended up in Bishopsdean to start with, the day I got on a bus just to see where it took me, as long as it was anywhere else than where I was. But Adam's daughter. His family – the wife he must have. I couldn't ask him to stay. I couldn't be part of his life. For a moment I'd felt my face ache with tears, and I made myself turn to him and suggest a game of noughts and crosses.

It was pitch-dark when we got off, the station tiny and windswept. The breath of the sea was in the air, and I could feel it nearby, restless, swirling. We were close to the edge. Tired, we dragged our bags through the quiet sleeping streets of the town, to the B & B I'd booked over the phone. A tired receptionist gave us a key, and it was then I realised I'd only booked one room.

Adam was standing behind me, looking at the rack of leaflets of tourist attractions. His eyes were tired, his hair standing up.

I turned to him. 'Um ... I'm sorry. I didn't think.' I held up the one key. It hadn't even crossed my mind, in the rush of planning. What must he think of me? 'I could try to get another ...' The receptionist had already gone, back to bed no doubt. 'I'm really sorry. What an idiot.'

He shook his head. 'It's fine. I just want to crash out. We can share a room for one night!'

But when we got upstairs, it was a double bed, not a twin. I paused again, drowning in embarrassment. Had I been thinking of us as a couple, that we were actually on a mini-break? He was most likely married to someone else! 'God, I'm sorry. I'm such a ditz today.' Me, who never forgot anything, I had finally been betrayed by my brain. This must be how the residents felt all the time.

He was already on the edge of the bed, taking off his shoes. 'Eve, it's fine. Let's just get some rest. We need to be up early.'

We stepped around each other politely. He let me in the bathroom first, and I got changed into my flannel pyjamas, glad that I always slept in the world's unsexiest garments. I got into bed while he brushed his teeth. I could hear every throat clear, every gurgle. The gentle rattle of the loo seat that made me blush. What was I doing? This was unprofessional, apart from anything else. He was one of our residents. Adam might be a young and handsome man, but he was still vulnerable. He had a brain injury, probably.

But then, so did I, in a way. Did Adam see me like that – a strange woman, a weirdo? Or was he possibly relieved to be with someone else whose memory didn't work properly? If we were both strange, did that make us normal together? One ordinary memory between us?

He came back out of the bathroom, dressed in the pyjama bottoms and T-shirt we'd bought him when he first arrived at Sunnyside. How easy it was after all to leave all your possessions behind – apart from five little objects of no real value. Maybe we didn't need all the anchors that we thought we did. Furniture. Houses. Family. Maybe we could just be people, in a certain place, in a certain moment. Together.

Adam sat down on the side of the bed, taking his socks off. I was so aware of every movement he made, the creak of the old bed springs between us. 'Are you warm enough?'

'I'm fine.' I moved over as far as I could to the side of the bed, as he climbed in. He cleared his throat again. Although I was doing my best not to touch him, I could feel the warmth of his skin just inches away.

'Eve?'

'Yes?' I held my breath.

'I – I want to thank you for everything you've done for me these past weeks. I tried to stay positive, when it first happened, but it was so frightening, not knowing who I was or why I was there. If I'd maybe done something bad. But you helped me. You were like – my home.'

He didn't need to say any more. I knew what he meant – that tomorrow, we might know who he was, and maybe who he was wasn't who he wanted to be. Tomorrow, all this could be over. Maybe we would never see each other again.

'Shall I put out the light?'

'Yes please.' Even with it off, the room glowed orange with a streetlight outside on the quiet high street of the town.

Under the covers, Adam's hand found mine and gripped it. 'Goodnight, Eve.'

'Goodnight.' He went off to sleep like that, clutching my hand, and as his grip loosened in sleep, only then did I let myself cry.

EVE

I woke up very early the next morning. It was as if my brain knew it was our last day, and wanted to spend as much time as possible with him. A lemon-yellow morning light was spilling through the gap in the thin curtains, and I realised, to my embarrassment, that our legs had tangled around each other in the night. I sat up. 'Um, morning.'

Adam yawned and blinked. 'Morning. What time is it?'

'Early. Not eight yet.'

'Good. We can set off to the beach before anyone else.'

'OK.' I averted my eyes as he climbed out of bed, even though he was wearing pyjamas. Half an hour later we were in the dining room of the small B&B, which was almost empty, eating cold toast and rubbery scrambled eggs. We didn't quite meet each other's eyes over breakfast, instead keeping them fixed on the TV, which showed Sky Sports as an apathetic waitress wiped a dirty cloth over the tables.

Since neither of us could drive – at least, not that we knew of – we were planning to catch the one bus an hour out of town to the beach. When we swung on, and took our seats on the torn leather benches, I experienced a sudden stab of happiness through the tightness in my chest. The sun was glinting on the navy-dark sea. We had the remainder of our snacks from the train, which Adam was already rummaging through in search of cheese and ham bites from Marks & Spencer, and we were trundling out of town on to a green-shaded country road. I was going to enjoy this day, no matter what. I knew it was something I would remember always, out of the flood of boring and hard days that stayed with me. I would try extra hard to press every detail of it into my head, like flowers between the pages of a book.

'Wow. I didn't expect it to be so . . . '

'I know. It's like . . . abroad.' Adam and I had got off the bus and hiked the two miles down the country road to reach the beach. Still early, it looked almost deserted, no cars in the car park. Far off in the distance, I could see a man walking two dogs. The beach was a small triangle of white sand, surrounded on two sides by sheer cliffs, and on the other by blue and navy sea, torn ragged by a stiff wind. At one side of the car park was a small shop, with buckets and spades hanging outside and signs advertising ice cream. We stood and breathed in the sharp sea air, tinged with frost after a hard winter.

'I must have come here,' he said, frowning. 'Recently. I wonder if I drove – the train didn't ring any bells. Why would I have come here, though?' I imagined him, standing here, bending down to lift a striped pebble – there were dozens of similar ones at our feet – putting it in his pocket. Maybe to place on his desk, or to give to the daughter he most likely had, the one the Lego had been for. Staring out at a wide dark sea, as wind ruffled the surface like a hand disturbing a smooth bedsheet.

Adam shivered. 'Cold still.' It wouldn't be tourist season for another few months, and he was right: despite the sunshine the day was chilly.

'Yeah. Wish I'd brought a better coat.' I only had a thin denim jacket on, and the wind cut right through me.

'Come here.' I hesitated as he held his arms open to me. For years, I had touched no one except to occasionally pat the hand or stroke the head of a resident. Usually when they had no idea where they were or who I was, a gentle touch to help anchor them to a world turned unfamiliar, terrifying. Dementia must be like living in a constant nightmare, where nothing makes sense. 'Eve. Please.'

I went to him. He was so warm I almost gasped, wrapped in a too-big duffel coat someone had left behind in Sunnyside. My face was muffled against his chest. 'Adam ... ' It wasn't even his name. Amazing to think I had known him all this time and I didn't know his name. I realised he was shaking. 'Are you cold too?'

'Not really. Eve ... I'm so scared.' He gasped out the last word. I pulled away to look at his white face. 'How can I go back to a life I can't remember? If I have a family ... what will it do to them, if I don't know them? I've been thinking my memory would magically come back once someone says, *Oh, you're so-and-so*, but what if it doesn't?'

I didn't know what to say. I knew more than most that memories did not just return, even when a person who loved you was begging and pleading with you. *Please, it's me. Don't you recognise me?* 'What else can we do, though?'

He shrugged. 'Run away? Look, that's France over there. We could ... eat cheese. Drink wine.'

'Sounds lovely,' I said, the weight in my chest growing heavier and heavier. We would never do that.

'Also, what if I did something bad? I have this horrible feeling ... I'm not going to like who I am.'

How could anyone not like Adam, his hands that stretched

over the piano keys, his kindness to the confused residents, his green eyes, his laugh? 'Of course you will,' I said. 'You're ... the best.'

'But you don't know me, Eve. Not really.'

I wanted to shout that of course I did, I knew everything about him, but he was right. He could have done anything in his past, and neither of us would know. Instead I just said, 'I'm going to miss you.'

'You too. Eve ... ' He gripped my face between his hands for a moment, my hair flying about us in the wind, and for a moment I felt his mouth press on mine, and lost my footing on the stony beach, and almost fell. He was kissing me! Oh my God. His mouth was so warm, his skin rasping mine, his hands in my hair. I pulled away. 'God, sorry, should I not have ... ?'

He was probably married. He must have kids, at least one. And what if, once he remembered who he was, he didn't want to associate with a lonely weirdo working in an old folks' home? 'Adam, I don't think ... '

'You're right. Sorry. Sorry, Eve.' He stepped away, running his hands over his face. 'God. This is so hard. I'm really sorry.'

'It's all right.' How could I explain that if we did that, I would never want to stop?

'Let's get out of here. I don't know, shall we get an ice cream or something?'

I was grateful to be on safer ground, but part of me, a large part of me, wanted to pull him back, wrap his arms around me again, rest my face against his stubbled cheek, breathe him in. 'Ice cream when it's cold?'

'You can have tea if you want. Come on, that little shop's open.'

Inside, the beach shop smelled musty and thrilling, a little damp, like wet feet dropping sand. An older lady sat behind the counter, painstakingly filling in a Sudoku in the paper (from the Japanese meaning 'single numbers', did you know?). 'Oh, hello there.' Her Kentish accent was a burr. 'Early, aren't you?'

'Beaches are nicest by yourself, don't you think?' Adam stepped forward.

She chuckled. 'Not much chance of that around here, love. Come back when there's a lick of sun and you can't move for tourists.'

Adam was scanning the chalk boards pinned to the wall. 'I'll have a ninety-nine, please. Eve?'

I didn't answer.

'Eve? Tea? Ice cream? Cake? All three? We are on holiday, after all.'

Again, I couldn't say anything. I just pointed. Adam followed my gaze. Behind the counter, stacked in a corner, were several storage shelves, with raffle tickets pasted on to them. Raffle tickets in the same colour as the one he'd had in his pocket.

'What's that?' My voice came out jagged.

The lady looked. 'Oh, just a sideline. I keep people's bags and that while they're at the sea, charge 'em fifty pee or so.'

'Is there . . . ?' I could hardly breathe. 'Is there anything there right now?' It seemed too much of a coincidence. After all, there must be thousands of tickets like that all over the country.

She frowned. 'Not much call for it right now, love, let me see. Oh! There's this old case. I dunno what happened with that, fella forgot it I expect, but I didn't like to throw it out in case it came back.'

'W-when was this?'

'Ooh, a few weeks back? I remember cos hardly anyone

171

brings cases to the beach, or comes at all this time of year. Let's have a look.' She bent and dragged out the small wheelie case, but I could already see that the ticket stuck to its handle was the same as the number as the slip of scrawled paper I had in my bag – 67.

We'd found the source of Adam's ticket.

RACHEL

Visiting the police station! So interesting. Wonderful atmosphere.

'I'm still not getting this. You're saying your husband's been missing for weeks?'

Rachel wanted to scream. It was the next morning, and she'd been talking to the desk sergeant at the local police station, through a pane of cracked glass, for almost ten minutes now. 'Yes.'

'But you never reported it.'

'No. I didn't realise he was missing – I thought he'd just . . . gone.' She'd decided to go with that explanation.

'So what changed?'

'Um . . . I think he may be in danger.'

'What kind of danger?'

Rachel turned to Mark, throwing her hands up in helpless frustration, and he took over. 'Mate, is DC Khan there? Raheem. He's a mate of mine – just tell him I'm here, please?' He turned to her. 'Got the photo?'

'Yeah.' She slid over her phone, which still contained the original of the framed shot on Simon's desk. It was the one she should have released to the police when he first went missing. Simon and Hannah on that beach he loved so much, him crouching down to put his arm around her, as they proudly displayed the sandcastle they'd made, sheltering it from stiff cross-Channel breezes. That day stood out in her memory because it was so unusual for Simon to take time off and not be on his phone all day. Sadly, she realised that if it was normal, she wouldn't recall it in such bright detail. It's only the exceptional days we hold on to, either the good or the bad.

The sergeant sighed and picked up a phone, muttering into it. For a moment, Rachel rested her head against the glass, thinking of Hannah at school, and who would pick her up if this dragged on. She would be off for Easter next week, meaning she'd be around all the time. Impossible to hide the truth from her. What a mess. Rachel had just realised how dirty the glass probably was, and lifted her head to see a woman in a Next trouser suit, her eyes tired but sharp, dreadlocked hair bundled on top of her head. 'Mrs Kempner?'

'Yes.' As Rachel followed the woman behind the sealed door, she didn't think now was the time to explain that, no matter what happened, she'd decided to go back to her own surname.

On TV, they always put you in a nasty interview room if you were a suspect. The kind with two-way mirrors and grey walls, a chipped table that maybe the detective would knock over in a rage if they thought you were lying. The one Rachel was in was quite dingy, but had carpet and no two-way mirror that she could see. Mark had not been allowed to come in with her, and she wished fervently he was here, his comforting solid presence. She sat opposite the detective, whose name was DS Irene Rusombe. She was taking it as a bad sign that Mark's friend, Raheem, wasn't the one interviewing her.

'So, you last saw your husband on the night of the fifth of March.'

'Yes. We had a row, and he ran off and . . . that was it.'

'You thought he was having an affair?'

'I saw a text on his phone and I assumed . . . I think I was wrong, though. I over-reacted.'

The detective wrote something down, which seemed to take an extraordinary amount of time. Rachel fidgeted. Why was she writing? Didn't they believe her? 'And you have no idea what might have caused him to run off like that?'

She shook her head. Lying to the police. That was a crime, wasn't it? Or was it just if you lied in court?

'And the fight you had, did it turn physical?' The detective's eyes were dark and calm.

'God, no! Nothing like that.' A flash across her eyes. Blood on the kitchen floor, soaking through paper towels. Simon stumbling back, terror on his face. Her mind raced through everything she knew from watching *Grey's Anatomy*. Head injuries could cause memory loss, yes. And the amnesia could be retroactive, meaning that people didn't remember what had happened to them right before it. If they ever found Simon, the incident could be totally wiped from his brain. 'Are you looking for him? I mean, he could be in danger, right? Those weird phone calls, the man who came to our house . . . ' She should have asked that sooner, she realised.

'Of course we're looking. We'll put an alert on the news straight away, now that we know he's missing.' Was that a pointed comment? Rachel tried to keep her face blank.

'So . . . can I go home now?'

'Not quite yet. Your daughter is safe?'

'She's at a friend's.' She'd had no choice but to ask Janine again. The story was probably all round the mums' WhatsApp group already – *Rachel's husband's been missing all this time! She's at the police station!* Rachel imagined the neighbours on their door-steps, drawn by the blue lights as police tore her house apart. She thought the gossip would go on for months, if not years. The cold-shouldering she'd get from the school mums. Maybe they'd even have to move. But it was always going to be this way. As soon as she'd let herself lose her temper that night, as soon as she'd done what she did, there was no going back from any of it. The last few weeks had just been – borrowed time.

The DS stood up. 'We'll let you know if we find anything. In the meantime, please just stay here.'

'Of course,' Rachel said, pretending to be helpful, suppressing her panic as best she could. What if they never let her out again?

EVE

Adam and I sat outside the shop on a picnic bench, staring at the case on the table between us. 'This is my stuff.' He sounded dazed, as I suppose you would be when you finally discovered a whole bag of things you didn't remember owning. Inside we'd found expensive clothes, neatly folded into squares. A leather toiletry bag with designer shampoo and aftershave. If I'd been on my own, I would have uncapped it and sniffed, trying to breathe in what he smelled of in his other life. There was also a ferry ticket to France, with a date for two weeks before. A few days after he'd gone missing. It wasn't the kind with a name on, unfortunately, so we still didn't know his true identity. 'I don't understand,' said Adam. 'So I came down here, and I left this luggage? I must have been planning to come back and pick it up, then, what – run away?'

I didn't say anything. It certainly looked strange, leaving your things all the way down here, at the edge of the country.

'I must have been in trouble,' he said, brow furrowed. 'If I have a family – and I was planning to leave ... ' The ticket was only for one.

I wanted to say something – that I knew he was a good person, that it didn't matter what he'd done or what mistakes he'd made in his other life, I knew him in this one and he was good, beyond good – but before I could, the shop owner came hobbling out the door. She started to speak, then collapsed in a fit of smoker's cough. 'Come quick!' she managed. 'It's you! You're on the lunchtime news!'

177

RACHEL

The wait at the police station stretched on for hours, during which Rachel sat in a marginally nicer interview room – it had a sofa and rug – and waited, clutching a cooling polystyrene cup of tea. It was now the colour of brown sludge. Soon, possibly in the next few hours, she might see Simon again. Would he remember what she'd done to him? There was a worse alternative too – they would find him, yes. But not alive. She looked at her phone again – Janine had texted and Hannah was fine apparently, doing 'crafts' with Jago, probably making a model of the London Eye from lolly-pop sticks. Janine had asked, *Everything all right???* Rachel didn't reply. No, everything was not all right, very far from it.

The door clicked open. She jumped, spilling tea on herself. 'Mrs Kempner?' A younger male detective.

'Oh. Yes?' She flicked drops of tea from her jumper.

'Can you come with me please?'

'Where are we going?'

He said nothing. She followed him down a corridor, which was hot and smelled of frazzled lights and beef stew. Posters flapped in their wake – burglary, domestic violence. All the things Rachel had thought were outside the scope of her life.

'Here you are.' He opened the door of another room – frosted glass, chipped wood – and she looked inside and saw, sitting on a sagging sofa – Simon. It was Simon.

*

He stood up. She looked him over in a flash – the clothes were his, which was confusing, because how had he got them? Had they taken him home first? He looked fatter, puffier, as if he'd spent the last few weeks eating unhealthy food. Off his usual regimen of protein shakes and low carbing. There was a mark on his forehead, healing now but still red and livid.

'I . . . Are you OK?' she said stupidly.

Did he recognise her? The police had said he'd no memory, didn't even know his own name. He was frowning. 'I'm sorry. My head's . . . a bit jumbled up. I don't know . . . '

Oh God, he didn't know her. It was surreal. And maybe he didn't remember what had happened. 'I'm your wife. Rachel.' It sounded so strange to say that, a line straight from a day-time soap.

'And I'm Simon?' He looked so vulnerable when he said it, so unlike himself, that for a moment she wondered if he was faking it. Even the lines of his face had changed, and he looked younger, at least five years younger. She realised he must have been permanently frowning for the last few years, weighed down by stress and worry.

'Yes. You're Simon, and we have a daughter, Hannah. She's seven.'

'I have a . . . ' He stepped back, and then he collapsed on to the sofa, and he was weeping into his hands. 'A daughter. Oh my God. I can't remember her! I can't remember anything.'

Rachel stood frozen. Should she comfort him, or was she like a stranger to him?

Detective Rusombe had stepped into the room, quiet and calculating. 'We think you should take Simon home now, Mrs Kempner. We'll come with you, see you settled in. Maybe being home will trigger some memory of what happened after he ran out of the house that night.'

The way she said it, Rachel wondered if the other woman knew it was a lie, that this wasn't what had happened. Or maybe she was just being paranoid? Maybe they accepted her story, that Simon had left her, and somehow lost his memory after that?

'Of course.' She swallowed. 'Let's get him home and we'll take care of him.'

As they led Simon out, her following in his wake, gulping in air after the small stuffy rooms of the station, she watched his frightened, helpless eyes, and she had no idea what was going to happen next.

EVE

He was gone. While we were on our way to the beach, his wife had turned up to report him missing, and the detective on duty had made the connection between this lost man and the one they'd found a few weeks earlier, and then it was on the news, and then the shop owner had called the police, and a car had quickly arrived to take us back. I knew I would be in trouble with Magda sometime, once this was all sorted out, taking Adam away without telling her. But I couldn't bring myself to care.

Simon Kempner. That was Adam's real name. Forty-three. As I'd thought, he had a daughter, who was seven. And he had a wife. Rachel. The evening we returned to Bishopsdean, I begged Raheem to tell me what was going on, when he came round to eat Julie's chocolate lava cake, but all he would say was that Simon's wife had come to the station, which was how they'd tracked us down. He was back with her now, as far as Raheem knew.

When I heard that, I sat down hard at the kitchen table. 'All right, Eve?' Julie looked at me with concern. 'You'll miss him, won't you?'

'I . . . he was a resident, that's all.'

'More than that. He was ever so handy lifting down the heavy pans for me.' She patted my shoulder and placed a plate of cake in front of me. I shoved some in my mouth. Hot, sweet, filling the emptiness inside me. I shovelled in some more. It somehow hadn't crossed my mind that it would be this fast. Even when the shopkeeper had come running out and insisted right there and then on calling the number on the TV screen, and a short while later the local Kent police had pulled up and taken us to the hotel for our cases, then driven us all the way back to Bishopsdean (which took something like two hours, during which time a shell-shocked 'Simon' and I didn't speak at all), and we'd driven up to the police station and he'd got out, even then I was going to unbuckle my belt and go in with him. Because that's what I did – I went places with him. I helped him.

But the police officer, a young woman called Toni, had stopped me. 'That's OK, miss, we'll take you home.'

'But ... '

'He'll be all right. They've a social worker waiting, and a doctor. And his wife, of course. They'll take it from here.' And they sent me home to Sunnyside, and Magda had opened the door and enfolded me in her floppy, perfume-scented bosom. Then immediately told me off – *I could lose my licence, Eve* – then hugged me again. *Oh, lovie.*

'Simon don't seem like a good name for him,' said Julie now, wiping down the counter with vicious swipes. 'He was just our Adam, weren't he?'

Raheem nodded, through his third helping of cake. 'What will happen now?' I asked him. 'He'll just – be at home?'

'S'pose so. They said he might need to be in hospital for a spell, depending.'

Julie tapped her spoon to clear it – bang, bang, bang. 'It's proper weird the wife didn't report him missing. Maybe she did something to him!'

I wished I knew more about her, his wife. On the news they'd shown Simon being taken out of the police station into a car. He'd got changed into the clothes from the case and I still had the ones from here, the things he'd been wearing in Kent, in a plastic bag at my feet. I knew the trousers would have sand in the turn-ups (which is almost entirely made of silicon dioxide, but I found I had no enthusiasm for facts right now), tiny fragments of the beach where we'd been together for the last time. I knew they would smell of him, that breath of grass and toffee I always wanted to press my face into when he was near. Maybe all I had left of him now.

That's the trouble with being able to remember everything. The people you've loved, the people you've lost, the feeling doesn't go away just because they're not with you. Even if they die, or are completely lost to you. Even if they've forgotten all about you. You still remember every little thing about them, all the while knowing that you will never see them again.

I walked out of Sunnyside in a sort of daze. Back in my flat. The door locked, alone. *Pointless* on TV. It used to be my happy place, but now I just felt like I had a hole beneath my ribs, open and raw. Empty. Without him. It was so stupid! There was no Adam, just a married man called Simon Kempner, who worked in stockbroking. I wasn't totally clear on the full story of how he'd ended up lost and running along the M25, or how he'd hurt his head, but one thing was clear. I had no idea who Simon Kempner was.

Trying to cheer myself up, I dusted the Museum, brushing away a few cobwebs, but it just made me feel worse. What good was it to have toy soldiers and snow globes and sepia photographs, when the people who'd owned them were long gone?

(Did you know *sepia* is the Latin word for cuttlefish? No? Why would you? Do any of these silly facts matter, the ones that silt up my brain?) I might do my best to remember them, the owners of these items, but no one else did, and when I died too it would all be lost for ever.

I had to keep going, even though my heart was in my ankles. Soon, I had to see Janet Marks's daughter, Colette. She was bringing her mother to Sunnyside to visit Mrs G. I had tried to explain what was happening, only to have Mrs G look past me in her vague way, then shout at me when I said it again. 'I'm not stupid, girl! I heard you the first time. I won't do it.'

'Come on, Mrs G, you must! She's coming all this way.'

She'd folded her arms. 'I don't care. Janet Marks, or whatever her name is now, she's no better than a common TROLLOP.'

I felt sure we were going to find out that Graham was the name of the man they'd fought over. Maybe he was still alive. But even with the solution of a mystery on the cards, I couldn't feel anything but empty. Even my quiz shows didn't cheer me up. For once it really did seem pointless, these little titbits of information like whose assassination had kicked off the First World War, or what slivovitz brandy is made from. What did it matter, all those facts and figures? No one cared any more. They could google whatever they needed to know in five seconds flat instead. Nobody but me. Maybe not even me any more.

Then, just as I was sinking into the depths of despair, I remembered something – in my unpacked bag from Kent. Was it still there? I pulled out my dirty clothes – a shower of sand falling on to the carpet – and there it was, the little plastic bag of Adam's (Simon's!) things. He might want them back, mightn't he? Even if the ring wasn't valuable it was pretty, and the Lego had been for his daughter. So it would be perfectly reasonable for me to find him and give them back. Wouldn't it? The only problem was, I didn't know where he was. A brief swoop back into darkness and then I remembered what Raheem had said – Adam (Simon!) would be going back to hospital at some point, having check-ups until they worked out why he couldn't remember. I could go there.

The hole under my ribs started to close itself and I felt as if the light in the room had been turned up. There was hope. No matter what, I might see him one last time, and after that – who knew what would happen?

RACHEL

'Wow! We have such a nice house.'

It was so strange, the way this new Simon spoke. Artless, wondering about everything. Admiring the house, when just before the incident happened he'd been complaining that it wasn't big enough, didn't have 'kerb appeal', a phrase she had never heard before she met him.

'Yes. It's – you always liked it.'

'Where is Hannah? That's her name, right? Will I see her?'

Hannah was still at Janine's, no doubt well on her way to building the Seven Wonders of the World out of toilet-roll holders and yogurt pots. 'I don't think it's wise just yet. I need to tell her you're … different. That you don't remember things.'

He nodded sadly. 'I didn't mean to forget her. I hope she'll understand that. Do you think you can still love someone you've forgotten?'

That was the question, wasn't it? Since Simon no longer remembered her, was he even her husband? Rachel approached the door, feeling in her bag for the key. 'I don't know.'

Rachel was still struggling to take everything in. All that time panicking, desperately wondering where Simon was, only for him to turn up on a beach in Kent. Dungevin again. Somehow, that place held the key to what was going on inside his head, an explanation for his strange behaviour leading up to his disappearance. Simon himself couldn't explain it because he still had no memory of who he was. All the time before that night, it had simply vanished. Had she done that to him? They'd said he had a head injury, but all the same the doctors hadn't been able to find any obvious damage that would lead to total amnesia like this. So ... maybe it wasn't her fault? But what then was causing it? Rachel felt jittery, like time was moving at once too slowly and too fast. He was here. He was back. Except ... it wasn't entirely him.

Simon followed her in, his eyes taking in everything. Rachel tried to see it as a stranger would – a tidy, welcoming house, stylishly decorated, framed family photos on the wall. Neat piles of intelligent reading material like the *Economist* and the *London Review of Books* (of which she had never yet read a copy). Farrow & Ball walls. Nothing wrong here. Not a trace of the confrontation between them that had caused so much damage. If he truly remembered nothing, this place must be a strange place to him. Not home. Just the bland and pleasant house of people he didn't know.

The police had let them leave with little fuss, but Rachel sensed they still had questions about how Simon had ended up running down the M25 with no shoes on and a head injury. She hadn't said that she knew how Simon got the injury. Could they tell she was lying? She just wanted to shut the door, take a breath and try to deal with this new Simon, who apparently had no memory of her at all, after ten years together.

'You must be tired. Would you like coffee?'

Simon blinked. He was still clutching the wheelie case he had apparently left in storage at a shop near Dungevin, several weeks before he went missing. Rachel didn't recognise it; he must have bought it specially for whatever he was planning. He'd bought a ferry ticket, too. Only for himself. She wanted to scream at him, *What were you up to? What the hell was going on?* But she couldn't, because he was injured, he was an invalid. And it was up to her to take care of him, because she was his wife.

'Coffee?' she asked again. Oh God, what if he had permanent brain damage? Would she find the strength and love to nurse him?

'I just – do I even like coffee? I can't remember. At Sunnyside we drank tea, gallons of it.'

'I can make tea if you prefer.'

Still he stood there, like a courier waiting for a signature. 'I don't know. This is all so . . . this is our house? I live here?'

'Of course you do.' It was surreal, the way he looked about him with a stranger's eyes. Part of her wanted to shake him. *Come on, you must remember! How can you forget? It's me! It's your piano! It's that table you spent two grand on!*

'I just can't remember it. I can't . . . Rachel, I'm sorry, I can't remember *you*.'

She didn't know what to say to that. To him, was she a total stranger, not the woman he'd spent ten years sleeping beside? The woman who'd done . . . *that* to him? Was their marriage, all the past good and recent bad of it, down the drain? 'They said it might come back. You just need to take it easy.'

He sagged. 'All right. I guess I'll have some coffee.'

'Coo-ee! Anyone home?' Just then, the door opened and the sound of light running feet made Rachel jump. *Oh no – she can't be here . . .*

Hannah burst through the door, her curls sticking up, closely followed by Janine Hewson-Taylor. 'Daddy! Daddy, you're home!' And she hurled herself into Simon's arms, and Rachel stared in horror as Simon, ashen-faced, stumbled away from his daughter, as if he had never seen her before in his life.

EVE

To my surprise, I found that going back to the hospital was kind of comforting. It reminded me of him, and of course it was almost impossible to be really lonely in a place like this, full of people. I told myself it would be all right. I might have helped Adam, but he had helped me too, shown me the world wouldn't end if people knew about my memory. I'd let him into my life, I could let other people in too. It was a habit just like everything else. I'd get used to telling them I never forgot anything, and maybe someone out there would be all right with it. Someone like Adam, who couldn't remember things at all, perhaps. They might even like my memory, if their own didn't work so well.

Maybe because I'd been here with him, even the hospital smell now had some pleasant associations to replace the old, bad ones. I had to remember that. Even if bad memories remain, sometimes you can bury them beneath an avalanche of good ones. I made my way up to the Neurology Ward, the plastic bag of things clutched in my coat pocket. I realised I should have kept one of them. Something to add to the Museum. The pen, probably, as that wouldn't be missed. After all, although Simon was alive, 'Adam' was certainly dead. And I would like to have one thing of his that he'd touched and kept close to him. I whipped the pen out and stuck it into the pocket of my jeans, then I knocked on the office door, and it was opened by Praj, who looked excited to see me. 'Eve! You came back!'

'Yes, I just ... '

'Mad news about Adam, isn't it? Simon, I mean! He still doesn't remember, even now he's home.'

'Oh, he doesn't?' I had wondered about that. As he'd feared, his memories had not automatically returned now he knew who he was. I thought of his daughter. Her father not recognising her. The way that felt.

'Not yet. Maybe, in time. I'm so pleased you've come to help us, though. Come in.' He was ushering me in before I really understood what was happening. 'We weren't sure you'd come back, to be honest. You didn't seem keen. But the possibilities inside your brain – they're amazing. Now, we know memories are stored in certain places in the brain. What we'd like to do is get a look at the same areas in yours. Who knows, maybe it'll be the key to treating memory loss. Dementia, head injuries. You could be our breakthrough, Eve.' He looked so excited that I didn't know what to say.

He thought I'd come back to help with the study. And why not? Maybe he was right. All this time I had been hiding from what I could do, helping people on their way to death to claw back the odd memory here and there, the name of a long-gone dog, the brand of sweets they'd eaten on their honeymoon. If Praj was right, maybe there was a way to stop the damage before it even began.

I was very nervous. My heart pounded in my ears, and my hands were so sweaty that when I reached for the handle on the MRI machine, they slipped right off. At least this time I was wearing my own clothes, not the gaping hospital gowns they put me in before, when they scanned my brain after my mother died (did you know that Japan is the country with the highest number of MRI machines per capita?).

Dr Praj gave me a thumbs-up. 'All OK, Eve?' I nodded because I couldn't speak. My breath was coming in short little puffs. I told myself I was doing this for Adam, but not just for him, to help all the other people whose memories had been lost to them. And who knew, maybe if they could look inside my brain, they'd see something different, some kind of switch they could flip that would turn me normal, let me forget things like other people did, like the password to the Netflix account or the name of your childhood teacher or the exact colour of the rug in your grandmother's house. I wanted to lose these things. I had too many, crowding out my brain. Because if you keep the good memories, the Christmas mornings, the snowball fights, the first kisses, you also keep the bad ones. Like blood lapping around a little pink shoe. Like the colour of twelve different bedspreads.

The machine was whirring now. Pulling me back into the dark tunnel, like a monster slowly eating me. Dr Zoe talked in my ear. 'OK, Eve, we're just putting you in now. You'll be able to hear us the whole time. We have to ask you not to move. Keep as still as possible.' Immediately I wanted to twitch, but I held my breath, and then I was inside. All around me were smooth plastic walls, like a coffin.

I breathed in and out. This was important. I had to do this. But then I forgot to count the seconds for a moment and it all came back.

They first noticed my strange memory about a year after the accident. If that seems like a long time, remember I was in foster care. Foster kids don't get a lot of attention, as a general rule, unless they're being bad. It was Natalie who spotted it, screwing up her face. *Eve, how come you know all the words of songs on the radio? What's the matter with you?*

I hadn't even realised this was strange. And I was about to find out my weirdness went a lot further than this.

'Eve? Are you all right? You've gone very quiet.'

I snapped back into the moment, the memory that was still being made, and I was inside the machine. I was in my thirties, decades away from that past day. I was in control. I focused on my breathing. 'Do you see anything?'

'Well, yes.' Praj sounded excited. 'It's amazing, Eve! You've got brain structures we've never seen before. The hippocampus is so much bigger than usual, and the occipital lobe – the bit that handles visual processing – it's, well, it's really dense. We're sure to get a paper out of this.'

'Eve?' It was Zoe. 'Can you hear us OK?'

'Y-yes. It's great.' I didn't sound very convincing. All I could hear was what Natalie had said, all those years ago. *Urgh, she's a freak.* At the moment Adam (Simon!) and I were the same, both a little strange, both not able to manage basic human functions. I couldn't forget and he couldn't remember. But he could be cured, surely, now he was with his family, and he would go back to being a regular person who could remember his name and where he lived and who he loved, but not the number of the bus that used to run past the first flat he ever lived in, or the exact position of the cigarette burns on the carpet in his fourth foster home. And I would still be me, Eve the freak. *Alone.* The word echoed in my mind, like a single stone dropped into a well, threatening to start another cascade of memory.

After a while, Praj said, 'Let's get you out now. We have some fantastic readings, but if you don't mind, we'd like to see you a few more times. Carry out some memory function tests, that kind of thing? I think you've got something really special going on! It could revolutionise our understanding of how to treat dementia. Are you up for it?'

'Sure. Fine.' All I wanted was to get out and go back to my flat, surround myself with my Museum and reference books and turn on *Pointless*, and let out some of the knowledge and memories that filled my head like an overflowing bin. It had been silly to imagine I might see Adam here, that things could go back to the way they were. He was home in his life now, and as I'd feared, there was no space for me there.

RACHEL

Watching Hannah hug her father, only to be pushed away, was definitely one of the worst moments of Rachel's life. Way up there with Christmas 1987, childbirth, and of course not forgetting the night of the incident.

Hannah was bewildered. 'Daddy, what's wrong? Where have you been?'

'Er ... Oh God, I'm sorry, I'm sorry.' Simon was practically cowering from her. Snapping out of her frozen state, Rachel stepped forward and steered Hannah away.

'Darling, Daddy is very tired and a bit confused. He's ... he sort of got lost for a while. You remember, like next door's dog.' In retrospect that was perhaps not the best comparison, but she'd had to think on her feet.

Janine cleared her throat – oh God, why was she still here? Taking notes to feed back to the WhatsApp horde? Maybe they had a secret group Rachel wasn't in, where they discussed her shortcomings. Her missing, brain-injured husband who she hadn't reported gone. Her child with non-matching socks. Her undone roots. 'I'll leave you to it, Rach. Call if you need anything.' And finally she was gone, leaving Rachel with the remnants of her family.

Hannah cried. She hardly ever cried, not even when she'd cut her hand on a bit of the food processor left on the draining rack by Mrs Cole, their cleaner, and needed three stitches. 'But why did Daddy not hug me?'

Rachel was cradling her on the sofa, both of them shaking with the violence of Hannah's sobs. Her face was red and wet against Rachel's Boden T-shirt. 'Darling, he's lost his memory.'

'He has to remember me! Mummy, he's known me all my *life!*'

'I know. I know. It's not very nice.' It was an unsettling experience, to see a man with the face of your husband just look right through you. He'd stared at the house, the pictures of them on their wedding day, on holiday, the day of Hannah's birth, as if he remembered none of these things. Was it even possible, a total amnesia like that? She thought if people hurt their heads they just forgot a few days, perhaps conveniently including the night of the incident. Not everything, even his childhood. The doctors couldn't find a reason for it. Was it possible . . . it wasn't real?

No. He would never hurt Hannah like that.

But he was going to leave you, a little voice whispered. Simon had bought a ticket to France, left a suitcase of his clothes in a small town in Kent, of all places. That, along with the holiday he'd taken from work, the threatening phone messages and the strange business with the house, all added up to one thing – he had planned to leave them with a pile of debt and run off.

When Hannah eventually stopped weeping, and Rachel managed to distract her with the promise of a Penguin bar – standards had really gone to pot around here – she went into the kitchen. Simon was standing looking out the French doors at the garden, very close to where the incident had happened. Her stomach lurched at the memory. The grass was too long. She'd have to ring the gardener – but they didn't have money for things like that any more. She'd have to rethink her entire life. 'OK?'

He turned, and for a second she saw him like a stranger, the way he must see her now. Handsome. He had always been handsome, those green eyes that had drawn her in on that day ten years ago, made her drop her hat on to the floor. His dark hair needed cutting, and he hadn't shaved in some time. 'I'm sorry. Is she all right?'

'I don't know. It's hard.'

'I keep trying and trying – I look at all these things . . . ' He gestured to the kitchen with its copper pans and stylishly mismatched crockery, the garden with the bird feeder and swing he had installed. 'I know I must have helped choose them, used them every day. But there's just nothing. It's so scary.'

She leaned against the kitchen island. 'You really remember nothing?' There was so much she wanted to ask him. *Why did you do it? Were you actually going to leave us? What the hell were you up to?*

'Nothing. I'm so sorry, Rachel.' Even the way he said her name was different. Like talking to a recent acquaintance, not a wife. 'What are we going to do?'

The question hung in the air. How could they carry on like this, forcing him to live with two strangers? Where else could he go?

EVE

'Isn't this exciting, Mrs G?' I forced on a smile, though inside I felt even grumpier than she looked. Sitting in her chair under a rug, she had a face like a slapped arse, as Magda would say. It was the next day, and Janet Marks and her daughter would be here any minute, but what had seemed like such a great idea a week ago now looked doubtful.

'Exciting? What do I want with excitement, at my age? All I want is to be left alone to watch *Doctors* and then die in peace. But you will insist on MEDDLING.'

'But it's your old friend, Janet!'

'That cow,' she muttered. 'I don't want to see her.'

I sighed. 'Mrs G, it's too late. They're on their way.'

'They're here,' said Julie, sticking her head in.

'See? They're here. Just have a cup of tea, catch up, and then they can head back. I got you some biscuits with chocolate on.'

'You better not let that cow have any.'

Shaking my head, I went out to the lobby to welcome our visitors. Janet's daughter Colette was a trim woman of about forty, with feathery blonde hair and too much pink lipstick. She was fretting about parking. 'Are you sure the car will be OK?'

'Yes, totally; there're no restrictions on this road.'

'Because I got a ticket once and I don't want another, it was ever so much hassle.'

'I promise, you'll be fine. This must be your mum?' Janet Marks was old and stooped, but she walked by herself, leaning on a flowery walking stick. She had a lovely beaming face, and I was amazed she and Mrs G had ever been friends. As she came in, she almost fell over something that streaked past the front door. A black cat, running fast.

Julie, who had come out to nosy, shooed him away. 'Bloody thing. He was begging round the kitchen earlier. Musta smelled the lunchtime salmon.'

Mrs Marks said to me, 'Hello, dear. I'm Janet. It's ever so good of you to set this up. I always regretted my falling-out with Jean.'

'Yes, she ... she said the same,' I lied. I leaned in. 'I'm sorry, she's a little confused. Please don't be upset if she seems ... ungrateful.'

Janet burst out laughing. 'Oh, that's Jean! She was always a grumpy goat. The boys flocked to her all the same – liked a challenge, I think.'

'Oh yes?' I tried to think how I could bring up Graham. 'Any in particular?' But it was too late, Colette had already marched into the lobby and was now fretting about where she could hang her coat because, 'It's wool, you know, it will soak up smells! Just soak them up like a sponge!' While Julie fussed around with coat stands and cups of tea, I dashed into the rec room to make sure Mrs G hadn't done a runner. Not that she could walk, but you never knew. Residents could get quite far when motivated by something they didn't want to do.

'They're here!'

Mrs G grunted. 'I won't see them.'

'Here they are!' Ignoring her, I ushered them in, pulling over a seat for Janet.

'Oh, Jean! It's me! Janet! Gosh, it's been ages.' Janet pressed her plump cheek to Mrs G's withered one. I held my breath, but Mrs G let her.

'It's you, then, is it?' she said grouchily.

'Yes, Jean. Come to make amends, after all these years.'

Mrs G sighed. 'I can hardly remember what we fought over, truth be told.'

Janet sat down, grasping Mrs G's hand in hers. 'I'm glad to hear you say that, Jean. It wasn't right, falling out over a fella. The tizzy we got into over him! He was handsome and all, but not worth that.'

'He didn't want either of us, in the end, did he?'

'Well no, Jean, he was gay, wasn't he? Like that Elton John.'

'He was?' Mrs G blinked.

'Oh yes. Don't you remember, he lived all those years with his special friend, Brian?'

Mrs G was frowning, trying to work it out. 'He was *gay*?'

'Very, Jeanie. Weren't we naïve, that we didn't spot it!' Janet let out a happy peal of laughter, and even Mrs G smiled. I almost laughed myself in relief. It was going to be OK. 'So, friends again?'

'I suppose.'

I leaned in. 'Janet, I don't suppose you know what became of Graham, do you?'

'Graham?' She frowned. 'Who's Graham?'

Oh dear, I hoped her mind wasn't going too. 'The man you fought over, who was gay.'

Mrs G tutted. 'You've taken leave of your senses, girl. His name wasn't Graham, it was *Colin*. Colin Tanner. Handsomest man in Leeds.'

Puzzled, I asked, 'Janet, do you remember any other Graham? A boy you knew, maybe?'

Janet shook her head. 'Oh no. And I can remember everyone from those days. You remember the dances, Jean? We loved those dances.' And they were off, reminiscing about the old days, and happy as I was to see Mrs G loosening up, her memories of the past intact, I was even more puzzled than before. If Graham wasn't an old boyfriend, then who the hell was he?

'Another good deed, young Eve?' Terry had come up behind me, painstakingly inching over the carpet with his walker. A book of trivia was tucked under one arm. 'You must be missing our Adam. He was a great help with the crossword, he was, even if he didn't know his own name.'

I wished people wouldn't keep bringing him up. It made it impossible to forget him for even one second. 'Oh no. Just – trying to be useful.'

'There's another way you could be useful.' He waved the trivia book at me. 'The South of England Pub Quiz League. Finals are tonight and we're a man down. Maureen's going in for cataract surgery – good job, really, she's been no earthly use at the picture round for months now. Imagine, she thought a map of France was Iran!' He shook his head in disbelief at such a mistake.

I tried to think of an excuse. 'But – wouldn't it be cheating? You know, because I ... remember things more than most people.' I could all too easily imagine the looks, having to pretend I'd forgotten a name or date sometimes, just to seem normal.

'Not a bit of it! I like to think we all have a touch of special memory, us quizzers. Can you name all the FA Cup winners, back to the year it started? Or even the year it started?'

I thought about it and drew a blank. We'd never watched

sport, back in the foster homes, and these days I had no cause to know about it. I didn't know something! 'No,' I said, suddenly excited. 'Ask me another.'

'How many players are there in the traditional sport of shinty?'

'No idea! Again?'

'Let's see, geography – what is the highest lake in the world?'

I'd left school at sixteen, so I didn't know this kind of thing. 'Terry, I don't have a clue,' I said proudly. 'I might be no use at all to your pub quiz team.'

'But you'll join? Since it's not cheating?'

I thought about answering questions, showing people the extent of my memory. Going public with the quirks of my brain. *Eve, you're such a freak.* I remembered my vow to myself – let more people in. Don't allow my memories to trap me, because what's happened in the past is no indicator of what will happen tomorrow. Things can change. They can always change. 'All right,' I said. 'You've got yourself a team member.'

RACHEL

Simon had been home for one day, and it already felt interminable. It was exhausting, having to explain to him where they kept the spoons and how they'd met and what school Hannah went to and when her birthday was, what he did for a living (Rachel hardly knew more than him), what his parents' names were and when they had died. It was like starting over with a whole new husband. He and Hannah stepped nervously around each other, like a pair of feral cats introduced for the first time. Hannah didn't understand what was going on, and kept bursting out with random displays of temper. 'I want pancakes! Daddy makes me pancakes!'

'Darling, he's not feeling well . . . '

'He's fine! He looks *fine*!' It was true, in some ways. Once he'd had a shave and put on some decent clothes, Rachel could see that Simon did look well. His face, which had grown thin with low-carbing and stress, seemed smoother, younger even, and there was an animation to him that she hadn't seen in years. As if he was . . . alive, somehow, despite his confusion and sadness.

'I'm sorry,' he said weakly, as Hannah stormed out of the kitchen and upstairs. 'I don't even remember how to make pancakes. Did I really do that?'

'Yes. It was . . . sort of your thing with her. Because you hardly saw her the rest of the time.'

He frowned. 'I didn't?'

'Well, no. You worked all the time. Like, *all* the time. Hundred-hour weeks. Holidays, weekends.' It was crazy what you could get used to, how a crisis could show you the fault-lines in your life, like an earthquake uncovering the unstable foundations of a house.

'Oh.' He looked down at the cup of tea he was drinking – he'd never drunk tea before, had he? He was always a three-espressos-to-wake-up kind of guy, and as the pressure mounted at work, he'd been using caffeine as a sort of legal stimulant. 'But she seems so – so funny and lovely. Why wouldn't I want to spend time with her?'

'I don't know. It was just – work. Work was everything.' And why? Not just for money – they could have lived on much less, like Rachel had as a child. For something less tangible. Pride, status. She knew that she was the same.

'What did I do there? It was stocks and shares, right – did I work with any bad companies? Oil, arms, that sort of thing?'

'I've no idea. Probably.'

'Oh.' He looked down at the table. 'I had this feeling, while I was at Sunnyside, that maybe I wasn't a very good person. My job, and the thing with the house ... Do you think it's true?'

The old Simon would never have asked anything so open, so guileless. She looked at him across the breakfast table, this man she barely knew and at the same time knew inside-out. 'Simon – have you any idea what you were doing? The ferry ticket, the case? You had money troubles, I know.' She needed to know what the situation was with the loan sharks, if more bailiffs would be coming after her. If Simon had broken the law. If he'd remortgaged the house with another firm, if there

203

were other debts outstanding. Anything could be true, and neither of them would know. She remembered that Mark was looking into it for her, and relief surged in her chest. He would sort it. He would help.

Simon sat there, the morning light falling on to his face. She'd thought she knew him inside out, his likes and dislikes, his every mood and expression. But right now she had no idea who he was. 'I'm sorry,' he said again. 'I really don't remember. It's all gone.' He fixed her with his green eyes. 'Maybe if you told me what happened that night – why was I in the car? I remember being scared.'

She swallowed. Her story for the police was that he'd run out of the house, left her, or so she'd thought (without his phone or wallet or shoes). If anyone looked into it, they'd see how flimsy it was. 'I don't know,' she lied. 'I don't know what was going on with you.'

Simon sighed. 'This is – it's awful. I can't remember my own daughter! It's not fair on her.'

'I just . . . we really need you to remember. That's the only way.' Although if he did, she could end up in prison herself. Rachel searched his face, so familiar and yet unfamiliar at the same time, but could see no sign that he remembered that night. What she'd done to him.

'I'm sorry. I'm trying. It's just so hard.' He massaged his head, right on the spot with the fading red mark.

'I know. It's not your fault.' She thought of her treacherous idea earlier, that he might be faking this. People did that, didn't they, to avoid being convicted of crimes? 'I just – if there's anything we can do to help you, we should do it.'

'There's something we could try,' said Simon, haltingly,

and his face changed, lightening somehow. 'The woman who helped me at Sunnyside, at the home – she was trying to bring my memory back. Maybe if I carried on working with her, I might remember?'

EVE

Terry's team were the A-team of quizzers. When they walked into the pub, people actually fell silent, nudging each other. Not that they could all walk. Doris, who was ninety-two, rode a mobility scooter, Terry was on a walker because of his hip, and even the sprightliest member of the team, Abraham, a mere seventy-eight, used a cane. Doris rolled up to the table and clicked open her saddlebag to remove exactly four black biros, new and uncapped. 'Don't touch!' she snapped, as I went to pick one up. 'New pens every time.'

'Doris is superstitious,' said Abraham. 'Don't mind her.'

'I won the 1957 Skegness Butlin's table quiz with a pen just like that,' she retorted. 'Now get us a sherry, we'll be starting soon.'

Intimidated, I watched them prepare. Terry went to buy the drinks, waving away my help. Sherry for Doris, a pint of bitter for him, and a tomato juice for Abraham, who liked to quiz sober, because 'the trivia rush is enough for me, dear'. I had a gin and tonic, which was a drink Magda liked, and I found it at first bitter, then refreshing. Doris wrote the answers down, and if it wasn't neat enough they squabbled among themselves to cross it out and be absolutely clear. In the interval, they would share two packets of crisps, one salt and vinegar, one cheese and onion, and have one more drink each.

'Any more and you lose the edge,' Doris said, eyeing me over her glasses. 'This isn't just a quiz for fun, dear. This is war. Us

206

against the Baron von Quislings. They won last year – it was a TRAVESTY.'

Abraham and Terry groaned. 'You have to let it go, Dor,' said Terry, a moustache of beer foam on his lip.

'I will never let it go, Terence. Not till the day I die, which admittedly might be soon. The capital of South Africa is not Johannesburg – or rather, it isn't one of them, because there are three! What kind of quiz is it when you can't trust the answers?' She glared at me and I agreed that it was a travesty.

'What's your team name?' I asked.

'*Our* team,' said Abraham, kindly including me. 'We always use the same one – Izzy Whizzy Let's Get Quizzy. Oh look, it's starting.'

After that, all non-quiz conversation ceased. The question master, a man with a beer gut and straggly beard, whose name seemed to be Neville, lifted the microphone. 'Welcome, folks. The quiz pot tonight is up to two thousand pounds! Everything to play for.' I blinked – that was a surprising amount of money.

'Doris wants it for a cruise,' hissed Abraham. 'Could be her last chance.'

'Shhh!' Doris glared at us. 'Listen.'

'Question one – which entertainer was born in Bristol, as Archibald Leach?' Doris had started writing on the word 'Bristol'. Abe and Terry didn't say anything out loud. They used a series of nods and taps to convey that they agreed with her answer. This was to stop other teams overhearing their answers and stealing them, I'd been told.

'Easy,' said Terry dismissively. 'Hope they get more challenging.'

I peered at the answer – Cary Grant. I hadn't known that.

I didn't get much chance to watch old films on Saturday afternoons, growing up in care homes.

I was beginning to get worried that I wouldn't be much help at all, but the next question was about the names of the band members in Little Mix. Abraham looked blank. 'If it's not a musical, I'm stumped.'

Doris pursed her lips. 'Did they do that one that goes "zig-a-zig-ah"?'

'That's the Spice Girls,' said Terry. 'I don't know this other lot.'

Julie's younger sister Katie (nineteen, pink bits in her hair, hates liquorice) was a massive fan of the band, and had talked about them non-stop when she helped out at Sunnyside over the Christmas break. I leaned forward and whispered. 'I know it. Jesy, Perrie—'

'Can't hear you,' said Doris irritably. 'Write it down.' She spun the sacred answer sheet to me and I filled it in as neatly as I could, aware of what a great responsibility it was. And for once, knowing a fact that others didn't wasn't a burden or something to be ashamed of. Instead it was fun, feeling my brain-filers work overtime, retrieving and celebrating every tiny stupid bit of knowledge I had in there, everything from the name of the first host of *Blind Date* to the literal meaning of the term karaoke. I was actually enjoying myself.

Two hours later, the mood in the pub was tense. I felt my brain expanding, allowing in not just new facts but new beliefs. Going out for a drink could be fun. Being a know-it-all wasn't always bad. Not everyone found my skills weird – some were fascinated by it, like Terry. 'Is it like that brain-training? You can get better at it?'

'Or Sherlock's Mind Palace?' asked Abraham. 'Is that how you remember things?'

I took a crisp from the half-time packet. Doris was keeping an eagle-eyed view on how many each of us had of each, even though I didn't really like cheese and onion. 'It's more like a big warehouse, storing films in boxes. When I think of a memory, these sort of invisible workers, they get the film out and very quickly project it. So I can literally see it all happening again.'

'Fascinating,' said Abraham, a dapper man in a cravat, who still lived independently. Doris was in sheltered housing on the other side of town, and determined to die there.

'No offence, but I couldn't bear those care homes. Too many people with no memory.' She shivered. 'There but for the grace of God . . . '

Each of them touched the wood of the table, superstitiously, and I saw how afraid of it they were. They couldn't even say the word – *Alzheimer's*. They'd take a heart attack or stroke or cancer any day over waking up one morning and not knowing something. 'I'll go to Switzerland,' said Abraham cheerfully. 'If I find myself forgetting the words to "The Surrey With the Fringe on Top", that's it for me.'

'I'll just stop eating,' said Doris. 'Life's not worth living without memory, if you ask me. You want to get out of that home fast, Terry.'

'It's not so bad.' Terry winked at me. 'Everyone's friendly. And we have our Eve to help us with things we forget.' All the same, I hoped he would get out again, go back to his own flat once his hip had healed. I couldn't bear to see Terry, so sharp and alive, fade away like Mrs O'Reilly already had and Mrs Burke was starting to.

'I wish I could help more,' I whispered, but none of them heard me, because the second half had started, and they were soon in an argument about which film John Wayne won an Oscar for (*True Grit*, incidentally, in 1970).

The next morning, I was actually feeling all right. All the excitement of the pub quiz, the spark of facts in my brain, had temporarily let me forget about Adam/Simon. I had almost convinced myself life could go back to normal now, the way it had been before he came. Peaceful, ordered.

Magda met me in the hallway, three pens in her hair. 'Has something happened?' I asked cautiously.

'You've got a visitor,' she said, and I couldn't read her tone.

Adam. Adam! I raised a shaky hand to pat my hair into place. 'Oh, who's that then?'

Magda pursed her lips. 'Come and see.'

In the office, a woman was in the spare chair, where Adam had once sat as we looked up Dungevin Beach on the computer. She had expensively highlighted brown hair, and wore white jeans and a navy T-shirt, several rings flashing on her fingers. She stood up. 'Hello, I'm Rachel.'

But she didn't need to say any more. I already knew that this was Simon's wife.

RACHEL

Eve, the woman from the care home, was not like she'd expected. Much younger, for a start – no more than thirty-five, surely. She was pale and timid, and seemed afraid of her own shadow. All the same she was pretty, in a fresh-faced, youthful way, her fair hair pulled back, her skin clear. 'Oh,' she said, when Rachel told her who she was. She saw a flash of something on the woman's face – guilt, maybe. Interesting. 'Is he – how is he? Simon?'

'He's not so good, Eve. That's why I'm here. Do you mind if we talk for a minute?'

Rachel told Eve everything, or almost everything. There was still quite a lot she couldn't, and wouldn't, tell anyone; apart from Mark, of course. 'So you see, we really need him to remember. We don't know what things he might have been mixed up in.'

Eve's grey eyes were clear and cool. 'Why didn't you report him missing?'

'Um ... I thought he'd just left me.' She explained about the message from Jess. 'Then I found out he owed money to some nasty people, and he'd taken leave from work – plus he was going to remortgage the house! So by that point I thought I might make it worse, if I went to the police.' It sounded very dodgy when she said it out loud. 'I was just so confused. I realise now I should have done it, of course.'

'He was here all that time and he thought no one cared enough to look for him.'

Rachel wondered why this woman was so annoyed. 'I know. I regret it. Eve – Simon seems to think you can help him get his memory back. And if you could, it would really save us.'

Eve said nothing for a moment. 'You said he was in trouble. What kind of trouble?'

'I don't know for sure. Money, I guess. He'd overspent, borrowed from people he shouldn't have borrowed from – and he was going to remortgage our house to pay them off, I think. Without telling me.'

A strange look passed over the woman's face. Pain. Why would she care? 'Oh.'

'Eve, please – will you help us? Help Simon?'

Again, the strange stillness. Then, she slid open a drawer in the desk she was sitting behind, and took out what looked like an airport security bag with a handful of objects inside. 'I think this is yours.' She fished something out and placed it on the desk, where it caught the light.

Rachel's hand stole unconsciously to her left ring finger. 'My engagement ring!'

Again, Eve seemed to wince. 'I thought it must be. How did he end up with it? Ad— Simon had it in his pocket, along with this other stuff.'

Rachel shut down the memory. *You can have this back, you bastard.* 'Um, I don't know. Maybe he picked it up from the house before he left.'

'He just walked out, didn't say a word?'

'That's right,' she lied, doing her best to meet that steady grey gaze. 'Thank you for finding it.' Rachel had always been nervous owning something so valuable, sure she'd leave it on the side of a sink or something.

'All right,' said Eve finally, after thinking about it for a long moment. 'I'll come with you. The rest of these things are his too.' Rachel glanced at the bag, but all she could see was a little heap of junk – a bit of Lego, a rock and a torn raffle ticket. Nothing of any significance at all.

EVE

Rachel and Simon lived in a huge house. Of course they did. I could tell from everything about her, from the rings on her fingers to the clean, expensive car she drove me in, that they were rich. Or he was rich – she didn't work, she'd told me, sounding vaguely ashamed of that. He worked in the City, moving money around from different accounts, and somehow getting very wealthy off the back of it.

Was it true, what she'd said? He had tried to remortgage her house without telling her? Maybe it was all a mistake – the man I knew would never do something like that. He was kind, he helped me, helped everyone at Sunnyside. He played the piano, he had a childlike joy in beaches and ice creams and Lego. He wasn't a cheat or a liar. I had agreed to go, of course – I couldn't turn down the chance to see him – but all the same, an uncomfortable itch was growing at the back of my neck with every mile we got closer. He was a real person now, with baggage, with a past, even if he couldn't remember. I knew where his house was, what his full name was. That he definitely had a wife and a daughter called Hannah. That he was a stockbroker, and maybe that he'd lied. Every single fact was filed away into my brain, never to leave, never to be forgotten, and with each one, like every tiny piece of Lego, the Adam I had in my head was erased a little bit more.

We parked outside the beautiful house, sitting on its own in a paved driveway, surrounded by neat trees and bushes. I could hear birds singing, children playing somewhere not far off. I was going to see him. Adam – Simon – was inside this house.

Rachel unlocked the door, calling out, 'We're here,' and there he was. Wearing normal clothes – a navy shirt in some thick fabric I wanted to run my fingers over, grey jeans – instead of ones from the Death Box. His hair neatly gelled instead of sticking up everywhere, and his stubble shaved off, showing the planes of his face. But it was him, my Adam. And he looked utterly miserable.

'Eve,' he choked out, and before I knew it his arms were around me, clutching me tight. I couldn't resist hugging him back for a moment, breathing him in – he no longer smelled of the cheap soap from Sunnyside – but I was very aware that his wife was there. His wife! And I had kissed him on that beach! Did it count as cheating, if he couldn't remember he was married? Of course it did. 'I'm so glad you've come. I'm so confused, Eve.'

Gently, I stepped back. 'It's OK. I'll try to help.'

'Mummy? Who's that lady?' Someone else had come into the room. A young girl, with his springy hair but fairer, dressed in pink tights and a striped bumble-bee dress. It must be Hannah. Simon's daughter.

RACHEL

It felt so surreal, to stand in a room with her husband, her daughter and a strange woman she had only met that day, and watch her husband rush to the woman as if she was his wife, and Rachel and Hannah the strangers. She tried to take charge, hustling Hannah upstairs on the pretext of tidying her room, while Simon and Eve remained in the living room to do whatever it was she did to bring memories back.

'Who is that?' said Hannah mutinously, as Rachel fished apple cores out from under her bed. 'Why is she here?'

'She's going to help Daddy remember things. You know how his head is poorly, so he's a bit confused.'

'But Daddy doesn't know her. He knows us!' Hannah couldn't seem to cope with Simon having a part of his life she knew nothing about. Rachel felt similar.

'It's going to be OK,' she lied. 'Daddy will be back to normal soon.' He wouldn't be, though, would he? If there was no medical cause to the amnesia, or at least not that the doctors could see, there was no way to cure him. Her life stretched in front of her, having to start again, with Simon knowing nothing about her or their history together. While she would be carrying the burden of their past, all the things they'd done to each other. Fear seized her throat. Maybe he would never remember. Perhaps they would have to start from scratch, a fresh slate. Would they even like each other, after all this? Without ten years of history, would Simon still love her?

'Mummy, I don't like things being like this! Daddy was away for ages, and I was really worried but you said he was working, and he wasn't, was he?'

'No. How old are these socks, Han?' She'd extracted a dirty pair from under the bed.

'I don't care about the stupid socks. You lied, Mummy!'

Rachel paused, for a moment thinking how lovely it would be to lie down on the little bed with its unicorn duvet, and go to sleep for five days. 'I know, sweetheart. I'm sorry. I was worried, too. I just didn't want to upset you.'

'Well, I *am* upset.'

'I am too, Han. I'm sorry.'

Hannah seemed slightly mollified by Rachel's honesty. She threw in one last salvo. 'AND you never took me to Legoland, after you promised.'

'Did I actually promise, though? Never mind. I'll take you at May half-term, how about that. That's a cast-iron double-promise.' She could hardly imagine that far into the future, a normal life that contained things like a trip to Legoland.

'And I want ice cream,' said Hannah, a born negotiator. Perhaps the Brexit department could make use of her. Rachel was saved from having to respond to that by Simon appearing at the door, knocking tentatively, as if this was not his own house, which just weeks before he had been disposing of without even telling her.

'Someone's here,' he said. 'Says his name is Mark?'

More surrealness. Mark in her kitchen, filling the space with his presence, his fleece and sturdy walking boots. Beside him, Simon was dwarfed, hesitant and lost. When Mark had arrived, for a moment Rachel just stood in the hallway, stared helplessly at Hannah, who was eavesdropping behind her on the stairs. She didn't understand what to do with this combination of people, or the fact that their family, once made up of three, now seemed to involve five.

Eve had stepped forward, quiet and tactful. 'Maybe we can go into the living room, Hannah? I'd like to see some of your Lego, if you don't mind?' Hannah had gone with her, casting terrible stink-eye at her parents. Now Rachel, Mark and Simon were gathered nervously in the kitchen.

'Do you want coffee, Mark?' Rachel felt so strange talking to him in front of Simon. Guilty, almost, which was ridiculous.

'I'll get it.' Simon was standing near the kettle. He flicked it on then looked helplessly at the cupboards. 'Er . . . mugs?'

'Left-hand cupboard there.'

'God.' He put his head in his hands. 'This is terrible. I don't remember *anything*. It's like . . . staying with someone you don't even know that well.'

Mark cleared his throat. 'All right. I haven't been able to find out too much more, I'm afraid. I made contact with this loan company, and we worked out a payment plan. So they should stop hassling you at least. The problem is: your money's all gone.'

'All of it?' Part of Rachel had been hoping they'd find a secret account or a savings fund or even a stash of bills under a floorboard. 'Where did it go?' She looked at Simon when she said it, but he seemed disengaged, as if they were talking about someone else.

Mark shrugged. 'You were very over-leveraged. Mortgage, cars, private school. It just got spent. It looks as if Simon's remortgage plan was never completed, which is good news in a way, as the house isn't at risk. The bad news is you still have all the debts it was meant to pay off.'

There was not even a flicker from Simon at his name. Rachel had once heard it was almost impossible not to react if you heard your first name, so even spies sometimes used their own ones. That must mean Simon really didn't remember.

She said, 'So . . . we're broke.'

'You're broke, yes. My guess is Simon got overwhelmed, and he couldn't take it, so he planned to run away.'

Simon seemed to snap out of a daze. 'Me. I was going to do that? Leave – Rachel, and leave Hannah?'

'We can't know for sure, mate. But it looks that way.'

'I'm sorry. I can't. This person – this Simon, it isn't *me*. It's not me! I wouldn't do these things! Please, will you get Eve for me? Please just get Eve!'

Rachel hesitated at the living-room door. Simon had gone out to the garden, and she could see him pacing there, his hands on his head. This had been a mistake. Of course it had been too much for him. If you had no memory of yourself, how would you cope with learning you weren't a very good person?

Inside the living room, she could hear Eve's soft voice intercut with Hannah's strident one. 'And I like to mix the bricks up, because it's a bolder design move than just having block colour, don't you think?' Rachel had to smile, to hear Hannah recite things she'd learned on daytime decoration shows.

'Good idea. Look, I can show you a way to strengthen the corners, so it doesn't fall apart. You can build higher that way.' Then the sounds of soft clicking, as bricks snapped into place.

'Not bad.' Hannah seemed to have come round to Eve. Rachel

heard her hesitate, then say, 'Eve . . . do you know what's going on with my dad? No one will tell me.' Rachel froze, listening.

'Well, he's . . . he can't remember who he is, Hannah. I'm sorry, it must be horrible for you.'

'Does he not . . . ? But Eve, he has to remember me?' Hannah's tone said, *You're being silly but also please tell me it's OK.*

Eve paused. 'You know, Hannah, brains can stop working like any other part of you, like your foot or your heart or whatever. It's not the person's fault. They just . . . sometimes they wake up and their memories aren't there. They've gone missing.'

'And do they come back?'

'Yes, sometimes.'

'But not always.'

'No. I'm sorry, Hannah.'

'But he's my dad! He has to remember me.'

'I . . . listen, when I was your age, or a bit younger, I lost my mum and dad. And it was horrible – I hated it. But it wasn't their fault. I know that, if they could, they would have been with me the whole time. It's the same with your dad. He doesn't want this to be happening. It's just . . . an accident, that's all.'

Rachel walked briskly in as if she hadn't heard a word. 'Hi! Eve, Simon's having a bit of a hard time. You wouldn't go and chat to him? Thank you ever so much for helping us.'

EVE

Hannah was wary of me at first. I didn't blame her, to be honest. She knew nothing about me, and here I was turning up at her house and hugging her father. I could imagine all too well how it was to be her, seven years old, bewildered by the speed with which her world had fallen apart. Her father looking at her like a stranger. All the same, I couldn't believe I had almost told her the whole truth about my parents. Why and how I lost them, and what it did to me. I saw something of myself in Hannah. A little girl of six or seven, who had suddenly found all the certainties of her life blown away. Like where she lived. Like having a mother or not. Like knowing the people you loved loved you back.

Look, it's Eve, come to see you. Theresa steered me across the room. We were in a strange kind of nursing-home place, except it didn't have old people in, like the one we'd visited my granddad in before he died. It had young people, but they were weird. Some of them bashed at their own heads or shouted or drooled. It scared me, this place, though Theresa just said this was what I'd wanted, and she'd tried to warn me.

I couldn't believe it at first. The man in the chair, hunched over, with his hair grown in strange patches, wearing a baggy tracksuit – that was him? That was my dad?

The Lego in my pocket felt knobbly. It was a little pilot figure with clip-on hair, because Dad always liked those best. I took it out and held it up, as if making an offering. Theresa pushed me forward, towards the man in the chair.

Daddy? It's me.

Simon was close to tears, pacing around the chilly garden with no jumper on. I rubbed my bare arms. 'Are you OK?'

'No, I'm not OK! That man, the detective – he said I did bad things. That I was broke, planning to run off and leave my family in the lurch. Eve – do you think I did it?'

I thought of the evidence – the fake ring, the ticket to France, the hidden suitcase. 'Simon . . . '

'Don't call me that!' He seized my hands. 'Please, Eve – that isn't me. It can't be. Maybe it was once, I don't know, but I'm different now. I'm Adam. Please. This isn't my home. These people – I don't know them. Can you take me back to Sunnyside with you?'

'You don't belong at Sunnyside. Look at you – you're young, fit . . . '

'I can't *remember*!' he cried. 'I don't know who I am. All I know is I was safe there. Happy, even, despite everything.' He was breathing hard, staring at me. 'Eve – I belong wherever you are. You know that, don't you? Where you are, that's my home. Not here.'

Home. It's a funny concept. Before I was six I had one, which I can hardly remember, except for the flower pattern of the wallpaper, which I would sometimes imagine faces in as I lay awake, listening to my parents talk in the kitchen, laugh sometimes, play music. After that, home was whatever foster placement I lived in or a children's home. A home that is not a home, like Sunnyside. Maybe it's the wrong word to use for a place like that.

Simon was holding my hand in both of his, and I could feel the pulse beating in his wrist. He looked so unhappy, so lost. I could do it. I could take him back to Sunnyside with me, tell everyone he wasn't ready to live with his family yet, look after him. See him every day, go on trips with him, sing around the piano.

But he would never be Adam to me again. I knew now that he was Simon Kempner, forty-three, a married man, a man who had done bad things. A man with baggage, with a past and with memories that already felt overwhelming to me. A dad, whose little girl needed him. I would not be the person to take someone's dad away.

I pulled my hand back. 'I'm sorry, Simon.' I deliberately stressed the name. 'I don't think I can help you any more. You belong here.'

'But I don't! Eve, I don't!'

For a moment, I was tempted. But I knew that what I felt between us – what he seemed to feel too, maybe – wasn't real. He could only remember the past few weeks of his life, an anomaly that he'd happened to spend with me. It wasn't fair. I wasn't really important to him, not to Simon Kempner of Little Sudbury, not in the vast scheme of his life, thousands of days instead of just a fortnight. If I let him come back with me now, at some point, when his memory returned, he would leave again. He would look around him, amazed – *What am I doing here, in this old folks' home that smells of cabbage, with this strange quiet woman who remembers everything?* – and he would run back to his real life, and I would be alone again. I couldn't do it.

'You do, Simon. This is your life. Your family. I'm just – no one. I'm sorry.' And I turned and walked away from him, right out of the house past Hannah with her Lego, ignoring the question on Rachel's lips, into the street and away.

RACHEL

Everything was a state. Eve had left without even saying goodbye, Simon wouldn't come down from one of the spare bedrooms, and Hannah had kicked apart her favourite Lego building – a sort of Sydney Opera House crossed with the Shard – in a tearful rage and also rushed off to her room. At least Mark was still there, although looking uncomfortable at the currents of tension running through the house.

'Be honest with me,' she said. 'How screwed are we?'

He shrugged. 'It's not looking good. If he doesn't go back to work soon, you'll be in trouble.'

'But he doesn't remember! I mean, he could be like this . . . '
For ever. He could be like this for ever; that was the thing no one had said out loud yet. Hannah could grow up and leave home and Rachel and Simon might be stuck here, virtual strangers. 'I still don't understand it. Why couldn't he have told me if he was planning on running? If things were that bad?'

Slowly, Mark shook his head. 'I don't think he was running, actually.'

'No?'

'I think he was planning to kill himself. I didn't want to say it in front of him, but . . . yeah.'

She leaned against the kitchen counter, winded. 'What?'

'He was getting desperate – you saw the messages on the phone. He'd borrowed too much and he didn't have the money to pay it back. He's got good life insurance, yes?'

'Well, yeah, we needed it for the house—'

'Did you know he'd increased it recently?'

Rachel shook her head dully. Of course she didn't. She knew nothing.

'Right. So he leaves stuff in Kent, of all places, right near the ferry port. I think he meant to get the ferry to France and then jump off it. If you die in international waters, a lot of red tape goes away. If it's recorded as an accident, you get the insurance money. He was trying to take care of you and Hannah.'

'But … why?' Her main feeling was confusion, a thin layer over the horror and pain she knew lay beneath. 'What could have been so bad? Even the debts, we could have sorted it out.' Why didn't he talk to her? Explain what was going on?

'People panic. They're ashamed to admit the truth, so it just gets worse and worse. All it takes is one missed payment – he'd probably already spent the bonus, then it didn't come – so you borrow some money, and it just spirals. The interest is huge. Likely he's been covering it up for ages, moving bits of money around to fill the gaps.'

She nodded, thinking guiltily of the holiday in Bali last year, the private villa with pool. She'd no idea how much that had cost. Thousands, surely. 'These people he borrowed from – there could be more, right?'

'Possibly, yes. I'm trying to find out, but it's not easy knowing where to start.'

'God.' She put her head in her hands. 'This is like a nightmare. There must be a way out.'

'The only chance is for him to remember what he did – everyone he borrowed from. And that's just going to take time.'

'But it might never happen?'

'No. The doctors said it was psychological, right? That means it could come back any time. Or never.'

The hopeless panic was back. She realised, uncomfortably, how much she'd come to rely on Mark. To be her saviour, this man she hardly knew. She drew in a shaky breath. 'Thank you. For everything. I know you didn't have to – that you've done more than . . . ' Oh God, she would have to pay him for his time. She had no money! It was just like being young again.

Mark looked at his watch. 'I should go. Getting late.'

She didn't want him to go. 'You could stay for dinner?'

'I think you guys need time together.' But she didn't want that. She didn't want to spend any time with this stranger who had the face of her husband.

'I'd like you to stay.' Her voice wobbled.

His eyes flicked upstairs. 'Rachel – you asked me to find your husband. I found him. My job's done.'

Her eyes filled with tears. *That isn't my husband.* 'But . . . I thought . . . ' She didn't know what she was trying to say.

For a moment he looked at her, his steady brown eyes seeing right through her. 'Maybe if things were different. But they aren't.'

And he went, lifting the large jangling keys to his Jeep (of course he drove a Jeep, a proper muddy one, not a Chelsea Tractor like the yummy mummies at Hannah's school). Rachel sat down heavily at the table, thinking about the ruins of her world – *hashtag living my best life! Hashtag contemplating eating cooking chocolate!* Her daughter crying upstairs. Simon bewildered, angry every time he couldn't remember some basic fact of his own life. She didn't blame him. It was at least partly her fault that he was like this, and anyway,

227

she'd made vows. She had to stick with him now, take care of him, no matter what.

For weeks now, Rachel had been desperate to have him home, to know he was safe and that she hadn't hurt him. Now that he was, and in theory her life was back to normal, she wondered why it was it felt like someone else's.

EVE

There are different types of memory. I learned this when I was little, when I first realised I wasn't quite normal. There's auto-biographical memory – the details of your own life, your name and your first crush and all of that. In me, that's unusually strong. The memories don't fade like other people's. Dr Praj described it as a computer with more storage than usual, so it doesn't need to compress any files. There's semantic memory, for facts and figures, like who's Prime Minister and the date of the Battle of Hastings. There's also procedural memory, how to cross roads and which way round knives and forks go. Adam – Simon – had retained that, but not his autobiographical one.

There are also different types of forgetting – bias, misattribution, and so on. If you think of a memory that's strong – where you were on 9/11, for example – it's often something that taught you an important lesson, which is why we tend to remember the bad moments of our lives rather than the good. Sucks, doesn't it? Who wouldn't rather hang on to the first kiss with someone you really like, the shaking in your legs and smell of their skin, rather than the time you sat on a wonky chair in middle school and fell right through it, getting wedged in there with your feet in the air? Just one of the many unfair things about memory.

Then there's what they call persistence. Memories that won't go away, that fly around your head like bats, which you can find yourself reliving at any moment, no matter how inconvenient.

That's what I have, except it's every moment. As if my entire life is an episode of PTSD. Sometimes I think we'd all be better off with no autobiographical memories at all. Not missing the people we've lost, because we don't remember they existed. And not having to live with who we are, the mistakes and the guilt of the bad things we've done in the past. When I think about it that way, I can hardly blame Simon for what he did – on the contrary, I think his brain found an excellent way to cope.

The day after I walked out on Simon, I woke up shot through with guilt. I had said no to helping him, to easing his pain and suffering. But I just couldn't. He was a stranger to me, was the truth, a married man, a father. I had let myself imagine something between us that wasn't there. It wasn't fair to cling on to him – I had to let him go, back to his life.

Instead, I was going to change myself. I would not let my life be ruined once more by something I couldn't forget, a person I couldn't let go of. I wasn't six this time, watching my mother bleed to death on a country road. I was thirty-four, a grown woman with a job and people depending on me. So what if I'd lost Adam? I had friends, and a place to live, and purpose. There were other residents who needed me, slipping further and further into dementia every day, their memories crumbling and eroding like cliffs. I could help them. I could change my life – go out like normal women my age, meet someone, even. If Julie and Raheem could fall in love even though her brother was in the EDL, then maybe someone would love me too, freaky memory and all.

I got dressed in clean scrubs. I blow-dried my hair with the hairdryer Magda had given me for Christmas, though I had to crawl under the bed to find it. It was very dusty. I even put on make-up, though I didn't really know how. I would ask Julie to show me some time. I'd tell Terry I'd join his pub quiz team permanently, if they wanted me, and together we would sweep the board of the South of England Pub Quiz League. I would have a life. I had to at least try.

I opened the door of my flat – and almost had heart failure, as something black and furry yowled at me. 'Oh my God!' It was that cat again, sitting on my welcome mat. 'Go away now, I mean it. Magda does not like pets! She'll have you sent to the pound.' I wasn't sure they had a pound for cats, but he wouldn't know this, seeing as he was one.

Having shooed him away, I crossed the lawn and opened the patio doors to the rec room. 'Good morn—' The cat streaked in past me, a blur of black. Little blighter must have been hiding in the bushes.

Magda, who was tuning the TV to *Homes Under the Hammer*, shrieked, 'Get it out of here, Eve! The Health and Safety people'll shut us down!'

I ran after him, dodging past chairs, but he was smaller and faster, and he bounded across the room, out of my grasp.

'Where's he going?' shouted Julie, who was carrying a tray of shortbread. 'Bloody thing better not go near my kitchen!'

It looked like he was heading straight for Mrs Gillespie. 'No! Bad cat! Stop.'

Too late. I saw him put up his paws, and with one leap he was on her knee. My heart failed. I could only imagine her rage, given how mad she got when people held her arm to help her get out of a chair. But to my surprise, she didn't look angry at all. In fact, she was petting the cat, running her shaky hands over his silky black fur. As I watched, he nuzzled his face against hers – and she let him!

'Mrs G,' I gasped. 'I'm so sorry. He just got in. Let me take him out.'

She frowned. 'Don't be daft, lass. I've only just got him back. However did you find him? He ran away the day they took me here – got out of his carrier and shot off, spooked, poor fella.'

'How did I . . . ?' I didn't understand.

'All that nonsense about pictures and letters, bringing Janet Marks here to see me, I didn't know what you were on about. How would Graham write a letter? He's a smart lad but he can't hold a pen in his little paws.'

Magda had come up behind me and was gaping, holding up her jewelled glasses to get a better look. 'What's going on, Eve?'

I stared at Mrs G, who for the first time had a smile of deep peace and happiness on her face, stroking and nuzzling the cat, who was purring like a lawnmower. The cat with dark shiny fur and green eyes. 'I think . . . we found Graham.'

'You mean . . . ?'

'Yes. Graham is Mrs Gillespie's cat.'

Later, I helped Mrs G up the stairs to bed. For once she let me hold her arm and bend down to undo her shoes. Graham was locked in the linen cupboard, shredding the pillow cases with his sharp claws, until we figured out what to do with him. 'I'm so happy he turned up, Mrs G.'

'Me too, lass. I thought I'd never see him again.' I wanted to ask why she'd never actually said Graham was her cat, which would have made him a lot easier to find, but there was no point. I couldn't imagine what it was like inside the mind of someone with dementia, any more than other people could understand how my memory worked.

'Eve?'

I paused. I don't think she'd ever used my name before, she usually just called me 'girl'. 'Yes?'

'I'd like to see my Jimmy now. It's been such a long time, and we parted on bad terms. Do you think you could ask him to visit?'

'He's in Dubai, Mrs G. It's a long way. Lots of . . . camels.' (Although, did you know, the country with the most camels in the world is actually Australia?)

'I know. But I have this feeling . . . that I would like to see him. Will you call him, please?'

She'd never said please before either. I was shaken, as I tucked her in, folding the duvet over her papery hands. 'Of course I will, Mrs G.'

'Call me Jean,' she said, just when I thought things couldn't get any weirder.

RACHEL

'Simon, can you grab some fruit for us? Hannah, stay close, OK?'

It should have been a straightforward trip to the supermarket, easier than usual given that Simon hadn't bought groceries in at least five years and it was usually Rachel on her own. She couldn't leave him at home, since he didn't know where anything was and seemed in the grip of some kind of breakdown, and certainly she couldn't leave him alone with Hannah, who trailed sulkily after her, and had insisted on bringing a stuffed unicorn which she hadn't played with since the summer before.

'What fruit?' He was so slow, this new Simon, where the old one had been snappy, moving at the speed of light, buying a house and growing sick of it, getting a new car and then looking for another one right away, making deals at all hours of the day and night.

'I don't know, whatever you feel like.'

'Bananas?'

Hannah rolled her eyes. 'I don't *like* bananas, Daddy. Why can't you remember?'

Simon rubbed his head. 'I'm sorry. OK, no bananas.'

She watched him move across to the fruit and veg, walking slowly. Hannah's eyes were on her. 'Do you want peanut butter or jam?'

Hannah scowled. 'I want Daddy to be normal again. I want him to remember what I like. I want to go to Legoland, all of us, like you promised.'

Rachel stared at the jam – why so many flavours? Apricot, strawberry, blackcurrant, lime. Who needed this much choice? – until the urge to scream subsided. 'We can't go to Legoland; Daddy's not well.' *And we're broke, surprise!* She'd been up late the night before, doing sums on a piece of scrap paper. They would have to take Hannah out of private school, barring a miracle. What would the school mums say about that?

And as if summoned by thought, when Rachel pushed the trolley into the next aisle, there she was.

'Janine! What a surprise!' Her heart sank. That was the last thing she needed.

Janine Hewson-Taylor's hair looked salon-fresh, honeyed with blonde highlights. She was wearing a camel coat that Rachel had tried on in Max Mara, but rejected as being too expensive even before knowing they were broke. 'Rachel! Are you all right? Hello, Hannah.'

Hannah said nothing, staring at her pink trainers – another regression. Usually she was polite, relentlessly chatty, no shyness.

'I ... well, I guess you heard about Simon?' Rachel wondered what version of events had got out there. Did people know about the debts, the bailiffs, Simon's disappearance that she hadn't reported? What must they think of her?

'A bit. He's back home now, though? All OK?'

'I ... ' She didn't know how to answer that. Her first instinct was to cover it up like she always had, pretend she and Simon were totally fine and just getting back to some quality family time, thinking of buying a little place in Norfolk for weekends. But what was the point? Her life, so carefully maintained, had fallen to bits all the same. 'Not really, no. It's such a mess. Simon lied so much, but he's in such a bad way – he still can't remember anything.'

Janine was nodding. Matter-of-factly, she said, 'Charlie's been having an affair, you know. For two years.' Hannah, almost out of earshot looking at cereals, swung her head around.

'What?' Charlie, Janine's husband, was something big in the City, in a similar incomprehensible job to Simon. 'Oh my God! Janine, I'm so . . . Wow.'

'It's fine. I keep telling myself I'll leave, then it's one of the kids' birthdays coming up, or we have a holiday booked, or it's Christmas or . . . ' She looked at Rachel intently. 'Rachel, this is your chance, you know. To change things. It's so hard to unpick your life. But if it's already unpicked . . . '

Rachel blinked. Was Janine Hewson-Taylor, queen of the PTA, telling her to leave her husband? She couldn't. Not while he needed her. 'I don't . . . '

Janine looked around her furtively, as if someone might overhear. 'I know, I know. It doesn't have to be right away. But – think about it. And don't be afraid to ask for help, OK? You've been through so much. Just know that, whatever happens, your friends will support you.' *Friends*. As Rachel watched her trundle away, she marvelled at the word. All this time feeling alone, had she actually had people in her corner and just never noticed?

Simon had come back now, and he bounced apples into the trolley, bruising them no doubt. Rachel sighed. 'Thanks. What's that?' He had a small box under his arm.

'Oh! I just thought . . . I know she likes it.' It was a small Lego kit, basic bricks and wheels, the kind of thing a younger child might play with. Hannah basically had an advanced diploma in Lego design. All the same, he was trying.

'Han? Look, isn't this nice? Daddy's bought you a present.'

Hannah came over, looking wary. 'Oh. Thank you.' Rachel smiled at her, relieved. *Pretend to like it, there's a good girl.*

Simon said haltingly, 'I'm sorry I forgot about the bananas. I'm just – things are very jumbled up in my head right now.'

Hannah nodded, taking the box of Lego. 'Can you . . . ?' she hesitated. 'Will you help me with it, when we get home, Daddy?'

'Of course I will! Of course!' The longing was so strong, the sadness, the confusion in both of them. Rachel had to turn away to stop herself crying, and pretend to be very interested in sugar-free granola, which, since she was likely to have less free time from now on, she would have to start buying instead of making from scratch.

As she moved through the rest of the supermarket, half-listening to the stilted conversation between her husband and daughter, Rachel found that she was thinking of what Janine had said about asking for help. About unpicking your life. About how hard Simon was trying for a second chance with his daughter, which might not come if he never recovered. And she realised that, when she got home, she needed to make a phone call.

EVE

It was quiet in Sunnyside that night. Charity, on night duty, was settled into the office, feet up on the desk and *Jane the Virgin* playing on the computer. She waved at me without taking off her headphones. I made my way across the rec room, with its silent TV and empty, sagging chairs. I imagined that each one represented a resident, because within a few years, surely all of them here would be gone from us. I'd seen it before. Moving into Sunnyside was like sitting in death's waiting room. I would say goodbye to each of them in turn, and all their memories, everything they'd ever thought or seen or known, would be lost the moment their hearts stopped beating. I did my best to remember them, but who was I doing it for? Would I really sit someone down, now or in the future, and pour all the memories I held out of me and into them, like cereal into a bowl? I knew that I wouldn't. Whatever I remembered would die with me.

I crossed the patchy lawn to my flat, walked in the dark up the stairs. Felt for the light switch. Dropped my keys into the little bowl I'd found in a charity shop, which I knew from research had been made in the Staffordshire potteries in the early 1930s. Took off my shoes (standard issue from Shoe Zone, 2013). I turned on the picture lights over the Museum. Each item represented a person I'd known here, who had gone. Mostly the residents who'd died – Mr Allen, who loved nothing more than Arsenal football club, had left behind an old match programme, which I'd taken when his kids cleared out his room. Miss Dunne, a huge fan of *EastEnders*, had owned a novelisation of the show about two of the characters falling in love and going on a road trip. She'd had no one when she died, no family, no kids, so everything had gone to the British Heart Foundation. I'd kept the tatty old book, making sure to put some pound coins in the collection box next time I passed the shop. I'm not sure if anyone would even have bought it, but you never know.

Not everything was from a resident. There was Aliya, who'd worked in the kitchen for a summer before going to university. She hadn't died, just moved on, but I wanted to remember her all the same, so one day when a bobby pin had fallen from her headscarf and I'd found it on the carpet in the hallway, I'd slipped it into my pocket. People didn't miss little things like that, did they? Was it strange? I just wanted to keep a piece of her, to remember our shy conversations about *University Challenge* and what questions we got right (I sometimes downplayed this, as I'd learned from Theresa that *no one likes a smartarse, Eve*). Aliya was a neuroscientist now. She'd sent Magda a photo of her in her lab, white coat on, her scarf a shimmering blue, and we'd stuck it up in the kitchen, proud of her. Just another one of the thousands of people I'd met in my life who I would never see again.

Beside a tin of old car sweets – mostly stickiness and powder now –and a potted cactus, spiky but enduring despite its erratic watering schedule, was Simon's pen, and I remembered the day we discovered where it came from. The sad dawning on his face that maybe he wasn't a good person. Was I a good person? I tried to help people and to make up for whatever I took, but I had stolen all these things as well. I told myself no one wanted them, but perhaps there was a son or daughter or husband or wife out there lamenting the loss of the dog-eared paperback or the picture frame with the smashed glass. Maybe I was as bad as Simon, in my way. A thief. A memory thief.

Noticing some dust on the collection, I turned around to hunt for my feather duster– and just then a rush of black zoomed past me, knocking over something and smashing it on the ground. 'Graham! What are you doing here? You were meant to stay in the linen cupboard.' He looked at me with his wide green eyes. I'd no idea how he'd got in, but cats had their ways. They were wily; they knew how to survive, to adapt. I'd been like that when I came here, seventeen and totally alone in the world. I'd have to learn it again.

'Come on, then.' I held out a hand to him, and he let me pet his head. 'What's this you've knocked over?'

It was James Gillespie's little soldier, his arm snapped right off. 'Oh, Graham. Look what you did.' As if he'd known this was his rival for Mrs G's affections – though he was hardly that, given that James hadn't seen his mother in three years. I remembered my promise to her. Something I could do, a small thing that might help.

'Come on, Graham. We have to make a phone call to the land of camels.' I picked up my phone and sat back on my chair, and Graham came and lay in my lap, and he was warm and smelled a tiny bit like yeast, and it was nice, not to be alone for once.

RACHEL

'For the last time, Hannah, go upstairs!' Rachel was sure she'd never shouted at her child this much before everything happened. She'd done her best not to, having been shouted at herself a lot as a kid. 'I'm sorry,' she said, as Hannah moodily stomped up the stairs. 'I just . . . I'm expecting a visitor, that's all.'

Silence. The slam of a bedroom door. Rachel sighed, then resumed her nervous pacing by the living-room window. She was watching out for a cab, her offer of a lift from the train station having been turned down. Was that a sign of things to come? Had she made a mistake, dialling that phone number?

Oh God. An engine. A taxi nosing its way down the road. Tyres on gravel. And getting out, struggling with a suitcase, was a short, plump woman with glasses on a string.

Rachel opened the door. 'Let me pay.'

'No, no, I've got it.' The woman handed the driver a tenner and straightened up. Her eyes travelled over the large, well-kept house, the cherry blossom tree, the BMW parked in the drive. Then they settled on Rachel. 'Well. Here I am.'

Rachel found she was suddenly out of breath. 'Hi, Mum,' she said.

There'd been no other choice. Simon couldn't look after Hannah – he barely knew who Hannah was. Simon's parents were dead, his sister Jennifer of the horses was away at a riding tournament in Canada, and Rachel's own brother, Dave, was thousands of miles away in Australia. They barely spoke, apart from cards at Christmas. And although she'd once had close friends – like Maura who'd introduced her to Simon in the first place – she realised that, somehow over the years, they had faded away. No, she had to face the fact that, for someone who never had five minutes to spare for herself, her life was actually a lonely one. Maybe she'd let her own identity be folded into the dough of daily life, gardening, cooking, shopping, school runs. Or maybe some part of her was ashamed of who she was now, the job she'd given up, her diminished life. So when it came to finding someone to look after Hannah, it was either a paid babysitter, which they could no longer afford, or ask her own mother.

Rachel had not seen her mother in years, not since Hannah was born and she'd been determined the baby would never experience the chaos of her own childhood, but she faced her now across the living room. She searched the older woman's face for traces of gloating, or vindication, or even judgement of the room's expensive trappings, the high-end wallpaper, the bank-breaking Swedish speaker system. Nothing but concern. 'Rachel, why didn't you call sooner?'

She cleared her throat. 'I didn't want you to see me like this.'

'Oh, don't be silly. It's always best to tell the truth.'

Rachel looked away. 'You do that now, do you?' She was ashamed of the barb as soon as she said it. It was just so hard, remembering all the bad times. Her father asking Simon for money, on their wedding day. Giving him some from her own savings, which he then lost in a gambling syndicate. Her mother scolding her for being stingy. *He's your dad, Rachel.*

Her mother set down her suitcase, an old-fashioned

non-wheelie kind, with a belt around it to keep it closed. She had also refused any help carrying it. 'I know you're angry. I know it was bad, what happened back then.'

'You knew, didn't you? That Christmas. That the money was gone. That they were coming to take our things.' She kept her voice low; Hannah was upstairs and Rachel was still trying to shield her from the worst the world could dish out, however futile it was. Simon was up there too somewhere, and it hurt Rachel's heart, to think of them in separate rooms, like lodgers in a shared house.

Her mother shook her head. 'We'd had letters, of course. Phone calls, even. But he said it was fine, he was handling it. Just a mix-up, he'd already paid the loans back, but they'd lost the paperwork.'

'And you believed him?'

'What else could I do? I'd no job, no money of my own. I had to trust him.'

And here was Rachel, thirty years later, a modern, educated woman, in exactly the same boat. She'd never asked Simon how they could afford the holidays, the designer clothes, the cars upgraded every three years. Because she hadn't wanted to know.

'How is he?' she muttered. 'Dad?' He'd had a stroke five years ago, she knew, and since then his memory hadn't been the best. She'd sent a card and a large cheque, but could not bring herself to go. It sounded awful when she thought about it. She hadn't even visited her own invalid father.

'He's . . . good days and bad days, you know. Doesn't always know me.' Her mother hesitated. 'He asks after you and Dave. I try to explain Dave's in Sydney, and I show him on the map how far away it is, but he forgets. Thinks you'll both be coming in from school any minute, asks me what's for tea.' She smiled, ironically. 'I found him halfway to the betting shop the other day. Old habits die hard.'

Rachel sighed. 'It's funny. Simon – I guess he was gambling too. It just wasn't down Ladbrokes.' Instead, he'd gambled with other people's money, vast sums of it, a much more socially acceptable form that was called stockbroking. And when that hadn't worked, just like her father, he'd borrowed more to try to hide it, panicking, until one day – the same as on Christmas morning, 1987 – bailiffs had come to the door. Rachel could remember every detail. The Christmas presents they'd removed. The TV. Even the cooker, so for Christmas dinner they'd eaten chips from the chip shop sitting on the floor. Dave had gone out and not come back for hours, drunk on cheap cider. Her mother had cried.

Now she said, 'There's no shame in marrying a gambler, love. It's an illness.'

Rachel fought back tears. 'But how can you . . . ? You stayed with Dad all this time, even after what he did.' And that was what she couldn't forgive. That her mother had chosen her father over Rachel and Dave, even when he swore off gambling month after month, and then a few weeks later Rachel would pass the bookies in her school uniform and see him coming out.

'I love him. He needs me now. And, pet – things were different for me. Rotherham in the eighties – it wasn't like your life here. You can do whatever you want, but I couldn't.' Was her mother telling her to leave Simon too? Did she even have that choice, when he was in such a state?

'I'm sorry. I – it was good of you to come.'

'Not a bit of it. I'm just delighted I can see Hannah. Your dad would love to as well. He can't travel far, but maybe, when all this is over ... '

'Maybe,' said Rachel vaguely, bending to lift the suitcase. Could she forgive everything, now she'd been through even worse? Now she knew how easy it was to turn a blind eye? 'Let me show you the room.'

'Nice that you have a spare room, isn't it?' said her mother as they went upstairs, having wrestled over the suitcase a bit.

'Yeah,' said Rachel, non-committal, thinking what was the point in having not one but two rooms empty, and never any guests? She was going to have to re-think a lot of things when this was over. If it ever was.

She settled her mother in the spare room – tasteful flowered bedspread and matching curtains, thick carpet, stylish furniture and an en suite – and closed the door, her mind racing. Oh God, her mother was in the house. Her mother, her angry confused daughter and her amnesiac lying husband. What a mess.

Passing Hannah's door, she heard voices.

Simon said, 'I see, so if you put it crossways you strengthen the corners?'

'Yeah. Eve taught me it.'

A pause. 'Eve is ... good at teaching people things.' Another pause. 'Hannah – I'm so sorry this is happening. I know it's not easy. I know I'm not ... the same. I'm trying, I really am.'

Hannah said nothing for a moment, and Rachel could see through the ajar door that her head was bowed, as she sat on the floor snapping bricks into place. Simon was perched awkwardly on her unicorn bed. 'Can you really not remember?'

'Really not. It might get better all of a sudden ... we don't know.'

'And when you were away, did you not think about me at all? Did I just fall out of your head or something?'

'I – something like that. But you know, when they found me, I only had a few things with me, and one of them was a Lego brick. I got it for you, but I never had the chance to give you it.'

'You mean ... you had something to remind me of you?'

'Kind of, yes. Even though my brain went funny, you were still there somewhere. You see?'

Another long moment of silence. Then Hannah said, in a tone Rachel didn't recognise, an older more mature one: 'It's OK, Daddy. I know you can't help it.'

Rachel crept away, not wanting to break the moment between them.

EVE

'Morning, Magda!'

'You're looking happier, lovie.'

I smiled at her. 'I know. I've decided to try and live my life. And we're having a visitor today.' I explained what I'd done – late last night, I'd got on the phone to James Gillespie in Dubai, and told him what his mother wanted. He'd promised to go straight to the airport and get the first flight, and it was amazing to me that he could be so far away yet arrive here later today. Maybe one day, as part of my new enlarged life, I would get to travel too.

Magda stared at me. 'You mean to say James Gillespie is coming here?'

'Yes! To see his mum at last, and be reconciled.' And she would be happy, and their relationship would be healed, and I would have done something good, helped someone, even if I couldn't help Adam.

Magda sighed. 'Well, lovie, there's just one problem with that.'

Mrs Gillespie was smiling, a strange sight to see. Her arms were neatly folded over the covers, her room in perfect order, her glasses placed upon the nightstand. 'When did it happen?' I whispered. Not that she could hear me now.

'In her sleep.' Magda squeezed my arm. 'It's the best way, lovie. They don't know it's coming, they just ... don't wake up. I've called the ambulance.'

I collapsed down in the chair in the corner of her room. 'I can't believe she's dead.'

'She was ninety and her mind was going. It's not a bad thing, Eve, to go this way.'

'But James is coming! They were going to make up! She'd just found Graham again.'

As if he knew his name, I heard a meow at the door and a black shadow slunk in. He leaped on to the bed, and sat by Mrs G, nuzzling her.

'Oh dear,' said Magda. 'I don't think the coroner will be impressed if we have cats snuggling up to dead bodies. You'll have to get him out of here.'

'I'll take him.' All this time searching for Graham, I felt a certain affinity with him. 'They had so little time together.'

'Maybe she just wanted to know he was safe. And the son – maybe it's enough, to know that she wanted to see him.'

'But . . . it's not the way I planned it.'

'Life isn't, darling. Time you realised that, instead of trying to keep it all neat and tidy.' She pushed her glasses up her nose. 'Only metaphorically, you understand. You still need to keep the cleaning cupboard tidy.'

'Yes, Magda.' She gave me another squeeze and was gone, yelling to Julie to hoover up the cat hairs on the stairs.

Graham regarded me with his deep green eyes. Mrs Gillespie was right, they were mesmerising. I felt that he understood what had happened to her. 'Oh Graham, she's gone. Maybe James would like to keep you. Would you live in Dubai? Is it safe for cats there? It looks very dry. I'm not sure you'd like it.'

Graham swished his tail, never breaking my gaze. What

was I going to tell James, when he got off his flight only to find it was too late?

'I'm so sorry.'

James Gillespie said nothing. He'd arrived off his flight into Gatwick, his face tanned but tired, his clothes crumpled. I'd never been on a plane, and I wondered what it was like, to soar so far above the world. If your thoughts became different, peaceful and faraway. 'It's not your fault,' he sighed.

'She was doing so well yesterday. Really happy to see Graham.'

'Graham. Huh. Is that his name – I never knew.' James's face was wary when I'd told him about the cat. 'She loved that monster. Once he bit me on the nose. I had to get a stitch!'

I wasn't surprised at such naughtiness from Graham. 'There's another thing he did. Again, I'm sorry.' I held out his little soldier. I had tried to glue the arm back on, but it was wonky enough that he'd surely be getting an honourable discharge from the infantry.

James peered at it. 'This was mine!'

'That's right.' I told him about finding it at his mother's house, how she'd kept it all these years.

He turned it over slowly in his hands. 'I'm really surprised by that. She's not – she wasn't sentimental, you know. When I told her I was moving to Dubai she just nodded, said something about the desert air being bad for my skin.' He rubbed his chin, which was admittedly a trifle dry. 'She wasn't wrong about that, incidentally. I tried to call her every two weeks, but it was hard. She never had anything to say to me. Even when I tried to talk about Dad, she'd shut me down.'

'I think . . . your mother had a disappointment when she was young. I think she never recovered from it – she found it hard to love, maybe.'

'That makes sense.' James sighed. 'I'm gay, you know. Not easy in Dubai, of course, but as long as you're careful . . . but Mum never really accepted it. She once asked me would it not be easier to find a girl, settle down. Have kids.'

I thought of Jean as a young woman, how madly in love she'd been with a man who couldn't love her back, and how she'd settled for Arthur Gillespie thinking that was just what you did. How lucky we were to have more choices nowadays. 'I think she regretted that, James. She was proud – stubborn. But I know she thought about you all the time.'

'Jimmy,' he said. 'People call me Jimmy, over there, or Jimbo. Kind of ironic. It was what she called me too.' He went to hand the soldier back to me.

'Keep it,' I said. The Museum would have a gap in it, but I knew I didn't need an object to remember Mrs Gillespie. She would stay with me for ever, until the day I also died, her grouchiness, her love of chocolate biscuits and Graham, the young woman in those pictures, arm in arm with Janet Marks. 'Take it. Remember her.'

'Thank you. If you like, I was thinking I might also take the cat?'

'Really?' I felt oddly upset by this. I'd liked having him on my lap last night, digging his claws into me and slowly shredding the chair cover.

'Yeah. I mean I'm not allowed pets in my apartment, and I don't know if I can take him overseas, and I think I'm mildly allergic – but she loved the beast, didn't she?'

'She did. And she loved you too, Jimmy.'

He didn't say that he knew, but he smiled at me sadly, and put the soldier gently in his pocket, so I hoped that he did, or at least that he would one day.

RACHEL

The days went on, the abnormal slowly becoming normal. Simon gradually learned where things were kept, and Hannah began to trust him a little more, and Rachel did her best to wade through the mess of their finances. She even began to like having her mother there – another adult to take the strain, whisk Hannah away to the park or soft play when things got tense, do the shopping and laundry. There was no question of Simon going back to work, not while he couldn't remember a thing. They would have to find a new way to live.

Then, as is so often the way in life, as you're meandering along, trying to make the best of things, solve daily problems like why there's a strange smell in the washing machine or where you put the potato peeler, things changed.

It was in the kitchen again. Scene of the worst moment of Rachel's life, which for a long time she could not go into without shaking, thinking of the blood on the floor and kitchen island, the heart-stopping fear of that moment: *Oh God, oh God, I've killed him.*

They were unloading the dishwasher, working almost in tandem in a way they used to back at the start of their marriage, but hadn't for years. 'Here you go.' She'd passed him a mug to put away, and he had reached out to open a cupboard, and suddenly he stopped and frowned, and Rachel realised he was standing in the exact same place it had happened. The incident.

'Are you OK?'

Simon stood against the counter on the other side of the kitchen island, near the cooker. His back to the plug socket where his phone had been charging that night. The dishwasher between them. Its door opened.

'Simon?'

A thin, pained sound was coming from him, like someone being choked. His eyes were wide and scared. 'Here. It was here!'

Panic rushed through Rachel. He was staring at her, eyes haunted. 'We had a fight. You read my phone – you started screaming and shouting.'

'Simon! Please . . . ' What was she asking? Please don't tell anyone? Don't say what I did to you?

'You took off your engagement ring and threw it. That's why it was in my pocket. You threw it!'

Rachel rubbed the empty spot on her finger, which she'd been doing obsessively ever since that night. 'I – I was angry.'

'Then you threw the phone at me – I leaned forward to duck– the dishwasher was open so I stumbled . . . ' He shuddered, looking down at the ground. 'I hit my head on the kitchen island.' He stared at the marble-topped island, hard as diamonds. 'That's what happened! I hurt myself. I was bleeding – I must have lost my memory just after. Oh God.'

Rachel was trembling. This was it, what she'd been terrified of anyone finding out. The reason she hadn't reported him missing. The truth she'd had to hide, no matter what. 'I'm so sorry. It was an accident. You ducked, you fell! I didn't mean . . . '

Simon was shaking. 'Oh God. Rachel. I remember . . . I can remember.'

'What can you remember?' Her heart was gasping in her chest, her lungs clawing in mouthfuls of air.

He shook his head, as if trying to clear it. 'I don't know! Bits, here and there . . . But it's so confused – why did you do it? What had I done?'

And suddenly, Rachel was just so tired of lying, of pretending, of holding up the whole crumbling edifice that was her life. Why not just tell him? Could things possibly be worse than they were now?

Wearily, Rachel began to relive the worst night of her life.

It had begun as a normal evening. Simon was late. Rachel sometimes played a game with herself – how late would he be? What excuse would he make – work, the trains, a meeting he'd apparently told her about but she'd forgotten, making her constantly doubt her own mind?

She heard the door slam as she was sitting in the living room, brooding over what she'd seen that afternoon, and he went straight past her into the kitchen. Didn't even say hello or ask how she was. Anger began to swell under her ribs, thinking of the woman she'd seen getting into the Mini outside her house earlier that day. The long legs, the swingy blonde hair. She got up, leaving her undrunk wine on the coffee table – she'd been too angry to even finish it. She'd sent Hannah to a friend's for a night, calling in an unearned favour, because she needed to confront this now. In the kitchen, Simon was plugging his phone in to charge, tapping away at it. 'You're back late,' she said. Her tone was crisped with frost.

'Hmm?' He didn't even look up. He hadn't even asked how his daughter was, or noticed she wasn't here.

'You're late. And you haven't even said hello.' Was that how it was now? He didn't bother with an excuse – didn't even speak to her?

He glanced up. His eyes passed over her, irritated. 'For God's sake, Rachel. I've been working all day. I don't need to come home to nagging.'

'Can't you put the phone down for one second?'

Exaggerated, he placed it down on the counter, still plugged in. 'Happy?'

'Not especially, no.' Her voice went wobbly with tears. To mask it, she flung open the door of the dishwasher and began to unload it, crashing the cups and plates together.

'You'll break something.'

'I don't care!' She wanted something to break, if she was honest. Maybe the smash, the sight of broken edges, would show him how badly things had gone wrong. She groped for a way to bring it up, the girl she'd seen at the house that day. Knowing that as soon as she did, her marriage would likely be over. Words failed her.

Simon sighed. 'Well, I can't talk to you when you're like this. I'm going to have a shower.' He left the room, and she heard his heavy feet on the stairs. Rachel finished with the dishwasher, then just stood there for a few minutes, vibrating with rage. Was this it? Was the end of her marriage approaching, seconds away?

She didn't know what made her do it. A similar impulse to smash things, maybe. She crossed the room – the four, five steps around the kitchen island – and picked up his phone.

Immediately, a message beeped in, popping up on the screen. She was surprised he hadn't turned the notifications off. An unknown number. *Have you told her yet?* And she knew, she just knew, it was from a woman. The woman in the Mini.

'Forgot my . . . ' Simon came back in to the room, shocking her. He'd changed into jeans and a band T-shirt, and that made her angry, that he still thought he was young enough to wear such things. To go with the young girl he planned to leave her for, probably. He'd come to get the phone, she knew. Because he wouldn't normally leave her alone with it. No wonder, with all the secrets he was keeping.

'What the hell is this?' She had his phone in her hand, pulling the charging cable out of the wall. 'Have you told her *what*? Her is me, I suppose? Who is this?'

'No, no. It's not what you think. Give me it.' Simon held his hand out.

'Tell me who she is! I saw her here! I know she was in our house!'

'Rachel, I . . . '

There might have been a moment then when he explained it all, and none of the rest happened. But he hesitated, and she saw in his face the lies he'd been telling her for months now. Maybe years. And rage filled her and she wrenched her engagement ring from her finger and flung it at him. 'You can have this back, you bastard!' Mechanically, he picked it up from where it tinkled on the tiled floor, slipped it into his pocket. 'Why, Simon? *Why*? Why did you have to do this? I just . . . I can't believe you, all this time, after all these years . . . I *hate* you!' And she pulled back her arm and threw the phone at him too.

Simon was standing on the other side of the kitchen island, near the door. He ducked forward instinctively to avoid the phone – he tripped over the open dishwasher door – he hit his head on the corner of the kitchen island, the marble work-top that had cost a thousand pounds alone. She could still remember the meaty crunch of it, as if someone had thrown a watermelon from a great height. A look of surprise and fear crossed his face, and then he slumped to the ground.

Then there was panic. *Oh God. Oh dear God.* She got him to his feet – he was conscious still, mostly, but confused, unable to talk – and she marched him out to the car in the dark, fearful of the neighbours, a tea towel wrapped around his head that was quickly red with blood. Hospital. They had to get to hospital, no time to lose. She didn't know why she hadn't called an ambulance. It would take too long, maybe. Or maybe she was just afraid of getting caught. She'd been drinking on top of everything else, probably shouldn't have driven, but she couldn't think straight. She pushed Simon into his seat, fumbled with his belt, then roared out of the drive and towards the motorway, heading to the nearest hos-pital, on the way out of town. But as soon as she stopped at a red light, Simon undid his belt and opened the car door and ran. Across the carriageway, into the night. She sat frozen for a minute in panic – should she get out? Leaving her car in the middle of a main road? Should she call the police? And then she just . . . drove home.

There was some blood on the kitchen island and the floor. She cleaned it up, filling the washing machine with tea towels, put it on. Scrubbed her hands until the red was gone. Thought about calling the police to tell them her injured husband had run from the car in the middle of the night. Didn't. And for the next day, and the day after that, she'd done the same. Nothing. And now look where she was.

When she finished, Simon was white-faced. 'I'm so sorry,' she said, voice wobbling with tears. 'I was so afraid. I thought I'd killed you, so I couldn't call the police. I should have. I see that now. I was just – I was so scared, and I thought you'd left me for that girl.'

'But I hadn't – I remember now. It was about the house, wasn't it?'

'Simon, I'm so sorry. If I could go back, I would do everything so differently.' He said nothing. What was he thinking? Would he call the police on her? It was probably a crime, wasn't it? Assault? A cold pocket settled around her heart, thinking how easily he could have died. She'd have been a murderer then. Manslaughter, at the very least. Years in prison, away from Hannah, her daughter growing into a stranger. Instead, here he was, returned to her, more or less whole, a miracle. 'Please,' she choked out. 'Please don't report me. I – it really was an accident.'

Simon said, in a low voice, 'I would do everything so differently too. I would tell you what was going on. Not borrow money. Sell the house. Down-size. I would . . . Rachel, I wish we could go back. But we can't, can we?'

'N-no. You mean . . . ?'

He sighed. 'Of course I won't call the police. It was an accident, and no more than I deserved. I remember that now.'

She was struggling to take it in. 'You really have your memory back?'

He made a frustrated gesture. 'I'm so confused. I don't know what's what, everything's so mixed up. But . . . I think so, yes.'

Rachel grabbed her handbag off the chair. 'We need to get you to hospital. Let them check it out.' Was this it – it was really over? If so, why didn't she feel any better?

EVE

I ran down the corridor of the hospital, the doors flicking closed behind me. The lift took too long, so I'd rushed up the stairs, and was now practically seeing spots. When I reached the Neurology Ward, I saw Praj. Breathless, I got out, 'He remembered? His memory really came back?' I had so much to tell him. Graham turning up, and the fact he was a cat. Mrs G dying, Jimmy Gillespie coming. My new resolution to live my life.

'Oh, Eve. What are you . . . ?'

'Can I see him?' When the news came in, that Simon had remembered himself, I knew I had to see him. All this time we'd worked towards it, and finally he was cured. What that meant for us, I hadn't stopped to think. I just knew I needed to be with him. If his memory was back, that meant he could make a choice on a level playing field. If he chose me now, if he still wanted me in his life – well, it would be real.

'Just be careful,' said Praj, as I pushed my way past him into the MRI lab. 'He's a bit confused – the whole of his life just came rushing back, boom!'

'What did it?' I couldn't see him. Where was he?

'Just being in the kitchen at home. Apparently that's where he got the head injury in the first place.'

So my memory techniques had worked after all. It had just taken a while.

I began to fret. I hadn't brushed my hair properly that

260

morning, and why was I wearing the same old jeans he'd always seen me in? I should have changed before rushing out of Sunnyside to the train station. But I didn't have time to panic much, because the ward door opened and Zoe came out. She looked cross, but I had learned that she just suffered from what Julie called 'resting bitch face', and when she saw me, she smiled. 'Eve! You're here!'

I barely acknowledged her, because with her was a tall, handsome man with a fashionable haircut, wearing expensive jeans and a soft navy jumper in a pattern that looked like a waffle. Adam. My Adam, the way he'd always been, even if he wore better clothes and had been given a shave and haircut.

I rushed over to him. 'Hi! Oh my God, how are you feeling? What's going on?' He was staring at me politely, but curiously. 'Adam, it's me!' I began to feel that hole again, curling through me like when you set paper on fire, blackening and disappearing. Because it wasn't Adam. I had forgotten that Adam did not exist.

His face cleared. 'Oh, I'm sorry, you have the wrong person. I'm Simon. Simon Kempner. I don't think we've met?' And he held his hand out towards me, as if it was the very first time he was seeing me.

Zoe and Praj were talking in quiet, but not quiet enough voices. I sat by the door of their office, and Adam/Simon sat there too, but had chosen the seat furthest away from me. My legs felt heavy with shock, and I knew that if I tried to get up, I would struggle to walk.

'Really unusual. No new head trauma since?'

'Police say no. That must mean—'

'It was psychological in origin. Traumatic amnesia! Fugue state, baby!'

'God, I told you, didn't I? I said it wasn't physical.'

'Yeah, yeah, I owe you a Twix.'

'Two Twixes, cheapskate. So what are we going to ... ?'

'Jesus, I don't know. It's a therapist he needs, not neurologists.'

'We could do a combined study. Eve and "Adam", two patients with disorders of the autobiographic memory. Could be fascinating. One who remembers everything and one who can't remember anything.'

Adam/Simon smiled at me with awkward politeness, like when you overhear someone having a row on the bus. 'I'm so sorry about this. My memory ... we have met?'

'Yes, you were ... After your accident, you lived in a nursing home for a while. Sunnyside?' How could he forget? I'd seen him only days ago. It was like some horrible dream. I kept expecting him to laugh and say, *Ha, gotcha, Eve, of course I remember you.*

He frowned and shook his head. 'They told me that, of course, but I can't ... I can remember everything leading up to the accident now – but then all I know is I was back at home in my kitchen, and the bit in between is just ... gone. Did we know each other well?'

I stared at my feet. Scruffy Converse (invented in 1917), frayed laces. I bet Rachel only wore expensive, polished shoes. 'I ... I was helping you remember.'

'Of course. Eve, right? They told me. I had some objects in my pocket and we tried to track them down ... ' He trailed off, embarrassed. 'Apparently I was going to run away or something. Go to France, I guess. I was in Kent when they found

262

me, they said. I don't remember all of it, but I think I did something. I was in some kind of trouble with money.'

I stared at him. 'I know. I was with you!' This was impossible. Somehow, in the short space of time since his memory had come back, he had forgotten me. I didn't understand. 'Don't you remember – Hamleys? The ring?'

He frowned, and the crease that appeared between his eyebrows was so familiar, yet everything else was so strange. 'I'm sorry, yes, they did say someone was with me. Do you mean Rachel's engagement ring? She threw it at me.'

Another thing he didn't remember? I said, 'It's fake, remember? We had it valued and . . . it's not real diamonds.'

His face changed. 'Oh my God. That's right. I . . . couldn't afford a real one back then, but I wanted her to think I could. So I . . . '

'She didn't know?' Even with what I'd learned about Simon Kempner, I was a little shocked. Poor Rachel, walking around with something she thought was genuine, but all the while was a big fat lie.

'I . . . No.' Softly, he looked at his hands. 'I'm really not a very nice person, I'm afraid. I'm sorry – I don't know why I'm telling you this. I got in trouble, you see. Money trouble. I borrowed some, to fill the hole. I thought I could pay it back. But then . . . the interest . . . it just kept getting bigger and bigger.'

'And they came after you.'

He stared down. 'They threatened to take everything. To go after my family too – Rachel and Hannah.' He said their names differently this time, as if he remembered them properly.

'So . . . what did you do, Simon?' Calling him that felt like another chunk was gone of whatever we'd had. If it was even real. If for him it had never happened, did that mean it never existed?

'I ...'

'I know it's hard. But please, I have to know.'

'I ... had a plan.' He was shaking. 'I was going to run away – or maybe jump off the ferry, I hadn't decided yet. I'd leave a note for Rachel – tell her to claim my life insurance. Settle all the debts. I just felt so totally hopeless. I hated myself. But then ... Rachel saw a message on my phone. It wasn't what she thought – she thought it was a woman, but it wasn't. Well, it was, but not like that. She lost her temper, threw the phone. But I fell. It was an accident. I ... ' His whole body shook with a sobbing sigh. 'I did this. It was all my fault. I was a bad husband, a bad dad. I let them down.'

I hardly recognised him, this crying, broken man, telling me these terrible things. I had to try once more. 'Simon – do you not remember anything after that? Sunnyside? Mrs Gillespie? Terry? Magda?' He looked blank. 'The Lego – the ring? The hotel? Kent? You really don't remember Kent?' How could he forget it, that sweep of jewel blue, the striped pebble shore, his hand in mine, ice cream on our lips, wind whipping our hair? I would never forget it, if I lived another twenty thousand days. Because out of every single day I could remember in crystal detail, that one would still be the best. 'Please.' I found myself saying it even though it was futile. The families of the residents sometimes begged them in the same way, frustrated tears running down their faces. *Please, Mum. It's me. You know me!* 'Simon – can you try?'

Slowly he said, 'I know I was in Kent when they found me, and I remember I went there to leave the bag – but not with you. I'm sorry. I don't remember that at all.'

264

'So!' Before I could run away or burst into tears or punch the wall or something, Praj and Zoe appeared in front of us, unnaturally perky. I could sense the tension between them, the excitement. 'The good news is we think we know what's wrong with Simon. And it's not the head injury.'

'The bad news is he doesn't remember anything about the last few weeks.'

'He ... won't remember me?' I stared up at them. Simon/ Adam still wore the same polite expression, as if we were discussing someone else.

Praj shook his head sympathetically. 'It seems to be a psychological trauma thing, as we suspected. Whatever was going on in his life before the head injury, the stress he was under, it was so bad that it triggered a fugue state. Dissociation. It's not unheard of, though quite unusual. He just ... forgot who he was. And now that he's come out of it, he's lost the fugue time.'

I thought of how happy he'd been with us at Sunnyside. Lighter, freer. Absolved of guilt, by forgetting himself. 'And when will it come back? The memory of me, of the past few weeks?' Maybe it was just like the first amnesia and would return when his memory was jogged. Maybe I could even help him again.

They exchanged a look. Zoe said, 'Eve ... in the studies we've found, the person rarely recovers any memories at all of the fugue time. I'm very sorry.'

RACHEL

'Everything's back to normal,' Hannah declared, in her 'Margaret Thatcher announcing war in the Falklands' voice. 'Daddy's OK, he's not poorly any more.' She barrelled her way into the living room, picking up the remote. No sign that anything had ever been wrong. They had told everything to DS Irene Rusombe, and no charges would be pressed, although Rachel felt strong disapproval of her decision not to call an ambulance or report Simon missing. That was something she'd just have to live with, knowing things could have been different. Had she done the sensible thing, not been paralysed by the fear of losing everything – and it was more than just fear of the police, wasn't it, it was the idea of everyone knowing her life was a sham, her husband was a liar, that she was violent and angry, it was the shame of it all, the desperate need to pretend things were perfect.

'That's right,' Rachel said weakly. Nothing felt at all normal. After his check-up, Simon had been brought home from the hospital in London. Rachel had held her breath, watching him and Hannah meet in the hallway, but this time he'd buried his face in his daughter's hair, weeping. Rachel had never seen Simon cry before all this. He was a manly man, buttoned down, keeping it all in. Which, it turned out, had not been the best approach. Hannah had disengaged herself, patting his shoulder. 'It's all right, Daddy. You're OK now.'

But was he? Simon was still hovering in the hallway of the house. Like a guest, not the person who actually owned the place.

To Hannah, Rachel said, 'I'm so sorry you had to go through that, darling. Daddy didn't mean to forget you, you know.'

'That's OK. I like that Granny came. She lets me have a bun from Greggs every day!' Hannah didn't appear to be traumatised by her father vanishing and almost dying and forgetting her. But how would they go forward from this? Simon had at least recalled the details of his debts now, but his memory was still damaged, and he was confused, sometimes angry when he couldn't remember things. He seemed to have no memory of his time at the nursing home, for a start. He couldn't work, and they still owed all that money, even with a payment plan. There would be major cutbacks to their lifestyle. She'd have to get a job again. She felt helpless just thinking about it.

Her mother, who was out buying groceries, was planning to leave the next day. Rachel had begged her to stay on in the spare room, but she'd declined. 'Your dad needs me; he can't be alone for long.' She'd pressed Rachel's hands in hers. 'Love, I know you're OK now. But we'd love to see you more. And Hannah. Maybe . . . '

Rachel had fought back tears. 'Oh, Mum. I'm sorry.'

'None of that. Just think it over and come when you can.' Would she go? It was too much to think about just now.

She still couldn't quite adjust to it. Was it really over? Had she got away with it, almost killing her husband, covering it up, not reporting him missing? What would come next?

She was just hovering in the kitchen, the scene of her crime, wondering what the hell to do next now that her life had been returned to her, when she heard the sound of tyres on gravel. Who was that? Her stomach tensed – not the bailiffs? Hadn't they agreed to stay away? It would be a while before she stopped associating visitors with the police, or with loan sharks, and her heart rate spiked.

'Mummy!' shouted Hannah from the living room. 'It's Mark.'

'It's good to see you.' She'd asked him in, but he declined, saying he wouldn't 'stop'. Instead, they stood on the driveway in the cold wind. Rachel had her arms wrapped around herself, shivering in her long cardigan, and Mark twirled his car keys round his fingers.

'I just came to check you were OK. He really remembered?'

'Yeah. I can't believe it.'

'Well, you're all right now. Back to your old life.'

He seemed to be saying something else but she couldn't get a handle on it. There was so much to sort out she couldn't think past the next hour. 'Right.' For weeks, all she'd wanted was to go back to how things were, living in blissful ignorance, worrying only about what was in the veg box that week and what to wear on the school pick-up. But now a strange nervousness curdled in the pit of her stomach. That life she'd fought so hard to hold on to, even when it had crumbled from the inside out – could she really go back to it?

A silence fell between them. She watched his large hands fidget with his keys. The back seat of his Jeep was covered in manila files – other women who'd come to him for help? New cases he'd be moving on to soon? Maybe that was all she was to him, another job.

'You'll be OK?'

'I . . . I don't know. But thank you. If it wasn't for you . . . God, I must owe you a fortune as well. Send me the invoice.' Though she didn't know if they had any money now.

He waved it away. 'We'll sort that out later. Take care of yourself. For what comes next.'

'What do you mean?'

'You know. After something like this, you can't just go back to normal, pretend it didn't happen. You need to think about what to do next. With your life, Rachel.'

Panic seized her, which was stupid, because she'd faced far worse over the past few weeks. Was Mark suggesting what it sounded like – that her marriage was permanently damaged? Simon had lied to her so much, about so many things, and she had hurt him then tried to cover it up. She pushed it away. 'I . . . I can't think about that now. It seems too overwhelming.'

'It's not so bad, you know. Divorce. I miss my daughter – Lucy, that's her name – but I see her every week or so. You don't have to stay in something just because you made vows.' She thought of her mother's constant refrain. *I married him, Rachel. I made my bed.* This idea that you had to pay for your past mistakes, even if you'd no way of knowing it was a mistake at the time. She thought about it some more. Hannah had been without her father now for several weeks, and she was doing fine. And as for money, for the house, all those details – people worked them out. People managed without cleaners and gardeners and yoga classes.

'I don't suppose you know a divorce lawyer too,' she said lightly. A joke. But he took it seriously.

'I know everyone, Rachel.' And for some reason, when he said her name, she got a shiver down her back. Not an unpleasant one. And for a second, a crack of light opened up, and she let herself imagine a future that was different from the one she'd planned. Where she didn't have to live with a man who'd become a stranger, who had in fact been a stranger for a long time. But inside the house, there was Hannah, a little girl who'd come close to losing her father for ever because of Rachel. She couldn't split them up again.

'I – Mark, I don't know. Simon needs me. He's not well. How could I . . . do anything more to upset our lives?'

His face closed. 'Of course.'

On an impulse, she seized his hand, squeezed it. It was as large and capable as she'd thought. She imagined him fixing fences, pushing a lawnmower in the garden at weekends. 'Thank you, Mark. I won't ever forget what you've done for me. I hope you know that.'

Mark looked over her shoulder. 'Listen, there was something I never told you. When you came into my office that day – I knew I'd seen you before.'

Rachel blinked. 'You had?'

'It's not as strange as it sounds. I was a copper, I'm good at recognising people – it happens more than most people notice. And you, I have definitely crossed paths with.'

Rachel was racking her brains. Where could she possibly have met him? 'I don't remember.'

'No, I don't think you even noticed me. It was in London – Islington. A summer day about ten years ago. You were walking along, wearing this dress with flowers on it. A big hat. You were smiling. I remember because you looked like a person in a magazine. Like you were so happy nothing could possibly add to it. I was there investigating a burglary, little old lady scared half to death by some thugs, lost her life savings, and I guess I was glad to see someone in a good mood.'

'Oh my God. You were the policeman. The one who smiled at me.'

'You remember?'

'Yes! Wow, I didn't even recognise you.' But maybe she had, in some distant echo of her brain. Maybe that was why she felt she'd known him for so long. Even if she didn't consciously remember it, that encounter, that flash of seeing him – every detail of that walk to the pub, every person she passed, every crack in the pavement – it was somewhere in her head. Maybe every single person was walking about with a lifetime of memories in those folds of flesh between their ears. For someone like Eve, who remembered them all, it must be overwhelming. 'Wow,' she said again. 'Isn't that weird?'

'Not so weird, like I say. It probably happens all the time but you don't realise. I just wanted to tell you that.'

'Thank you.' It made her sad, for some reason, to think of that hopeful young woman, in a flowered dress, heading out in the sun, not even knowing she was about to meet the man who'd change her life. Make her a mother, a wife. Make her rich. Then make her go through all of this.

He looked away. 'Rachel, it was ... good to get to know you. I mean that.'

'You too.'

He stepped forward suddenly and gave her a rough hug, and she breathed in the smell of his old Barbour jacket. Leathery, comforting. There seemed to be nothing and everything to say, so after a moment she stepped back and he got in the Jeep and drove off, without looking back.

EVE

I trailed back to Sunnyside, which had never seemed less sunny to me. I saw it as it really was – an ugly red-brick building set in a rectangle of half-dead grass. Inside it was filled with people who had lost themselves, who would never find a way back as Simon had done. Who would never remember more, only less and less with each passing day.

As I approached the front door, I was barely aware of where I was, nursing inside me the feeling of that moment when Adam (Simon! He was Simon!) had looked at me and not known me. A very particular pain that I hadn't experienced for almost thirty years. I saw someone hunched outside, smoking a cigarette in the cold. A woman of about forty, with a smart camel coat and nice handbag. She was crying, her face shiny with tears. 'Are you all right?' I said. 'Carol, isn't it?' Mrs Munroe's daughter.

She scrubbed at her face. 'Oh, yes! I'm sorry. I can't . . . '

'Eve,' I supplied. 'I help look after your mum.'

'Right. She's not doing so good today. She . . . she didn't know me at first. I had to say, "Mum, it's Carol."'

Mrs Munroe had always been one of the sharper residents, capable of completing the Countdown Conundrum on a good day, and my heart sank to hear this. She too was going, disappearing into the fog. Soon, she wouldn't remember anyone.

'It's the disease,' I said gently. 'It's not really her. I'm sure she loves you very much.' Did I even believe that? Simon didn't know me, and I'd felt no love there. Nothing at all. It was as if we'd never met.

'But she didn't know me! She looked at me and it was like . . . polite confusion, like I was the tea lady or something.'

Silently, I passed her a tissue. Working where I do, I always have a ready supply of them, to mop up tears, or indeed other bodily fluids as the occasion demands.

'I'm sorry,' Carol said, wiping her eyes, smearing mascara. 'Today was just a bad day. And I know that, even if she does recognise me again once or twice, she won't get any better. I don't know what to do.'

'There's nothing we can do,' I said. 'Just remember her as she was. Hold on to her that way.'

She nodded, but I could tell I hadn't really helped and I wasn't surprised. What comfort was there to give for this terrible loss – the erasure of all your time together, gone from the brain like wiping a computer's hard drive? I went inside, leaving her to the cigarette and the rain.

My flat, which had once seemed so cosy, looked gloomy and empty. No one else ever there to move a cup or dislodge a speck of dust. Pacing around, I found myself looking at the Museum. Such a lot of clutter, and the dust it collected was crazy. Did I really need it? I wasn't going to forget any of the residents or the people I'd known in my life. I wasn't going to forget Simon – more was the pity. But they would forget me. Even Magda and the others, Anthony and Charity and Julie, they didn't love me, they just worked with me. The residents, they didn't even know who I was half the time. And the only person who had truly mattered, Adam, did not even exist.

It all seemed to build up inside me, suddenly, the years I had worked here, trying to hold back an unstoppable tide with my stupid techniques, an old song, a broken object, a string of questions. Meanwhile, dementia just kept going, ravaging through the residents, washing away their memories, their pasts, everything that made them who they were. What was the point? Why would I bother getting up tomorrow, handing out biscuits and pills? A disease like this could not be beaten. Before I knew it, I was sweeping the Museum – so carefully looked after for so many years – into black bin bags. It all went in: the snow globe, the sweet wrapper, everything. I lingered over the pen, Adam's pen. *Simon's*. A cheap, leaking thing that had led us to find out how low he'd stooped. We had found who he was, and in the process lost him. Lost us, if indeed there had been an us.

The Museum, my life's work, came to two and a half bin bags. I tied them up and left them by the door. Then I threw a few things into a hold-all – toothbrush, pants, a few jumpers – and left the flat. I heaved the bags into the large bin by the gate and set off into the night, without looking back.

RACHEL

It was getting late. Hannah was in bed, and her mother had retreated to the spare room, perhaps to tactfully allow Rachel and Simon to talk. But what would she say to him? Rachel walked around the ground floor of the house, touching things from time to time, making sure they were solid. The spice rack, specially built to hold forty spices. The framed pictures, original art from local artists or pieces they'd seen on holiday. The polished brass mirror in the hallway that she'd spent three full days bidding for on eBay. Her house, her belongings, which she had hoped would hold the chaos at bay. Doing the right things – maths tuition, milk deliveries, regular dentist appointments. And none of it had helped, ultimately. Things had still fallen apart, her husband lying to her, herself hiding a terrible secret. Maybe it had been the same for her father. Maybe he too had gone to sleep every night gripped by fear, hoping for a miracle where it would somehow all be OK, only to wake up and find the waters rising higher and higher around his neck.

'You OK?' Still dazed, she walked into the dining room, where Simon was standing, staring at some framed photos on the wall. Hannah as a baby, their wedding. So many smiles it was almost blinding. She'd put them up, despite him insisting it wasn't classy to have photos of people in the house. Arty black-and-white shots only were acceptable. 'Do you want something to eat?'

'What is there?'

She hadn't got as far as meal-planning. 'Hmm, I don't know. Beans on toast, maybe.'

Simon frowned. 'Do you eat bread? I seem to remember ... '

'Oh. I didn't, for a long time. I guess I started again.' It occurred to her that she had changed too, in the short time Simon had been away. Her old self emerging from the shiny shell she'd been, as if worn away to her essence. He was still frowning at the pictures. 'What's wrong?'

'It's just – we look so happy here.'

'People always look happy in pictures.'

'No. Not if you really look.' He turned to me, his green eyes serious. How she had loved those eyes, once. Back when they first met, she had actually felt her knees give away when he turned them on her. 'Rachel. We haven't been happy like this for a while, have we? When I remember it, I get this horrible sad feeling. Like you're ... standing on a clifftop miles away, shouting to me, but I can't hear.'

She looked at the pictures, the wedding shot blurring at the edges. The old Simon would not have said that to her. Would never have been so honest. 'I ... no. I guess we haven't.'

'Why is that? What did I do?'

She sighed. 'I don't know if you did anything, as such. You worked a lot, and I was here all the time. So it was a sort of ... disconnect. I usually went to bed before you even got home. You hardly ever saw me, or Hannah. And recently, I guess, with the money worries, you stopped talking to me at all. It was ... Simon, I was really lonely.'

'So was I,' he said bleakly. 'I was just so trapped – I hated what I'd done, who I'd become. But I couldn't see a way out, and every day it just got worse and worse.' He rubbed his hands over his face. 'I lost it all, didn't I? Our money.'

She decided to be kind. 'I think you just . . . got into bother.'

'I was stupid. And greedy, I suppose. I thought I could just borrow a bit, tide myself over, but then things kind of . . . spiralled.' The same word her dad had used, when he sat weeping on the stairs – they'd taken all the furniture – on that Christmas morning. *I'm sorry, kids. Things just spiralled.* 'You know I never even wanted to work in finance. I hate it, in fact!'

'Do you?' Rachel had never known that. 'What would have you wanted to do instead?'

'God, I don't know. Be a musician, maybe. Apparently, I used to play the piano at the old folks' home, not that I can remember.' He made a noise, half a laugh. 'Rachel, there's so much I never told you. The ring you threw at me. It's not even real, did you know that? It's a fake diamond. I gave you a fake engagement ring. When we met, I wasn't anywhere near as well-off as I made out. It was all a show. Because that's what I do, apparently. I lie.'

'It's fake?' Rachel was startled. It had never occurred to her it was anything other than a real diamond. She thought of how she'd shown it off back then, madly in love and newly engaged – had people known, laughed at her behind her back? Would someone properly posh, instead of just pretending like she was, have known it wasn't real? 'Oh.' She realised she'd never put it back on after Eve gave it back to her, so she supposed she hadn't really missed it after chucking it at him that terrible night. She wasn't even sure where it was – in a drawer somewhere? How strange, to lose something you'd valued so much, and not even notice.

'I'm sorry, Rachel. I'm a liar. I hurt you, and Hannah.'

She took Simon's hand, and it felt like a stranger's. Not the same hand that had curved around her waist the first night they kissed, on that warm summer evening, half-drunk on each other, or cradled Hannah's bloody newborn head, reached out to pick her hat up from the floor, that first day a decade ago. 'It was as much my fault, you know. I was the one saying let's upgrade the car, let's go on holiday, getting facials and hair-dos and all. And I left you on the motorway, for God's sake! I didn't even try to find you.' A chill still ran through her when she thought about it. How close they'd been to complete dis-aster. If he'd fallen an inch either way, if no one had picked him up running along the motorway, if a car had struck him. She'd thought she was living through the worst thing she could imagine, but somehow, the three of them had emerged alive. Home. Free. Maybe, they needed to take this as a second chance they hadn't earned.

He almost smiled. 'Just an accident. I probably deserved the phone thrown at me. But I never had an affair, I swear.' Again, the eyes on her, like a searchlight. 'Rach. I wouldn't blame you, if you . . . '

She thought of Mark, the comforting smell of his Barbour jacket. 'No. But since you've been gone, I've sort of had . . . feel-ings. For someone.'

He nodded. 'Mark. Is that who you mean?'

'He helped me,' she said, as if that was an explanation. 'Eve . . . '

He frowned. 'She helped me too, I think. She tried to get my memory back, and when it came – I found out I wasn't very nice. And now I can't even remember her. I mean, it's the

279

bare minimum, isn't it? Remembering someone who tried to save you.'

'You had feelings for her?'

'I can't remember.' He shook his head in frustration. 'How can I have feelings for her when I don't even know her? All I know is – when I think of her, I feel safe. Like I'm home.' He looked around him, at his actual home. 'This place – I don't feel anything. Just sad.'

This was such a strange conversation. 'Part of you will know her. Even when you forgot us, forgot Hannah – you had that little Lego brick with you, in your pocket? Some bit of you was thinking of her?'

He nodded. 'Maybe.'

She saw how painful it was, losing bits of himself. 'Simon,' she said haltingly, 'how can we get past this? Everything we've done to each other?'

There was a long silence between them that seemed to go on and on, that seemed to stretch across the ten years they had known each other, a marriage, a child, two houses, many cars, many more lies. She might have said something to break it, break everything, if he hadn't cocked his head to one side and frowned. 'Is that the phone?'

EVE

Memory is a funny thing. When we're fully immersed in it, it's like we're living it again, just like the first time it happened. PTSD is when your brain can't tell the difference between a memory and the real thing. When time loses meaning and the moment goes on and on for ever, and you never escape.

A few miles away from where I stood, the zoom of cars on the motorway never stopped, the constant buzz fading to background noise. I wore only my thin jacket again, and I was shivering in the cold wind. When I thought of my little flat, cosy and clean, I wanted to cry. Why was I here? It was like a bad dream. Like living a terrible memory, over and over, until it becomes reality.

Where I found myself was a place of no significance. A stretch of country road not far from the M6, near a Midlands village called Ashley Bridge. The nearest city, Wolverhampton, was fifteen miles away. I had taken the night coach there from Bishopsdean, a journey of six hours squashed up the whole time beside a large man who watched cat videos on his phone without headphones, then a taxi to this stretch of road, bracing myself. The driver had been confused. *Here? Are you sure?* I was sure. As I stood on the grass verge at the side of the road, hardly any traffic passed. It was a quiet place. Nowhere, really. It was the place my mother had died, and I had lost my father for good.

*

Daddy, it's me. A panic was rising in me. The man in the chair in the nursing home looked like my dad – tall, broad-shouldered, wearing his diamond-patterned jumper – but the expression on his face wasn't one I recognised. There was no love, no smile for me. His eyes were flat and cold. A red and grey scar ran along his head, over his ear.

Dad? It's me! Eve!

Nothing. He got up from the chair he was slumped in, pushing himself up on shaking arms. He brushed past me, roughly, and the Lego man I had brought dropped to the floor. *Take her away.* And finally, I understood. He did not know me. My father no longer knew who I was.

My memory, the curse and blessing of my life, only began working the way it does after the accident, when I was six years old. I wish this wasn't true. I wish I could remember every moment of my mother – Diana Mahoney, thirty-one years old, sang in the kitchen in the mornings, peeled oranges for me in one long bright strip – but instead all I have are the blank facts of her life, a handful of hazy memories. A yellow dress. The smell of roses, that years later can still stop me in my tracks. I don't remember the sound of her laughter or if she drank tea or preferred coffee, what her favourite song was, what she felt like when I hugged her. She has been dead for twenty-eight years, killed when the car we were driving in hit a pothole on this road, flipped on its head, crushing the two front seats. I, aged six, buckled into the back, was totally fine, my hair full of shattered glass but not a mark on me. My father – David Mahoney, thirty-two years old, worked in Sainsbury's but was studying at night to be a teacher, born in Cork – was not killed in the accident. He survived,

282

but had terrible injuries. Traumatic amnesia. He lived another eleven years – dying when I turned seventeen, the event which sent me running from my last foster home, eventually fetching up at Sunnyside – but he never recovered. He never learned how to dress himself, or eat without spilling, or tie his laces. And although I visited him once a month – or whenever I could persuade my latest foster family to bring me – he never once remembered who I was. Whatever happened to his brain in those fateful seconds, when the soft tissue of it broke against the hardness of bone, it ripped me out of his memories. All the stories, the Lego houses, the hugs, six years of love, they were all gone in less than a second. I have come to realise that this is the greatest cruelty of life – that everything we are, everything that lasts, is dependent on that one weak globe of bone and flesh.

My name is Eve Mahoney, I'm thirty-four years old, and I remember everything that's ever happened to me since the age of six. I had lived a half-life for seventeen years, hiding away, ushering people out of the world, blank and empty as white paper. I had fallen in love with a man I thought was perfect, kind and handsome and empty, with no baggage. The truth is everyone has baggage. I have fleets of it myself, more than Heathrow Airport. The man I loved did not exist, and my crippling memory was not going to change or disappear. I was not going to wake up transformed, as Adam had, becoming Simon again with one flash of memory. I was stuck like this, always, as Eve the weirdo, doomed to be alone, because who could be with someone who never forgets? And so now I had to decide what to do with the rest of my life.

RACHEL

It was handy, she had to admit, having her mother there. There was someone to take care of Hannah while she and Simon bundled themselves into the car and dashed off. It was just like that terrible night, the two of them driving furiously, except now there was honesty between them. Except now they were going to try to help the woman who'd taken care of Simon when he was lost.

The decision had been automatic when they'd heard Eve was in trouble, that she'd run off from Sunnyside. Everyone was worried because she'd left home without telling anyone, thrown out most of her possessions. They had to help her, like she had helped them. And so they drove.

'How will we find her?' Magda, the care home owner, was in tears when they arrived. A glamorous, plump woman in black, she appeared to have – was it really five pens stuck into her hair? 'She's like a daughter to me. She doesn't know about the world – she's lived here since she was young! She's not like other people. What will I do?'

'We'll help,' said Rachel in what she hoped was a soothing tone. 'She can't be far.' The home was in uproar, old people crying and wandering bewildered in the hallways, a scowling woman with long acrylic nails shouting, 'Not in there, Ms Jerman, back to your room!', and a young man with white make-up on chasing about with a clipboard. 'Where's Terry?

Where's Miss Cole?' And everyone they passed seemed to know Simon, except they called him Adam. They asked how he was, if he'd play them a song on the piano, if he'd help with the crossword or lift something down off a high shelf.

Simon passed by, bewildered. 'I'm sorry ... maybe later ... I need to help Eve now ... '

'You don't remember them?' Rachel whispered, as they fought their way into the office, Magda trotting beside them.

He shook his head, wild-eyed. 'It's like ... I did all these things in a dream or something, and I just can't remember.'

'Well, they remember you. And they like you. They really like you.'

'Do you think so?' He seemed puzzled by that, and she remembered what had upset him most about his loss of memory, apart from the pain of not knowing his daughter. The idea that he was a bad person – so bad that his brain had shut down to avoid being Simon any more. Here, as Adam, it seemed he had found a way to be good. To be loved, and needed, and appreciated, in a way he wasn't in his own life. Rachel's heart ached.

'Oh God.' Magda shut the office door behind them, breathing hard. 'Eve's the one who holds this place together; it's just madness without her.'

'So you've no idea where she went? She didn't leave a message or a note?' Rachel tried to take charge.

'Nothing. She's hardly gone anywhere in seventeen years! I told her to get out in the world, but I didn't mean like this!' She looked at Simon. 'Adam, lovie, did she ever say anything to you? A place she might go?' There was an awkward pause. Magda flushed. 'Simon, I mean.'

285

'I'm sorry, but … my memory came back, and now I don't remember being here.'

'You don't?'

'I'm so sorry. The doctors say it was a fugue state – but I know you took care of me really well here. The thing is – I think I might be the reason Eve went. I – she came to the hospital to see me and I didn't know her.'

Magda paled. 'Oh, lovie. Really?'

'I can't help it,' said Simon miserably. 'Before, I didn't know my own family, and now I don't know any of you!'

She laid a hand on his arm. 'It's not your fault, love. I just wish we had some clue where she'd gone. Maybe there's something in your things – you know you never came back for the stuff you had while you were here. Most of it was junk, of course, but you never know. I have it here from when we cleaned your room.'

She gestured to a box of photocopier paper, with a sad collection of objects in it. A jumper with angry-looking kittens knitted into it. What appeared to be a woman's blouse. Some cheap socks and a worn-down bar of chemical-smelling soap, a basic toothbrush. Was this how he'd lived here? This was the life she'd condemned him to, by not reporting him missing. By being such a coward.

'What's this?' Simon picked up a small notebook, A5-sized with the logo of an incontinence pad company on the front.

'Oh! You kept a little notebook while you were here. Trying to get it all straight in your head.'

Simon flicked through it, frowning. The pages were filled with what Rachel recognised as his strong blocky handwriting. Funny how that hadn't changed, even though he'd been a different person here. 'Look, there're pages about Eve.'

Rachel peered over – the heading said, *Eve Mahoney, 34, lives at Sunnyside. Orphan.*

Magda made a noise in her throat. 'God love her, her parents passed away. So sad.'

Rachel found herself remembering a conversation she'd heard through a door. Eve talking to Hannah, trying to make her feel better. 'I know where she is,' she said.

EVE

I didn't need to check the address, of course. I remembered it from the day she took me there for tea, right after my fourth foster placement broke down. We ate Kimberley Mikados, and I licked the jam off the biscuits, and that was when Theresa said that thing about *can't you just forget, Eve.* She didn't mean it unkindly. For all her brusque, chain-smoking ways, Theresa had always been kind to me. It wasn't her fault it was so hard to place a strange, intense girl, who never forgot a thing.

It was a small house, pebble-dash, with a cheap PVC door and a rail in front of it, as if the person who lived there struggled to walk. I rang the doorbell, then heard a hoarse cry of, 'It's open, don't expect me to get up.' I turned the handle and went in, the fug of the overheated house settling around me, cigarettes and damp laundry.

'Hello, Theresa.'

'Eve.' A harsh, raspy voice I knew all the way down to my toes. A forty-fags-a-day voice. Sitting in an old patterned armchair was a small, stooped woman. She wore a large hairy cardigan, cheap knock-off Uggs, and a beanie hat, as if she was cold despite the cranked-up heating. Her hair was grey and straggling, and she had glasses with clear frames. Theresa had aged. An oxygen tank sat beside her chair, a walker parked up. 'You came back, then, did you?'

My eyes filled with tears. 'I did. I'm sorry it took me so long.'

*

Theresa instructed me where to find the tea and milk, barking orders in between bone-wracking coughs. 'Not that cup, use a decent one.' Eventually we were sitting opposite each other, her on the old torn armchair, me on the sagging velvet sofa. Had I known anything about Theresa's life – had I cared, as a selfish teenager? Had she ever been married, or was this it, a life lived alone, revolving now around the metre-square of her armchair? She coughed again. 'Are you going to tell me what brings you here, after all this time?'

'I just . . . ' I didn't know how to explain it. 'I felt it was time. To see where it happened.'

She nodded; she knew I meant the accident. The moment that had divided my life in two, at the age of six. 'And?'

I shrugged. Being at the accident site had not brought them back, my mother before she died or my father before he was altered. All I had were the same bad memories, the blood on the road, the sparkle of broken glass. The silence. 'Is there anything you know – anything you didn't tell me back then?' Theresa had been my social worker since the day of the crash, when I sat on a hospital bed for hours, mute but unhurt, until she came briskly in with her smell of cigarettes and Trebor Extra Strong Mints. She had never lied to me, even from that first moment. *I'm sorry, Eve. Your mum is dead.*

'I told you everything. Your dad I just – I was trying to shield you as long as possible. I took you when you asked to see him.'

Had that been the right decision? I didn't know. Maybe it would have been better to let me believe they both died that day, rather than know my father was alive but had turned into someone else. That the love I had banked on, the air I breathed, was suddenly gone and I was alone in the world, or as good as.

'When he died . . . ' I began. Theresa had come to tell me that too, in my last foster house, perching on the edge of the set of two bunk beds that filled the room I shared with three other girls, all of whom cried or screamed or scratched at their arms in the night. *Eve, your dad passed away. It was a heart attack. Quick, in the end.* 'Theresa. Did he remember me before he went?' I was embarrassed asking the question. What did I think, that his brain injury had healed itself in the moments before death? That whatever blood vessel or speck of flesh had stored his love for me had magically rejuvenated?

Theresa just sighed, then coughed again. 'That's not how it works.'

'I know. I just . . . I hoped.'

Another storm of coughing. She waved a hand at the sideboard, stacked with framed photos of children. 'Open that up.' I knelt on the old nubbly carpet, looking at her questioningly. 'There's a tin in there.' I reached into the cupboard, and took out a biscuit tin. Peek Freans, of course.

Theresa rooted through it, her nails yellowed with nicotine. 'These were in his room when he passed. I was going to give you them, but you'd taken off by then.' I had run, not even saying goodbye to her, washing up in Sunnyside like a plastic bag in a river. I had never stopped to think that Theresa, who'd looked after me for eleven years by then, might have missed me or might have been worried. Inside the tin were pictures – my mother, a baby that must have been me. Gently, I touched her long-gone face, her eighties perm and sweatshirt. There was something else in the tin too. Colourful, knobbly. I pulled it up. It was a small Lego house, green base, yellow and red and blue bricks, a roof made of flat red tiles.

'He made this?'

Theresa shrugged. 'Musta done.'

I digested that. He had made this after he was injured, kept it safe with his meagre handful of possessions. His hands had remembered building houses for me. 'What is this – you're trying to show he remembered me after all?'

Another chesty cough. 'I'm just giving you it. Up to you what you do with it.'

There was a lot I wanted to ask her. Does love die when we forget someone, or is it there all the same, hidden in the folds of our brains? Is it our fault what we forget, or what we remember? If my father didn't know who I was, how could he possibly love me? But I knew that Theresa did not have the answers, and besides, she wouldn't tell me even if she did. She had always believed in working things out for yourself. 'Can I keep this?'

'Knock yourself out. Save my niece a job when I finally pop off.' She coughed again, her thin chest sucked in. 'Not got too long, as you see.'

'I'm sorry.'

'Not your fault.'

I wanted to say I would come back to see her, but in truth I had no idea what I would do next. I closed the cupboard door, making one of the pictures shift slightly, and as I righted it I recognised with a jolt that these were foster kids. Boys, girls, tall, young, black, white, smiling, miserable. The kids Theresa had looked after. There was me, sullen in a too-big jumper handed down from some forgotten foster sibling. How strange, to find that, when I thought myself alone in the world, someone had my picture in their house all this time, remembering me. Like family.

RACHEL

It was a strange journey the next day, zooming up the M6 with Simon, trying to find the woman that he ... cared for? Loved? Rachel had no idea what their relationship had been, and Simon couldn't remember. She was driving, him trying to navigate on her phone. They hadn't talked about what they were going to do if and when they found Eve, just that they had to go to her, because she needed them. Because they had broken her, between them, Simon with his forgetting, Rachel by taking him back, by hurting him in the first place, by leaving him to stew in a care home, though she hadn't known it.

'Next junction,' said Simon. She changed lanes, grim and determined.

When she'd first guessed that Eve had gone back to where she'd grown up, they hadn't known where to even start looking for her. All they had was it was the Midlands, a big place. But Rachel had known the answer, which turned out to be the same as to every other problem she'd had recently. Ask Mark. And Mark had delivered, once again.

On the phone, when he heard her voice, she'd thought he sounded hopeful. Vulnerable, even. 'Rachel? Is that you?' But then she'd explained the situation and he'd switched back to his usual brisk, professional tones. He'd quickly learned, via a mate in CCTV with the British Transport Police, that someone looking very like Eve had left Bishopsdean on a coach to Wolverhampton. That was where she'd grown up, and where, they learned, her parents had been in a catastrophic car crash that killed her mother and injured her father so badly he'd lived in a care home for the next eleven years, his memory gone. Eve, just six at the time, had gone into foster care. It cut at Rachel's heart – not least because, if Simon had not recovered his memory, or if he'd been killed, that could have been Hannah. Eve had helped them, despite what it must have cost her. Now, they would help her. And Mark was very good. In less than three hours, he had found her.

'Thank you,' Rachel had stammered, when he'd called her back with the news. 'I'll let everyone here know.'

'All right.' There had been a brief moment of silence, and it could have gone either way. She almost asked him to go with them. But no, it would be too strange, her and Simon and Mark too, and anyway, she'd asked him for enough already.

Now they were almost there, and Rachel had to think what to say. How to persuade the woman her husband was maybe in love with, but had maybe forgotten that he was, to come back to her life. It was so strange, when this whole thing had happened because she thought he'd fallen for someone else to start with. And now she found that, if that was how things were between Eve and Simon, she didn't mind the idea. She wanted Simon to be happy. She owed him that much. But he couldn't remember Eve – how could they find a way back from this?

'Next turn,' he said, and Rachel flicked on her indicator.

How strange life was, she thought. A few weeks ago she had no idea who this woman was – their lives would never have intersected in the normal course of events. Eve was bedpans and sedatives and wiping drool. Rachel was Instagram and the school run and blouses from Boden. She'd done her best to seal her life off from pain or suffering or poverty, but trouble had come to find her anyway. And now who knew what lay ahead.

A lone figure was standing in the country graveyard, hands rammed into the pocket of a denim jacket, hair blowing in the wind. Rachel went to open the car door, but Simon put his hand on her arm. 'Let me.'

EVE

'Hi, Mum. Hi, Dad.' I felt silly saying it out loud. They weren't here, after all. They had been gone for a long time, Mum for twenty-eight years, Dad for seventeen. All that remained of them was in my memory, and before the accident it had been just ordinary, fallible. I only had scraps of them, diminishing every year.

What would they think of me? Standing here in this lonely graveyard, once again too cold in my inadequate denim jacket, all alone in the world? My only friends were my boss and co-workers, and a bunch of older people with failing memories. I had been in love just once, with someone who wasn't real. I had been nowhere, achieved nothing except a dusty collection of junk, currently on its way to the rubbish dump. Most likely, they would be disappointed in me.

I heaved a deep sigh. I had hoped that, in coming here, I might find some answers about what to do next with my life. How to live with a memory that crippled me every minute of every day. And I had found nothing. It was stupid. I should just leave, go somewhere warm, have a sandwich, and think about what to do to next.

That was when I heard the car.

'You're here! I don't ... ' Simon. It was Simon, here at my parents' graves. 'What are you doing here?'

It was Simon, who did not remember me.

'Are you all right? Rachel and I came to look for you.'

'Why?' I kept staring at the worn, moss-covered stones, afraid to look at him and see no recognition there.

'Magda was worried. We wanted to find you.'

'I'm all right.' Did he remember me? Was everything OK now? Was that even possible? 'How are you?' I risked.

He shrugged. 'Not so good. I have all these memories – my entire past flooding in all at once – and then there's this ... hole in them.'

Oh. 'So you don't ... ' It was fine. I hadn't expected it. The doctors had said he wouldn't get that time back, hadn't they?

'I'm sorry, Eve.'

'I'm not ... I don't really matter in the scheme of things.'

'That's not true, is it? You helped me, when no one else could.'

'Did I, though?' I stared at the graves in front of us, grown over with grass and weeds. A shared headstone, the plainest kind, grey slate. *Diana Mahoney, 1959–1990. Beloved Mother. David Mahoney, 1950–2001.* 'Are you happy, in the life you got back?'

Simon paused. 'Not really.'

Tears blurred my eyes, for the waste of it all. Love, and happiness, and joy, all spilled away on the ground, the same way memories died. 'You were happy at Sunnyside. I know you were. But it wasn't real, was it? This is your real life. You just have to make the best of it.'

A pause. 'Can't I do that with you in it?'

'No!' My voice was so angry it shocked me. 'You don't remember me, Simon. I mean nothing to you. Literally nothing.'

'That's not true.' He fumbled something out of his coat pocket – an expensive wool coat that he would never have worn at Sunnyside. 'I kept this notebook, apparently. And look, all these pages' – he rifled through them – 'they're all about you. Your childhood. What you like and don't like. Your favourite biscuit, your favourite colour, the songs that make you cry. The TV quiz shows you prefer. The way you take your tea, the exact colour of Caramac bars. It's everything, Eve. Everything I know about you.'

'*Knew,*' I said. So what if Adam had cared enough to write this down? Adam was still gone, and pages in a cheap promotional notebook were not the same as knowing me, remembering me. He was still a married man, and I didn't want whatever stilted friendship we could develop in future. I wanted everything, and I couldn't have it, so I would have nothing. 'It doesn't matter. This makes no difference.'

He sagged. 'Please, Eve. If not for me then come back for your friends. People miss you. They need you.'

'No.' My voice was quiet, bleak somehow. Lonely.

'They do!' Simon pulled out a phone, scrolled through dozens of anxious WhatsApp messages on a group called *Find Eve*. 'They all want you back. Magda, and the staff, and the residents, and the doctors – not just for your wonderful brain, Eve. For you. So please – will you come with us? If you want, I'll leave you alone after that. But don't throw your life away because of me. I'm begging you.'

I thought about it for a long time. Sunnyside, the only home I'd known for most of my life. However much I might wish I could go back to being six, my parents alive, being loved and wanted, a place in the world that I filled utterly, that was not going to happen. You can't turn back time. Simon would not remember me. Adam would not come back. Like I'd told him to do, I'd just have to make the best of it.

'I'll come back,' I said. 'But not with you.'

'But . . . '

'No, Simon. Rachel is your wife. Your place is with her. I need to just . . . forget about you and move on. So please, let me do it. I'll get the bus back.'

His face was bleak. 'Are you sure?'

'Yes.'

'I really am sorry, you know.'

'I know.' But it didn't make any difference.

Is it true? Anne – my foster mother – was standing over me, hands on her hips. Natalie was in the background, staring daggers at me. *Told you I'd get rid of you.* I stared at my dinner plate – I remember it was a plastic one, with a drawing of a train on it. When I ate my potatoes and beans I mashed them up and pretended it was a field. I remember this. I remember everything. Anne was wearing a T-shirt with the Little Mermaid on it (she was obsessed with Disney, saving up her foster payments to go to Disneyland Paris) and had a plaster around the fourth finger of her right hand, where she'd cut it slicing potato waffles.

You remember everything – like, what we had for tea two months ago?

I mumbled, *Mince from a tin and sliced bread toast.*

She gaped. *It's not natural, that.*

Natalie said, *She's not natural. She's a freak. You should get rid of her.*

After a moment, Simon nodded sadly then picked his way across the muddy graveyard, to where Rachel sat in the car, a white shape between the windscreen, and after another minute or two they drove off. Out of my life, for good.

RACHEL

It was late when they got home, both of them deflated. They'd found Eve, and she was all right, but she had firmly shut them out of her life. And why shouldn't she? They'd brought her nothing but pain.

Rachel switched off the engine. Inside the house was their child, their life together, built up over ten years.

Simon sighed. 'I guess this is it. It's really over. We're back to normal, whatever that is.'

'So . . . what now?' she risked. 'I don't want to go back to how things were. Never talking, both of us so alone. Fighting all the time, living separate lives. Lies, secrets.'

'I know. Neither do I.'

'It's going to take a lot, Simon. I don't know. Therapy, maybe. Months of it. We'll have to get to know each other all over again. Right now, I feel like . . . you're this person I know everything about, how you put the toothpaste on the brush, what pants you own, all of that, but I also know nothing. I don't know you at all. We have to start again.'

He said nothing for a while, sitting there in the car on their expensive driveway. The cherry blossom shed petals over them like confetti on their wedding day. 'Do we have to?'

'You mean . . . ' When he'd gone, and she'd had to cope on her own, she'd been terrified at first. Having no husband undermined the entire foundation of the life that she'd been building so carefully since the day she took the coach to university from her parents' terrace in Rotherham, cutting them off as effectively as being orphaned. But she and Hannah had been on their own for weeks, and honestly, it wasn't much different from all those times Simon was working in London, hardly coming home. She knew she didn't love him, not like she had that first day in the pub, when he'd knocked the breath from her lungs. She cared for him, of course, hadn't wanted him hurt or confused, was sorry he'd been injured and had to learn difficult truths about himself. But that was all.

'You're right.' She was surprised by how steady her voice was. 'We don't have to do anything we don't want to do.'

A long silence, in which many things were said at the same time as nothing at all.

'Will Hannah be all right with it?' he asked, after a while.

'She's so resilient, that kid. I honestly think that if nuclear Armageddon came, she'd be leading the scavenger bands.'

'How will we tell her?'

'Just that Daddy isn't the same since he came back, and he loves her very much, but he'll live somewhere else now. I mean, if that's OK. To be honest, we might have to sell the house anyway, what with the debts.'

He bit his lip. 'I'm so sorry, Rachel. I'm such a dick. The man I am ... it's not who I want to be. I think maybe that's why I forgot. My brain couldn't take it any more. Being the person I am. Was.'

'You did some dick-ish things in the past. It doesn't have to define you. We can change. People can change. I have to believe that. Where will you go?'

He scratched his head. 'I have no idea. I doubt I can work in finance again. My memory's still shot; it might never fully recover. Serves me right, I guess, for trying to always have more than I needed.'

Inside the house, through the lighted window, she could see Hannah and her mother watching something on TV. Laughing together. A sight that would not have been possible weeks ago. 'How about we sell this place and get smaller flats? Use the rest to pay off the debts. And I can go back to work. We don't need all this anyway. Two guest rooms! No one even comes to stay.' How easy it all was, discussing the practicalities of dismantling their lives.

Haltingly, he said: 'So – that's it, then? Just as easy at that.'

It was over. Her marriage was over. 'Just as easy as that,' she said, and he leaned over the gearstick, awkwardly, and pressed her into his arms, breathing into her hair, and she knew that they were saying goodbye.

'Where's Dad?' The next morning Hannah wandered into the kitchen in her *Frozen* pyjamas, rubbing her eyes.

'He's ... he's gone away for a bit, darling.' It was amazing how easily the truth could cut through lies, like a knife in melted butter. Simon and she had admitted things weren't working out. He was going to stay at a hotel for a bit, the cheapest one in town. There would be no more five-star luxury, not any more.

'Again?' Hannah opened the fridge.

'He has a few things to sort out.' They'd thought it was easier if Rachel explained it. Simon still felt awkward around Hannah, knowing that he'd forgotten her, that he'd let her down and planned to possibly jump off a ferry without even saying goodbye to her. 'Han-ban, you know how your friend Kitty's parents ... '

'You're getting a divorce? Can I have this yogurt?'

'Ye— No, you can't, it's full of sugar.'

'Are you getting a divorce?'

'I don't know. I think for now, we just won't live in the same house as each other. I'm sorry, darling. It's just that with Daddy being so poorly, we couldn't really . . . get back from it.'

Hannah nodded, her curls bouncing. 'Will we see Mark again, in that case?'

'What do you mean?' Rachel stared at her.

'I like Mark. I like Daddy too, but I suppose I'm used to him not being here.' She said it so matter-of-factly, it hurt Rachel's heart. Simon was not a bad husband or father. He had always loved Hannah – he'd just allowed his work to swallow him whole, eat him up till there was nothing else. The pursuit of money, of status. And she had let him do it.

'You know Daddy loves you very much. He just . . . hurt his head badly. He's not really the same now.' And to be honest, neither was Rachel.

'I know.' Hannah's gaze had flicked to the high cupboard, which Rachel had christened the Treat Cupboard, something that her younger, working-class self would have sneered at. 'Can I have a biscuit instead of the yogurt, then?' It was an all-or-nothing negotiating tactic she sometimes tried, which Rachel was ashamed to say often worked, when she was too worn down to say no again.

'You cannot.' She was back to being In Control Mummy, who planned meals and enforced bedtimes. 'Things are going to get back to normal around here, young lady. No trips to Greggs. Homework done on time.'

'But Daddy won't be here?'

'Not . . . all the time.'

'Will we see Granny more?'

'If you like.'

'I do. *Granny* lets me have biscuits.' Of course she did. However, Rachel reflected, as she shepherded Hannah towards the fruit bowl, maybe a little refined sugar was a small price to pay for having your mother back in your life.

'You should ring Mark,' Hannah said, through a bite of apple.

'Should I? Why's that?'

'He likes you.' She had wandered into the living room and switched on the TV, deftly manipulating the three different remotes, and called back: 'I bet he's missing you, right now.'

Was he? Rachel eyed the landline. Thought about dialling Mark's number, hearing his comforting Northern tones. Telling him that he'd been right, divorce was not so very difficult after all, sometimes. Could she? Make a stand, try for happiness, admit to the world that her life was a mess after all? Rachel paused, her hand hovering over the phone, trying to make a decision.

EVE

I had been back at Sunnyside for a week when Magda told me, rather than asked, that I was going out that night. I hadn't been sure I would ever come here again, but when my taxi drew into the car park and I saw the familiar red-brick building with the straggly roses outside I just thought, *Oh yes, I'm home*. And that was it. I was.

I'd been nervous about seeing Magda, after taking off like that, but she pulled me into a hug, knocking the breath out of me. 'I was so worried! Don't do that again.' Then she started to cry. 'Oh, lovie, you did give us a fright.'

'I'm thirty-four years old, Magda,' I said gently, wiping Rambling Rose from my cheek.

'I still worry,' she scolded, and I knew what this reminded me of. Something I'd not had for years. A mother. Magda was like a mother to me, and so was Theresa, and even Rachel in a way. 'Listen,' Magda said, smearing mascara over her face, 'I know you think you're an odd one ... but we're all odd ones here. We need you. You help every single one of us, Eve. Not just the residents. Me, finding my phone and my tax returns and I don't know what. Anthony with his studies. Julie, Charity. You listen. You remember – that's something everyone needs, to be remembered. So as long as you want it, your home is here. All right?'

'All right,' I mumbled, trying not to cry.

'Good.'

After that, things had gone more or less back to normal. Dishing out pills, refereeing the TV remote, reminding people who I was, who they were, in a hundred different ways. And now, right in the middle of lunch clean-up, my scrubs spattered with custard, Magda said we were going out.

I'd been looking forward to a quiet evening with *Pointless*. 'What? Where?'

She shook her head, dislodging a pen. 'Can't tell you. Just put on something nice, OK?' I didn't have anything nice. I thought of my empty flat, the Museum all thrown away, and felt a pang of loss.

'Magda?'

'Yes, lovie?'

'Do you think ... maybe you could help me?'

I had no idea what floodgates I was opening. Within fifteen minutes not just Magda, but Julie and Sharice, Charity's daughter, were at my door like a SWAT team armed with hair straighteners, eyelash curlers, make-up, a choice of dresses, and more.

Magda peered round her. 'Looks different in here without all that junk.' I was trying not to think about the Museum. While Julie did something unspeakable to my hair – she had already singed my ear four times – and Sharice painted my nails, Magda held up a selection of dresses, each one shorter and more spangly than the next.

I was beginning to panic. 'Please – just make me look like me? Like me only better?'

Magda sighed as I rejected dress after dress. 'That is all we have, Eve. You can't go in your scrubs, or your usual schoolboy get-up.'

'Is there nothing else?'

'There's this old thing, but it's sort of plain . . . .' She held out a yellow print tea-dress, simple and pretty. A day dress, really.

Something twanged in my memory. 'Give me that one. Please, Julie, can you just . . . ?' I detached myself from the red-hot poker she was torturing me with and, shutting the bedroom door, I wriggled out of my jeans and hoody and into the dress. A summery dress, yellow, with green and blue flowers printed on it. Flared sleeves and buttons down the front, a full and swingy skirt. I looked at myself in the mirror. A woman in her thirties, with fair hair, grey eyes, a mildly burned earlobe, a yellow dress.

And she came back to me. Just like that, like a gift, like something you spend your whole life searching for and then you give up and suddenly there it is, just dropped into your lap.

Eve, we're going on a picnic today. It's sunny, and Daddy doesn't have to work. It's going to be so much fun! And she laughed, and the sound was high and free, like a child's laugh, though my mother was thirty-one at this point. The oldest she would ever be. I was in my single bed, and she'd come in to draw the curtains, wearing a yellow dress instead of her usual jeans. The sun made a bright square on the carpet, and the day was in front of us, full of hope and promise. And I was happy. I wonder if that was the last time I was truly happy, and normal. But I was not the person I am now, and there is no going back.

Magda hammered on the door. 'We'll be late!'

'Coming!' It was true I did not have my mother or my father. I did not have Adam. But I still had my memories, and

Sunnyside, and friends, and a job I loved, and tonight I was going out. That was a start, at least. 'Let's go,' I said, opening the door and tucking my arm through Magda's.

I still didn't know where we were going, but we were now on the high street in town. It was late, lots of the shops just lowering their shutters and closing up. I thought how sad it was to see so many shut down for good, their windows obscured with paint, and sometimes a few sad unsold goods sitting in there, waiting for whoever bought it next to open the place up and find them. But if you saw it in the context of history – if you looked at the photos in Bishopsdean Museum – the town had always been changing. Once there were stalls selling eels and offering trips to the water springs, and a whole bevy of rat-catchers. There had been video rental shops and newsagents and laundrettes. I bet back then the video rental shop owners and the rat-catchers had felt bereft, their industry dying under them. But there's always something else coming. There are always new memories to be made. In that context, maybe it wasn't such a terrible thing that Simon had gone. Maybe now my brain knew how to make friends with people, how to care for them – well, maybe it would be easier the next time.

I stopped in front of the alley where Mr Spitz's shop was, suddenly slapped in the face by memory. The day I'd gone in there with the ring, I'd felt so hopeful. I'd just met Simon/Adam, and I was happy to know him and maybe be able to help. Little did I guess that by finding out who he was, I'd hurt both of us. He would learn he wasn't a nice person – and the ring wasn't even real! – and I would learn ... that I needed him. That I'd let myself need someone after all this time, and they had gone

307

away. And I had turned my back on him when he asked for my help. It wasn't a good feeling. But at least I had tried.

We turned a corner, and suddenly I realised where we were going. 'What . . . ?'

'Go on.' Magda nudged me forward.

'What is this?'

'Come and see,' said Sandra proudly, greeting me at the door of the Bishopsdean Museum. I followed her in the door, puzzled as to what was going on. The place was full of people, dressed up in suits and frocks, more than I had ever seen here before.

'Oh my God.' For a moment, I didn't understand what I was looking at. It was the Bishopsdean Museum, same as usual, but instead of the snuffboxes and fossils and broken bits of pottery, the cases were filled with my things. My Museum. There was Mrs G's snow globe and the pen from Wise Buy, its ink leaking out.

Sandra smiled. 'It was that lad who found it all, Anthony. In the bins. He brought it to me, and I got the idea. The community fund loved it, so I got together with Mary from Age Concern and Sandeep from Contact the Elderly, and we made this – a Memory Museum.' I peered at the little printed cards by the display cases. Each item was floodlit like a proper museum exhibit, like a diamond or a priceless Anglo Saxon helmet. There was something overwhelming about seeing a scabby free biro treated in this way. On one I read: *Jean's memory. This snow globe was purchased by Jean Gillespie on the Isle of Wight in May 1964.* On another: *This hair clip was part of a set sold in Woolworths during the 1980s. It was bought by Anne Sheringham sometime in 1983 or 1984.*

All the memories of the residents. Here behind glass, with lights, with labels. People were walking around, sipping glasses of white wine, eating from bowls of crisps. I recognised some of the residents' families, and Raheem and some of the police officers, Amanda from the toy shop and Mr Spitz, holding a small glass of sherry and looking through his magnifying glass into a cabinet. Julie was there, her nails three inches long and painted lime green, blowing kisses at Raheem. Anthony was there, in his Goth get-up, and so was Arjang, his hands thankfully fine. I'd heard he passed his exams with top marks, and had already been offered a job playing piano on a cruise ship. Terry was there with the pub quiz team, Doris on her mobility scooter, and he confided in me that he was going to stay in Sunnyside even though his hip was better. 'The truth is, lass, I was lonely in the flat on my tod. Even if homes aren't always nice, it's company. And that's what matters.' I told him I agreed.

Praj and Zoe were there, out of their white coats. I realised that they saw people like me every day, who'd been knocked on the head in car accidents, or when they skied into trees, when things landed on them or they landed on things, or whose neurones had been tangled in toxic proteins like ivy choking a tree. Brains are fragile. All they are is flesh and blood and wiring. The things we take for granted – our memories, our identities – are all held in the smallest space you can imagine. And, like anything fragile, they are all the more precious for it. Zoe, flushed and happy, hugged me and made me promise to come back and see them next week. I saw Praj kiss her as the crowd closed back around them, and I was glad for them.

I saw Keith and Rosemary too, debating when would be a good time to burst into song (I hoped she had not brought her tambourine), and Charity and Sharice, arguing over the length or lack-of of Sharice's skirt. I saw Magda chatting to the mayor,

309

in her best Mafia-widow frock, her hair stuck through with ornate chopsticks instead of pens. Everyone was there.

Well. Almost everyone. 'I can't believe you did this, Sandra.'

'It was you gave me the idea. Why should a museum be just old things? Why not things from our lifetime, that people have loved? It's a new way of looking at it, darling. The council are very excited. The mayor's going to make a speech.'

There were posters on the walls about forging connections between the university and Sunnyside. Sending students to record the oral histories, the memories of our residents. Applying for more funding for a continuous, rotating display of the town's history on a personal level. 'After all,' the mayor said pompously in her speech, 'what is a town without its people?' I was pleased, of course – it showed that I hadn't been crazy all these years, keeping these things in my living room. That it did matter, the powder compact someone bought thirty years back, or the letter they carried in their breast pocket when they went off to war. That people mattered, however small their lives had been, however obscurely they'd ended. But I couldn't shake the feeling that he should be here too.

Adam.

Simon.

Whatever his name was. He'd changed things for me, and now he'd gone.

That was when I saw him.

EVE

The first time I met Adam, the mysterious man with no name and no history, nobody looking for him, it was in Sunnyside Independent Living Centre, with a suspicious smell in the air and Daniel O'Donnell on the stereo.

The first time I met Simon – properly met him, I mean – was in the Memory Museum, a new pop-up exhibit in the centre of Bishopsdean, which started because of my strange habit of squirrelling away bits and pieces from the residents who died. Simon looked like Adam, yes, but he moved differently, held himself more stiffly. He drank beer while Adam drank tea, and wore a smart black jumper and grey jeans instead of cast-offs from the Death Box. His face was more watchful, slower to smile. He was weighed down by his memories, whereas Adam had been free, light. But then again, Adam wasn't real, and Simon was.

I stepped forward. What was he doing here? My wine glass felt wet and slippery in my hand, and I worried I was going to drop it, so I set it down on one of the high tables Sandra had brought in for the party. 'Hello.'

'Hi, Eve.'

When he said my name, I was filled with stupid hope. 'Do you—'

He cut in. 'I'm sorry. I still don't remember my time with you. I don't know if I ever will. My brain just . . . wasn't working.'

'Oh.' I felt the pain of it all over again, of seeing no recognition in his eyes. The way the children of the residents must feel, when they see that their mother or father doesn't know them. A pain you never really get used to.

'I really am sorry. I know that . . . that we were close.'

My chest hurt. 'But it's all gone. I remember it and you – it just never happened for you.' The waste of it, all those conversations we had, all those days together. Standing on the beach, his hand in mine, our faces pressed together. Gone in the wind.

'I'm sorry,' he said again. He looked sad.

I swallowed the lump in my throat. 'It's OK. I'm glad you remember your daughter. Your . . . wife.'

'Eve – Rachel and I are going to split up. We should have before, but we were both too scared. Something like this puts it all in perspective.'

I wasn't sure why he was telling me this. 'I'm sorry to hear that.' A lie, because I wasn't, and he didn't seem sad about it, but I knew the protocol was to say I was.

'It's fine, really. Eve . . . When I was Simon, I had a lot of things. A house, two cars, a family, stuff . . . you know, a pasta maker, of all things! Who would ever use a pasta maker? But when I was Adam I had nothing, not even my name. Not even shoes. But you helped me. I know that you did, even if I can't remember. Because that's the thing.' He stepped closer to me, putting his beer bottle down beside my glass. I saw drips of moisture inch down towards the surface. It was loud at the party, and he had to stoop to talk in my ear. He smelled different from Adam. Like expensive aftershave and fancy washing powder. He said, 'Even if I don't remember the details, I remember the feelings. That hasn't gone. I know you were important – maybe the most important person in my life. I know you were home to me, for a time. I know there was something between us. I can feel it, somehow. I remember you made me safe. I remember salt wind, and the feel of your heart beating.'

'But you don't *know* me.'

'You don't know me either. Not as Simon, anyway. You don't know all the things I've done, the women I've kissed, the parking tickets I've racked up. That's why I came here tonight, to try again, even after what you said in the graveyard. Because you don't know me, and I don't know you. Not really.'

I took a deep breath. 'I know you like bourbons but hate custard creams. I know you stir your tea four and a half times, in a counter-clockwise direction. I know that when you play the piano the residents remember themselves. And when you think about something, you get a crease just there, between your eyebrows.' He was so close I could have touched it.

'Well, that seems like enough to start with. And you know, we can always make new memories.'

'What do you mean?' I stammered.

'I mean ... the things we did together have gone. But I'm not.' He paused. I was sweating into the yellow dress. It was almost too much, the hubbub of the party and the people and all the memories and him. Almost, but not quite. 'Can't we start again, you and me? Meet for the first time? And this time, I promise, I won't forget.'

I thought about it for a long time, standing opposite him as the party went on around us. I thought how it felt when he hadn't known me, and the possibility it could happen again. About how it was for all the residents' families, on the day their mother or father first had no recognition in their eyes. It's a basic thing, isn't it? Recognising someone. I thought how it would feel if I got to know Simon as well as I'd known Adam, and then he forgot me again, or I lost him, in the way that people do lose each other, to death or disaster or just the end of love, swept away unless we hold on tight. Even if he and Rachel were splitting up, what interest would he have in me? A weirdo like me. I thought how pretty she was, Rachel, how shiny her hair, how expensive her handbags. Simon was a serious man, with a proper city job and a fancy car and a knowledge of wine, most likely. I was . . . me. An orphan. A freak-show. I only knew him at all because of his accident. His fugue time had been to me the best time of my life. There was something wrong about that.

The man in front of me, he had the same face as someone I had loved. But that person did not exist.

Can you love someone when you don't remember them? Does love die along with memory cells, those delicate neurones built of dreams and flesh? Where does love go when one end of it disappears, like a dropped telephone, when that person dies or leaves or just forgets you? I've asked myself that so many times over the years, seeing the residents lose themselves day by day. The truth was, I didn't know the answer. I didn't know if I could feel for Simon what I had for Adam. Simon was a stranger to me, a man who'd lied and deceived and hurt people, run from everyone including himself. He didn't know me either. The odd quirks of my brain. All I knew was he was here in front of me, standing so close I could feel his breath on my neck. A stranger who wasn't a stranger.

'What do you say, Eve? Can I get to know you as myself? You might not like me. I think I have some pretty bad qualities. But maybe you will.'

314

I took a small step back, the better to look at him – his shorter black hair, his green eyes, the wool of his jumper that was so much more expensive than the home-knitted one with delinquent kittens on that he'd worn at Sunnyside – and I held out my hand. 'Hello, I'm Eve. I work at an old folks' home, though we're not supposed to call it that. I have a weird memory, I don't forget stuff. This exhibit was kind of my idea.'

He smiled and took my hand in his – so big and comforting. 'Hi, Eve. I'm Simon. I'm a soon-to-be-divorced man who went broke and almost tried to kill himself. But on the plus side, I am apparently quite good at making pancakes.'

'I love those. Pleased to meet you, Simon.'

'And you too, Eve.'

TWO MONTHS LATER

RACHEL

'Mummy, where is this place?' Hannah had her face pressed to the window, leaving smudgy marks on the glass.

Rachel stopped the car. 'This is where I grew up.'

'Here?' Hannah sounded doubtful. 'It's so small.'

'Yes, well, not everyone is rich, you know.' Hannah would have to learn that soon. Life was changing – Hannah was still trying to trust Simon again after he'd forgotten her. He had recovered, but still had headaches, moments when names and numbers and facts just dropped out of his head, like pennies down a sofa. Money would be tight. They were putting the house on the market, and Rachel was going back to work. Hannah was almost eight, and already self-sufficient. There was no reason for Rachel to be at home, obsessing over sourdough starters and homemade granola. She was looking forward to getting back to it, all the lipstick campaigns and sex scandals and glossy adverts. To the lighter side of life, after so much darkness.

She drove slowly up the street, looking for a parking spot, secretly hoping there wouldn't be one so they'd put off getting there a minute longer. Hannah piped up, 'Mummy? How come Mark didn't come with us today?'

'He had to work, darling.' A tech company suspected one of their staff was leaking information to competitors, and Mark had gone in to install hidden cameras and find out who it was. She was pleased he had a big case. Maybe he could even afford an office with space for a proper filing cabinet. And perhaps

319

even an assistant, now he'd discovered Eve was quite handy at finding things out herself. A chance to use her skills outside of the home, perhaps.

Mark was not living with her and Hannah. Not officially, anyway. Not yet. Rachel smiled to herself at the thought, at the day they'd just spent the four of them, Hannah and Lucy, Mark's daughter, a sweet quiet girl who loved *Harry Potter.*

'Mark's like Colbumbo, isn't he, Mummy?'

'Columbo. I suppose he is a bit, yes.'

Hannah didn't let up. 'Mummy? When I go round to Daddy's, will Eve be there?'

'I don't know. Maybe.'

'Is she his girlfriend?'

Rachel also didn't know the answer to that. Simon still seemed to remember nothing about his time at the old folks' home, but the shy, softly spoken woman who'd cared for him appeared to have lodged under his skin all the same. Rachel could see it in the way he talked about her, gentle and caring. He hadn't spoken to Rachel like that in years, or vice versa. Their relationship had been something greedy and passionate and loud, suited to the people they were at the time. Shouting at the tops of their lungs to drown out the thoughts in their heads. Things wouldn't be easy for Simon and Eve – her memory brought with it all kinds of issues, and his was still patchy, leaving him prone to confusion and distress. But they were taking care of each other. Maybe that was enough.

'Come on,' she said, finally reversing into a parking spot and turning off the engine. 'Get your seatbelt off.' She took a long time locking up the car, trying to delay the moment for as long as possible.

320

'Mummy, what are you *doing*?'

'Nothing. Are you ready?'

'I've been ready for like an hour.' Hannah rolled her eyes.

'All right, miss, you're seven, not seventeen.' She looked Hannah over. Who wouldn't love her? The unruly curls, her small tapping foot in glittery frog-adorned green shoes. She was already different to when Simon went missing, a little taller, her face a little older. Changing day to day, and all Rachel could do was try to look, and listen, and remember.

'What are we going to have for lunch, Mummy?' Hannah trotted down the street beside her. It was so run-down, paint peeling from the doors and window frames, rubbish drifting in the gutters. She'd turned her nose up at it for so long, but it was home. Where she came from. She knew which family lived behind each faded door, had played kerbies with their kids all those years ago. This was the real Rachel. Not the one who'd dropped a hundred quid on getting her hair done.

'I don't know.' It would be something cheap, baked beans or spaghetti hoops on the kind of spongy supermarket bread Hannah had never even tasted, or an oven pizza. For 'afters', maybe a bought trifle or a tinned pudding. It didn't matter. 'Whatever it is, you'll eat it. OK? Here we are.'

It was still strange to ring the doorbell, when for years she'd stuck her key in the lock and gone in. The familiar anxiety touched her, a ghost from the past – would Mum be crying because Dad had lost the mortgage money again? Would the TV be missing or her bike repossessed? She held tight to Hannah, gulping in air.

'Ow, Mummy.'

'Sorry.'

Someone was shuffling to the door, and then it opened, and there he was. Stooped and grey, wearing a holey patterned jumper and slacks. He had glasses on a string round his neck, which he peered into. He looked so old. She hadn't seen him in so many years, had spent so long being angry at him, but she realised now there was no point. The past was the past, and could not be changed, but the future still could.

She swallowed. 'Hello, Dad. Hannah, this is your grandfather.'

EVE

'Ready?'

'Ready.'

The wind was high already, whipping sand into our faces. Out to sea, the water was boiling and swelling, swoops of grey and glinting silver as the clouds scudded past. He scanned the horizon, as men do, with his hand shading his eyes. 'There's a bit of weather coming in. We better do this soon.'

After Mrs G's funeral – a fairly prosaic affair in the crematorium, with Janet Marks and her daughter in attendance, worrying about parking at the graveyard, plus a procession of residents with walkers and sticks, and Mrs Burke convinced she was at her own wedding in 1972 – James Gillespie had gone back to Dubai, taking Graham with him in a cat carrier, which Graham had loved about as much as he loved being locked in the linen cupboard. There'd been a long delay at the crematorium, and some trouble getting his mother's ashes on to the plane, so in the end James had asked me if I would scatter them.

'After all,' he said, hefting the mewling, rocking cat carrier, 'I have something to remember her by with Graham. Thank you, Eve. I'd lost my mother for a long time. Thanks to you, I got her back before she died.' He'd paused to wipe his eyes, his allergies already kicking in. 'This bloody beast. I'll certainly never forget her, anyway.'

Scattering someone's ashes seemed a big responsibility, and I'd been nervous the whole way down on the train, in case the lid came off the jar and dusted everyone in Coach C with a fine mist of Mrs Gillespie. But now here we were, on a windy clifftop, clutching the urn. 'Which way's the wind going?'

'Westerly,' he said, squinting. 'Chuck them out that way and they won't blow back in our faces.'

'I should say something.'

'If you like.'

I cleared my throat, feeling stupid. 'Hi, Mrs G. We've brought you here to this beach, because it's where Simon found himself again, and because it's the most beautiful place we could think of. That didn't involve taking you on a plane anyway, which is apparently quite hard. We hope you like it. It's very windy and wave-y, so you should have a lively time. I hope you're at peace, wherever you are. Graham and Jimmy are fine, don't worry. And Simon is fine too, I think – you know him as Adam, but he's really Simon. Oh, and I'm very fine as well. Bye.'

'That was more of a postcard than a speech,' he said, pulling on the draw strings of my anorak. 'Get a handful.'

When we opened the urn some ash blew out, and blinking, I quickly emptied it into the wind, where it was carried out to sea and vanished in the mist and fog. 'Bye, Mrs G,' I said. I wondered if my parents had wanted to be cremated, if they had actually been buried in those graves I'd visited or if those were just memorials. Theresa might know. I was going to see her in a few weeks, and I would ask her to tell me everything she knew about my mother, my father, where I came from. Everything about me.

He – the man I still had to get used to calling Simon – dusted off his hands. 'That's that, then. Let's get in somewhere dry before it tips it down.' He paused. 'Are you what you said? Very fine?'

324

'More than,' I assured him, tucking my arm through his. 'I'm extremely fine indeed.' As we made our way down the cliff path to the car park, I bent to pick up a pebble, striped like the first one, which we'd given to Hannah.

'What's that for?' he asked, unlocking the car.

'To remember this place. And today. Would you like one too?'

'Eve, it's OK. I don't need anything to remember you by,' he said, smiling. And we got into the car, with rain in our hair and salt on our skins, and drove away.

ACKNOWLEDGEMENTS

Huge thanks to my endlessly supportive agent Diana Beaumont, and my wise and kind editor Maddie West, for all their input into this book. Thanks as well to everyone at Marjacq and Sphere, with an extra-big special thanks to Cath Burke.

LETTER

The idea for this book came to me in two distinct parts. First, I read an article about fugue states, and how people can slip into them and then out again with no memory of what they've been doing in the time between. Some people never come out of them, and must simply start new lives somewhere elsc. I also came across an article about people who remember every detail of their lives – a real condition called hyperthymestic syndrome. They can almost watch days of their past unfold again, like a film in their head, but the condition can be crippling too, as it's very hard to do anything without being flooded by memories. (If you are interested, the memoir *The Woman Who Can't Forget*, by Jill Price, is fascinating). I put these two ideas together – a man who can't remember and a woman who can't forget – and came up with this book.

I also wanted to write about dementia, something that many of us are likely to experience either ourselves or with our loved ones. As a writer, the idea of forgetting, of not being able to work any more, has always been terrifying to me, and there's a family history of it. By the time I was a teenager my grandfather was already in a home with Alzheimer's. He wasn't sure who we were most of the time, but he remained loving and cheerful, able to play the violin and offer us Polo mints from secret pockets. His main concern was that we had enough petrol in the car, even though he hadn't driven in years. Even when we weren't going anywhere. Then there were his rare moments of lucidity – often funny amid the loss. While he was in hospital once, someone whispered sadly that he reminded them of 'Sam', who was my aunt's ancient, three-legged dog. Gramps, who everyone thought was totally out of it, piped up: 'Oh, so I'm a dog, am I?' Most days he didn't recognise his children, but that day he knew who Sam was. This book is partly in memory of Gramps, and everyone else who lives with this condition.

I'd love to hear from you if you've read this book. I'm on Twitter @inkstainsclaire, Instagram @evawoodsauthor, and online at www.evawoodsauthor.com. Drop me a line!

Lots of love,

Eva x

THE UNMISSABLE, UPLIFTING BESTSELLER

'So likeable, smart and wise. A bittersweet read about love, life and friendship that makes you stop and think long after you've finished reading the last page' TASMINA PERRY

'Entertaining, funny and full of wisdom, I loved this book'
KATIE FFORDE

'I read this recently and loved it SO much. I cried buckets, but it's ultimately a really positive, uplifting book about making every day count' CLARE MACKINTOSH

'A joyful, wise read' ROSIE BLAKE

'It's a gorgeous book - funny, touching, sweet, sad and profound'
DAISY BUCHANAN

'You'll laugh and cry ... heartwarming' BEST

'Uplifting' INDEPENDENT

'Will make you laugh while it tugs
at your heartstrings' THE PEOPLE